Also by Kate O'Shaughnessy

The Lonely Heart of Maybelle Lane

Lasagna means I Love You

KATE O'SHAUGHNESSY

Alfred A. Knopf
New York

THIS IS A BORZOI BOOK PUBLISHED BY ALFRED A. KNOPF

Visit us on the Web! rhcbooks.com

Educators and librarians, for a variety of teaching tools, visit us at RHTeachersLibrarians.com

Library of Congress Cataloging-in-Publication Data is available upon request.
ISBN 978-1-9848-9387-1 (trade) — ISBN 978-1-9848-9388-8 (lib. bdg.) — ISBN 978-1-9848-9389-5 (ebook)

The text of this book is set in 12.5-point Goudy Old Style.
Interior design by Jaclyn Whalen
Text and photographs on pages 352–360 courtesy of Kate O'Shaughnessy

Printed in Canada

10 9 8 7 6 5 4 3 2 1
First Edition

To Gammy,
maker of books, lover of animals,
baker of pink cookies

THURSDAY, JUNE 8

Dear Nan,

You died on a Tuesday.

Given how much you hated Tuesdays, it makes sense it would cement its place in history as the worst day ever.

Uncle Bill gave me this notebook—the special one you got for me—right after your funeral. That was about a month ago now. I like the cats and the laser beams on the cover, and I've already stuck a Jets sticker on the back. I think I've read the letter you wrote for me on the first few pages over thirty times. I even have parts of it memorized. I'm sorry it's taken me so long to write back. Maybe you weren't expecting me to write you a letter. Maybe you were hoping I would fill the pages with thoughts about the new hobby you asked me to start.

I know learning how to knit tiny sweaters for stressed and featherless rescue parrots helped distract you after Mom died. I know that's why you want me to start a hobby. (For the record, I couldn't care less about ferret-racing or palm-reading, but thanks for the suggestions.)

So much has happened that I don't have any space in

my brain for a new hobby, no matter how much you think it will help. I've been dreading writing to you about what's been going on because almost none of it is good news. But I need your advice, which is why I'm writing you this letter in the first place.

In fourth grade, when we were doing that essay project, Ms. Lee (my ELA teacher—do you remember her?) told us that using lots of interesting details and dialogue could help make our writing feel real. And if I make it real enough, maybe you'll find a way to answer me back. You even said yourself, if anyone can find a way to communicate from the afterlife, it's you. All I know is that I need to feel like that's possible right now really, really badly.

So I'm going to try to write about it exactly like it happened.

The first piece of bad news is that your funeral wasn't anything like what you wanted it to be. There were no disco balls, no open bar, no karaoke. It was so serious. So *final.* You would have hated it.

Uncle Bill made me wear black. When I told him it wasn't anything like what you would have wanted, he said, "If it'd been the funeral Ma wanted, Elton John would have performed."

I crossed my arms. "Then you should have hired Elton John."

He rolled his eyes at me. "Aw, c'mon. Not you, too."

I can't remember much from the actual funeral. Crystal and her family came, including her grandparents, two of her cousins, and her four-day-old baby brother, Charlie. Crystal sat next to me and never once let go of my hand, even though she hates how my palms always get so sweaty. What I can remember most is how swollen and puffy my face felt, and that the "visiting area" smelled like old soup and stale coffee.

Uncle Bill and I went straight back to our apartment after the funeral was over. That leads me to my second piece of bad news.

I flopped down on the couch without taking off my shoes, which I know is a bad habit. But even the idea of reaching down to slip them off seemed like too much effort. My whole body was buzzing with exhaustion. Even my brain. Most of all my brain. "I could sleep for a million years."

"Yeah. Hey, Mo, can we talk?"

Uncle Bill had his shoes on, too. He also still had on his suit jacket, even though it was a muggy, too-hot-for-May day. He kept rubbing the palm of his hand back and forth across his shaved head.

"Talk about what?" As you know, Uncle Bill always rubs his head when he's bluffing in poker and is about to lose big. The fact that he was doing it now was making me nervous. "Is everything okay?"

He stopped rubbing his head and started pacing. He'd been acting weird all day, but I'd chalked it up to funeral stuff and being sad. I waited for him to say something, but he just kept pacing.

"Uncle Bill? What is it?" I asked again. "Are you sick, too, or something?"

"No. God no. It's not that. It's . . . listen. I love you, Mo. You know that, right?"

I nodded. I wasn't entirely sure where he was going with all this, but if I close my eyes and try to remember, this is when the pit in my stomach started. The pit that hasn't gone away since Uncle Bill and I had this conversation.

"Okay." He sat down on the edge of the coffee table facing me. "So I'm Army, right? I'm a single man in the army. A single man in the army who barely scraped by with a high school diploma."

"Yeah," I said. "And?"

"I've been over this backwards, sideways, and upside down. I haven't slept in days thinking about it. But I keep coming to the same conclusion."

"What conclusion?"

"That I'm not the right person to take care of you."

"What?" I sat up, and it was like the exhaustion I'd felt only moments earlier slipped off like a blanket. My heart was pounding now. "What do you mean?"

"I've got no other skills. No other ways to make money. I made a commitment to our country, and I'm on a real path for the first time in my life. If I agreed to be your guardian, I'd have to give it up. And then what? Without the army, I wouldn't know how to take care of you. Of us."

"But what about the money Nan left you?" I asked.

"She said she'd made sure you could afford to take care of me. She told me that."

"The money won't last forever," Billy said. "But listen, we can split it. You can use your half for college. You'd be the first of us Gallaghers to go. Wouldn't that be something?"

"I already have a college fund," I told him. "Nan's friend Rose left it to me."

He rubbed his face. "Of course you already have a college fund."

My face got hot. He said it like it was a bad thing. "What's that supposed to mean?"

"Nothing. Forget I said that. The bottom line is that this is just the way it has to be."

"But there's no one else but you," I said.

"I know." He rubbed his face again. "I know that. And I'm sorry. But there are probably a lot of good families out there who would love to have a kid as great as you. Who are a lot better equipped to take care of you full-time than your ol' uncle Billy."

He smiled and pretended to knock me on the chin, but I couldn't smile back at him.

How could I? I could barely breathe.

So, that's what happened. That's the biggest, baddest news I have for you. I know you planned everything based on the fact that Uncle Bill was going to come back and live with me. Here, in New York City, in our apartment.

But I guess life doesn't always work out the way you expect it to.

I have so much more to tell you, but my fingers are cramping up and I need a break. I can't remember the last time I wrote this much by hand.

Before I go, I need you to know one more thing: My heart isn't nearly as big as you said it was in your letter. My heart isn't a mansion, or a skyscraper, or the size of New York City. It's small and hard, like a lump of coal. Okay—maybe it's not *that* small. But I do know for a fact it's only the size of our apartment. The apartment that fit you and me and our lives perfectly, like a hug. The apartment I'll probably have to move out of soon and will never see again.

This is why I can't make any promises about starting a new hobby. I wouldn't even know where to begin. *How* to begin.

Unless my hobby could be inventing a time machine, so I could travel into the past to live with you. Before all this. Would that work?

Love,
Mo

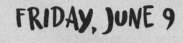

FRIDAY, JUNE 9

Dear Nan,

Okay, I rested and iced my hand with an old bag of peas I found shoved in the back of the freezer. I'm ready to tell you the rest.

A few days after that terrible conversation, Uncle Bill and I went to our first meeting. Maybe he thought it would be easy to hand me over to the city, but apparently it's not easy at all. It's a whole big process.

I know I should try to be positive, but it was awful. Everything about it was awful. The front door of the building was made of glass, and it was cracked, like someone had swung a baseball bat at it. It was all taped up, in multiple neat layers, like a different someone had tried to fix it as carefully as possible. But the tape looked worn and old, like it'd been put up a long time ago.

The meeting itself was awful, too. I met my caseworker for the first time. His name is Rowan. He seems nice enough, but he was distracted, and his clothes were wrinkled and oversized. His pants were too big and it looked like he slept in his shirt. And he seemed tired, like I was one of a hundred kids he'd had to meet with that day. I've been to one other meeting with him since that first one, and he was all wrinkled and tired again. You would have nicknamed him Rumpled Rowan and made it funny.

But it's a whole mess, because apparently you were never listed as my official guardian. I didn't know that. Did you know that? They asked a lot of questions about other people in my life, relatives, and all that. I guess they want to see if they can get me a place to stay with someone I know before they drop me in with strangers.

"My mom died when I was little. That's why I live—lived—with my grandma in the first place," I explained.

Rumpled Rowan tapped a pen against a stack of paper on the table in front of him. "Well, then, obviously it can't be your mom, because . . ." He trailed off, motioning at me with his hands, like he was trying to point at the words I'd just said. "So what about your father? When was the last time you had contact with him?"

I'm starting to get the feeling that people don't like to say the word "died," do they? Like they think it might be contagious or something. News flash! I wanted to tell him. It is contagious. It's the most contagious thing in the world. But instead I only shook my head and said, "No. It can't be my father, either."

"Why not?"

I wasn't sure what to say. That I hadn't seen him since I was five? That I can barely remember his last visit? What I

8

can remember is him taking me out, right after Christmas, for a hot dog that he put way too much mustard on. I remember him stealing twenty dollars from your purse when he dropped me back off, and the Christmas card that he signed "Johnny" instead of "Dad."

"I haven't seen or talked to him in a really long time," I finally said.

Rumpled Rowan made a note. "Okay. Even though he's not on your birth certificate, we still have to try to find him."

"I wouldn't want that," I said quickly. "To stay with him, I mean. Even if you did find him."

Rumpled Rowan made another note. "Okay. Good to know. Is there anyone else you feel a connection to? A favorite neighbor? A friend of your grandma's?"

First I thought about your poker-night friends. They were always nice to me, but no offense, the idea of asking to go *live* with any of them makes me want to crawl out of my skin.

I can't stay with your online pen pals. Roger, for obvious reasons. (I doubt they'd let a kid move into a maximum-security prison, no matter how innocent you think Roger is.) And not grandDAMN09496, either, mainly because I don't know her real name or where she lives. Or if she's even a she.

Then I thought again about Rose. With her cats and her six-floor brownstone and all her fancy furniture. Her rare-beetle collection and her booming laugh that seemed too big to be coming from her frail body. I wish it could have been her.

"My grandma's best friend in the city was an older lady," I finally said. "She left me money for college. But she's gone, too."

"Okay. Don't worry," he told me. "We'll figure something out."

Everyone at Wallace has been really nice, and they haven't made me come back to school after . . . after everything. I have some take-home work, but not much. I'm glad I don't have to face anyone. I'm not sure I could. Even Crystal. I haven't told her about any of this yet. She calls me every single day to check on me, and usually texts throughout school even though she's not supposed to. And every day, I almost blurt it out. There's only another week left of classes before summer starts, and I know my chance to tell her while she's still here is slipping away, because she leaves for China the day after school ends. She's been looking forward to this trip to see some of her second cousins for three years, ever since COVID ruined and rescheduled it again and again.

And now that they can finally go, without complications, I don't want to be the reason it's ruined *again*. Because I know if I tell her, she'll feel bad and sad for me while she's away. I can't let my bad news be a rain cloud over her summer.

And to be honest, I don't want to say the words out

loud. *Foster care.* Because if I say them out loud, it'll make it real.

Wish me luck with all of this. And maybe wish that Uncle Billy starts feeling overwhelmed enough to call this whole thing off. Half the time, I hear him muttering about forms and certificates and files he's trying to find in your room. Maybe he'll get so annoyed and fed up that he'll throw up his hands and say, "You know what, forget it, I'll stay."

Love,
Mo

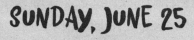

SUNDAY, JUNE 25

Dear Nan,

Well, it happened.

Uncle Billy did get fed up with all the meetings and court dates and the waiting we've had to do. Except it didn't end with him telling me he was going to stay.

Instead, he told me the city could take it from here.

"It's ridiculous," he complained as he packed up his stuff. "It's, like, a fifteen-thousand-step process. What will they want next, a vial of my blood? An organ donation? I have to get back. I've already requested three extensions."

I could tell Rumpled Rowan was annoyed with him, or maybe mad, because at the meeting where Billy told him this, he kept sighing and shaking his head. He said they hadn't found the perfect placement for me yet, and he asked Billy to do his part. But Billy wouldn't budge.

"I'm going to get discharged if I don't get back as soon as possible," he said. "I'm sorry. It is what it is."

Packing was the worst part. It was like playing the game "What would you take to a desert island?" but real, and ten times more depressing. I wanted your paper-mache parrot sculpture, your pink robe with the patched-up elbows, your phone case with the fake diamonds I made for you in second grade. I wanted your chipped "What happens in Vegas stays in Vegas" coffee mug with the lipstick stain. I wanted everything. But apparently, it doesn't work that way. I was only able to keep what fit into my worn-out pink duffel bag, plus a big black trash bag of clothes, because Billy had already thrown out your suitcase. I didn't cry until Billy took our all-year Christmas tree down. I cried so much I'm amazed I didn't wrinkle up into an old prune.

The day before we said goodbye, Billy handed me his wallet. "Here. This is for you."

It's the wallet he's had forever, the one you gave him. I flipped it open. It was empty. "I don't understand."

"It's my lucky wallet," he said. "It's made of football leather. From an actual Jets football. Ma gave it to me when I was sixteen. I want you to have it."

I ran my fingers over its pebbly leather. I don't have anything to put inside of it, but I guess it's nice he gave it to me. He must love this wallet if he's kept it since he was sixteen. Maybe it's his way of trying to show me that he cares about me. Or at least I hope it is.

Now I'm writing to you from my first "placement." It's an apartment, about ten blocks north from ours. The woman's name is Ms. Schirle. There's one other kid who's like me, Pedro, but he hasn't said a single word to me yet. He's six. And then there's Ms. Schirle's actual son, Kyle, who's six months older than me. They're okay, I guess. I only moved here about a week ago, two days after school ended. Even though I wasn't there for the last day, it still felt like fifth grade ended and catapulted me into a new dimension. Like that book about the girl whose parents had buttons for eyes. Except for me, there's no way back into the right world.

For the past few days, I've been trying to work up the courage to send Crystal a text. Because I need to tell her, don't I? She's my best friend. I wrote out the message explaining it all to her at least ten times. But then this morning, when I finally pressed send, the text wouldn't go through. Then I noticed I didn't have any bars of service. I guess the cell phone bill didn't get passed from your name to Uncle Bill's. I think it's fate telling me I was right to not ruin Crystal's trip.

I'll write more soon.

Love,
Mo

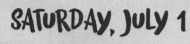

SATURDAY, JULY 1

Dear Nan,

I've never believed in ghosts or angels. Not until this morning. But I'm starting to suspect if anyone could make the impossible happen, it'd be you.

It happened right after another meeting I had to go to. Ms. Schirle brought me to a new building, and a woman met me in the waiting area and introduced herself as Moira. She said she was my new caseworker.

"What happened to Rumpl—I mean, to Rowan?" I asked.

"He was only assigned to the first sixty days of your case," she said. "Which has been transferred to my agency. So now you got me."

Moira has pale white skin with tons of freckles, big red curls, and a silver nose ring. She was also wearing a pair of ratty Converse sneakers, so I considered calling her Old Shoes in my head. And I did, at first. But as the meeting went on, I changed my mind. The way she listened, and looked right at me, made me feel . . . I don't know how to describe it. Like she actually wanted to hear what I had to

15

say. I don't think Old Shoes is a nice enough nickname for someone who makes you feel that way.

There were a few other adults who I was introduced to during the meeting. One of them is apparently my representative for . . . something? I can't remember. It's hard to keep straight. (If there's one thing I'm learning about being in foster care, it's that there are a *lot* of meetings. And strangers I have to talk to. And people who "represent you" for different stuff that I don't fully understand.) They asked if I was interested in therapy, and my answer was obviously a big fat no.

"Gallagher girls don't need therapy," I told them, repeating what you'd said to one of your hospice nurses. "We work things out ourselves."

"Okay," Moira said. "But I want you to know that's a service we provide."

Moira asked a lot of the same questions that Rowan did. Even though I'd been over it all with Rowan, and I was now staying with Ms. Schirle, she kept going on about whether there was anyone I liked well enough to see if I could live with them. Really, anyone.

"They can be friends of your grandma's, or friends of yours," she said.

For a second, I let myself think about Crystal's family. Because that would be amazing. A permanent sleepover. Crystal wouldn't just be my best friend; she'd basically be my sister.

But if I'm being honest with myself, I know that would never work. It's already jam-packed at her house, especially now with her cousin, and, of course, baby Charlie. Both of her parents had bags under their eyes at your funeral because of Charlie. How could I ask them to take care of me, too?

The whole meeting was making me itchy and sad, and I wanted it over with. So I asked to go to the bathroom, hoping it would end it. And it did.

"Sure," Moira said. "It's right down the hall. This is probably a good time to wrap things up for now anyway."

When I got there, someone was using it, and they were taking a long time. So I sat on the floor outside to wait my turn.

The hallway was quiet and empty. Too quiet and too empty. Whenever I'm alone is when I miss you the most. Sitting there in the quiet, I would have even listened to that boring NPR radio station you like and actually paid attention—that's how much I needed to be distracted. So I looked around. Across from where I sat, there was a low bookshelf. I tilted my head sideways so I could read the spines. They were mostly picture books, the hard-paged ones meant for babies. But there was one that didn't look like the rest of them. It looked like—I leaned forward and squinted—a cookbook.

That's when the spooky thing happened. No—the amazing thing.

Because as I stared at it, it fell out of the bookshelf. *Plonk!* It was like a ghost had touched it. Like *your* ghost had touched it.

In fact: make the lights flicker three times if you can read what I'm writing. I'll wait.

Okay. I put my pen down and waited a few minutes, but no lights flickered. Still, I think it was you. If you are a ghost, I hope that when you're not keeping an eye on me, you're busy haunting the people at your health insurance company who kept telling you "No, we don't cover that," like you always promised them you would.

After the book fell, I picked it up. Of course I did. You think I'd ignore a sign from you, Ghost Nan? No way.

On the cover it said *Georgie's Family Cookbook*. It didn't look like something you could buy in a bookstore. It looked homemade. I flipped through it. Along with recipes, there were tons of pictures of a family glued to the pages. Gathered around picnic tables at Rockaway Beach, presenting a big Thanksgiving turkey in a cramped kitchen, eating off paper plates on the stoop of an apartment building. So many smiling faces.

There was one recipe that caught my attention more than all the rest. It was for something called Grammy's Egg-Lemon Soup. It wasn't the ingredients I was interested in, but the story.

Here's what Georgie wrote:

> This is my favorite recipe of my grandmother's. Whenever one of her grandchildren was sick, Grammy would make a big pot of her egg-lemon soup. She'd spent time in Greece as a

girl, and told us the recipe was inspired by a Greek soup called avgolemono. She'd bring us a steaming bowl, and the room would fill with the bright smell of lemons and salty chicken broth. She'd sit on the edge of our bed and press a wrinkled hand to our cheek while we had our soup, and she'd tell us stories about her childhood.

It's such a simple recipe, but somehow it always felt so special. We were allowed to drink the soup, for one. No spoons when you're sick. And it was the only time we were ever allowed to eat in bed. I used to pretend to be sick so Grammy would come over with a pot of soup, just for me.

Reading what Georgie had written, I imagined myself in my bed, in our apartment, my old Jets comforter tucked snugly around me, the twinkle of the Christmas tree lights bouncing off my bedroom doorway. Even though I've never tasted it, I swear I could almost smell the aroma of Grammy's soup in the air.

But it wasn't her hand I imagined on my cheek. It was yours.

Right then, I knew I had to make it.

And to make it, I needed the book. It looked dusty and forgotten, like no one had touched it in years. So after I used the bathroom, I slipped it into the band of my shorts and covered it with my T-shirt. I know I shouldn't have, that it was wrong to take it, but I'll put it back exactly where I found it when I'm done with it. I promise.

I'm going to copy down the recipe on the next page so you can see it, too.

Don't get excited, because I'm not saying that cooking's going to become the hobby you want me to have. I don't think we turned the oven on once in my whole life, did we? In fact, when Uncle Bill and I were moving out, I found all your winter scarves in there.

But I want to make this soup. So I'll start there, and that'll have to be enough.

I'll let you know how it goes. Ms. Schirle hasn't seemed very excited about the idea of me cooking. But I'm wearing her down, bit by bit. Just like you taught me.

I love you, Nan. Go, Jets.
Mo

GRAMMY'S EGG-LEMON SOUP
Makes one large bowl for one special grandchild

3 cups chicken broth
1 ½ tblsp. lemon juice
1 t. lemon zest
2 eggs
Salt and pepper to taste
⅓ cup rice

Cook rice for 20 minutes in simmering broth, covered, until tender, then add juice and zest. In medium bowl, beat eggs well. Slowly whisk a few spoonfuls of hot broth into the egg mixture. Gradually add eggs to the pot and heat through on a low flame, stirring constantly and being careful not to let the eggs curdle. Season to taste and serve.

*

Soup-maker beware: the eggs in this recipe will curdle if you aren't very careful! Grammy could make this soup without even looking at the pot, but it took me a number of tries to get it right. Start with a tablespoon of hot broth mixed into the beaten eggs and continue adding tablespoon after tablespoon. I probably add about a cup's worth of tablespoons before I dare mix the eggs into the soup. Only then does it come together smoothly. —Georgie

SUNDAY, JULY 9

Dear Nan,

I'm happy to report I was *finally* able to make Grammy's Egg-Lemon Soup.

Ms. Schirle told me I could only use the stove if she was there to supervise me, but whenever I asked, she was always busy.

Finally, after I asked for what must have been the fiftieth time, she threw up her hands and said, "For god's sake, Maureen! You can do it yourself. Just be careful with the stove top."

That's another thing about Ms. Schirle. She keeps forgetting to call me Mo. I've told her again and again that I don't like to be called Maureen, but that's pretty much all she calls me. Maybe she's doing it on purpose. I don't know.

But back to the soup. It was like I sprinkled magic in with the ingredients, because everything came out perfectly. (I know. I was surprised, too.)

The sharp smell of the lemon juice and the warm, salty steam of the rice cooking in chicken broth filled the whole apartment. It was so comforting. That's the word I thought of as I ate it. So warm and wonderful. I've had it for every meal since I made it, even breakfast, steaming hot. And it's summer—you know how I only ever want to eat Popsicles and frozen grapes in the summer.

I think it turned out so well because I followed Georgie's advice, and I read a bunch of instructions online about making soup, just to make sure I would do everything right.

Since then, I've been on a tear. I've been cooking so much I haven't had time to write.

I've made five recipes from Georgie's cookbook. Most of them have little stories about how and why the recipes were favorites of her family's. One of them—a vegetarian curry stew—didn't turn out so well. It got all lumpy and the sauce separated. That's a cooking word I read about on the internet, and it describes when the liquid part and the solid part of a sauce aren't mixed together anymore. Like curdled milk, sort of. But you know what? I still feel like I learned something (which is: don't boil coconut milk for too long. It might separate).

And okay, you were right. With every recipe I make, I feel like I've finished a project and given my brain a break from only thinking about how much I miss you.

Maybe cooking *can* be the hobby you said I needed.

Pedro's been eating everything I make. He sits at the small table in the corner and scoops whatever I make into his mouth with a serious expression on his face. He never says whether he likes it or not, even when I ask. He just gets up, puts his dish in the sink, and walks away.

Kyle is a different story. He complains about the smells and how hot I'm making the apartment by turning the oven on. He says everything I make "looks gross," so he won't try it. Not a single small bite.

When I moved in, I took his bedroom, since it's recommended that girls and boys don't share rooms. Apparently, Ms. Schirle had wanted to foster another boy, so they could put him in with Pedro. Instead, they got me. The room Pedro's in was already set up for sharing, with bunk beds and everything, so that's why Kyle had to move out of his room, instead of Pedro moving in with him. Kyle's made it clear that he's not happy about the situation.

"Guess what?" I asked him, after he'd come in to complain about it for the tenth time that hour. "I'm not happy about it, either. It smells like a dirty hamster cage in here."

And you know what he did a couple nights later? He snuck in and put my hand in a bowl of warm water while I slept. I woke up right as I started to pee.

I didn't wake up Ms. Schirle, because I knew she'd be upset. Not with Kyle—but with me. Because who wants to deal with an eleven-year-old bed wetter? (But to be extra clear, it was NOT—MY—FAULT.) I washed my pajama pants in the bathroom sink and slept in my jeans, my hands tucked carefully under my pillow.

Nan, I've been wondering—

Oh no—I have to go. Kyle just got home from the YMCA, and I don't want him to see my journal. I'm keeping it a secret. I want it to be just for me.

(And for you, too. Obviously.)

Love,
Mo

SUNDAY, JULY 9
(LATER)

Dear Nan,

Everyone's asleep, except for me. I'm sitting in the bath-tub, with the bathroom door locked. I realized right as I was falling asleep I didn't get to say what I was wondering about earlier, in my last letter. I know how much you hate cliff-hangers, so I forced myself out of bed.

Here's what I was wondering: do *we* have any family recipes?

Strawberry jelly and Marshmallow Fluff sandwiches don't count. Neither do SpaghettiOs, even if you heat them on the stove instead of in the microwave. Or Chips Ahoy dunked in heavy cream. A family recipe has history. Lots of steps and special tips, and a story about when and why it became important.

I wish I'd known I liked to cook when you were still around. You would have probably made a joke about it, something about me finally being useful for once, and then you would have spent the rest of the day trying to figure out where else we could cram your winter scarves.

But did you have any recipes? Maybe one your mom

or dad used to make? Or your grandma? Or anything you used to make for Mom or Billy, when they were little?

I wish I'd thought to ask before. When I still had time with you. I'd do anything to have a family recipe of my own, of *our* own, to hang on to. Even if it was a simple one. Even if it was just one.

You would have liked the strawberry cheesecake cups I made this afternoon. Other than strawberries, it also had cream cheese, graham crackers, vanilla, and lots of sugar in it. A boatload of sugar. Serious Pedro almost smiled after eating one. Or at least, he wanted to. I could tell.

Anyway, it's getting late. I should go.

I love you,
Mo

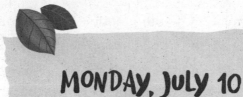

MONDAY, JULY 10

Dear Nan,

I miss you.

Those are the only words inside my brain today.

I miss your witch's cackle of a laugh. Your long hugs with your big, soft arms. The way you threw popcorn kernels at the TV during a Jets game. I even miss your stinky feet and your weird yellow toenails (sorry) and your bellowing snores.

I just miss you.

I miss you, I miss you, I miss you.

Mo

WEDNESDAY, JULY 12

Dear Nan,

Uncle Bill and I talked over video chat yesterday. It was the first time we've talked since he left.

Ms. Schirle let me take the shared laptop into the bedroom so we could talk in private, which was nice of her. Usually she only lets us use the laptop in the living area so no one ends up hogging it too much.

For the first five minutes, I'm pretty sure he asked, "How are you? Are they treating you good?" like, ten times. What was even more annoying was when he started saying stuff like "Wow, cool bed! Is that your bed?" And, "Wow, what a big room! Do you have it all to yourself?" It felt like I could have shown him a dead earthworm and he'd say, "Wow, what a cool pet!"

"None of this is mine," I finally snapped. "You made me get rid of everything that's mine."

The look on his face changed, and I felt bad then, because what if it makes him not want to talk to me at all? I promised myself I wouldn't snap at him again.

He cleared his throat. "So, what's up? Your email made

it sound like there was something you wanted to talk about."

"Yeah," I said. Then I asked *him* about a family recipe, too.

"No," he said. "I can't remember Ma ever cooking. Not even when I was little."

So it was just as I feared.

"What about other family?" I asked. "Cousins? Your aunts or uncles? Anyone?"

We'd already been through this during some of the meetings, but I hoped that maybe asking him again—and specifically about a recipe—might jiggle something loose for him.

Uncle Bill wrinkled up his face as he thought. Then he sighed. "Sorry, kid. Not that I know of. Like we've talked about, I don't even know how much 'family' is left. Ma didn't really keep in touch with them."

"So you don't have anything?" I asked. "Not a single family recipe?"

I'm embarrassed to admit it, but my voice got all shivery and full like I was about to cry. Over a stupid recipe.

Uncle Bill looked panicked for a second before he said, "You know, I have one recipe I could share with you. It's for something called ranger pudding. There's a funny story to go along with it. If you want."

I did want. I wanted it so bad.

"What's the story?" I asked, leaning toward the screen.

"Well, it was my buddy's birthday," Billy said. "And

30

when you're on active duty, you get something called MREs, which stands for Meals, Ready-to-Eat. They're terrible. Worse than Ma's 'cooking,'" he said, using air quotes. "That I can promise you."

He grinned, and I grinned back at him. It felt good to talk about you with him.

"Anyway, in one of the MREs there's this—"

Someone over his shoulder called something to him, and Billy looked away from the screen. I couldn't hear what the person said. When Billy turned back to the camera, he said, "Listen, Mo, I gotta go."

"Can you tell me the rest of the story first?" I asked. "Please?"

"I'm sorry. I don't have time."

"Then can we talk again soon?" I asked.

"Yeah, maybe," Billy said. "We can try."

"Don't forget to email the recipe," I said. "And the story, too. Will you send it later today? Or tomorrow?"

"I'll try, okay?" Uncle Billy said. "Okay. See you, Mo."

I sat at the computer for a minute after he logged off. I wished he'd had time to tell me the rest of the story about the ranger pudding. I wished talking to him had made me feel better instead of worse.

Later, in bed, I was feeling even crummier, and I couldn't figure out why. Our talk hadn't even gone all that bad. It had actually been kind of nice. But no matter how much I tossed and turned, I couldn't fall asleep, so I went to get myself a glass of water. And I don't know why I did it, but sitting there, in the dark kitchen, I slowly pushed the glass off the table.

When it hit the floor, it didn't shatter into a million pieces, like part of me was hoping it would. It only clonked down with a soft *thunk* and spilled water everywhere. I immediately felt stupid, so I mopped up the water with paper towels and put the glass in the dishwasher.

But when I got back into bed, I couldn't help wondering . . . did the glass have invisible cracks now, even though it looked okay? Would Ms. Schirle pull it out of the dishwasher, and right then it would decide it had gone through too much, and shatter in her hands? Or would it break in serious little Pedro's hands and hurt him?

I couldn't stop worrying about it, so I crept back into the kitchen, took the glass from the dishwasher, and slipped it deep into the trash.

I hope you don't think something's wrong with me. It was just a weird moment.

> I love you. I miss you.
> Mo

MONDAY, JULY 17

Dear Nan,

Billy didn't end up sending me the recipe or the story for his ranger pudding, even though I emailed to remind him. I really wanted to try it, though, so I looked up a recipe online. If you can even call it a recipe.

Here's what the instructions said:

"To a small bowl, add 1 hot cocoa packet, 1 coffee creamer packet, 1 sugar packet, and 2 single-serving packets of Nescafé instant powder. Mix together with water to make a thick paste. Whip well and serve."

And wow, was it gross. No—gross isn't enough. It was stupendously horrendous. It tasted like sandy, sweet mud. My guess is when you're deployed, you don't have a lot of options. Maybe Billy's recipe was better than the one I found. For his sake, I hope it was.

In non-cooking-related news, Kyle and I are in a war of our own.

As you know, I'm not one to let things slide without retaliation—I'm your granddaughter, after all. So in response to the warm water trick, I thought I would leave him a little gift, tucked under his covers. All I needed was black craft paper, scissors, and a lot of patience. I spent hours making them look as realistic as possible. I made about twenty of them.

I hung around his and Pedro's door at bedtime to watch. Kyle kept telling me to leave, but I stayed put. And it was worth it. When he flung back his covers, all the color drained from his face.

I can't believe how realistic my little paper spiders looked. It took everything inside of me not to laugh. But I didn't, because I wanted to savor the moment.

He crashed backward, tripping on a bin of Legos, and they went flying everywhere.

Finally, I did laugh.

I stopped when Ms. Schirle came running in. She was already in her pajamas. "What's going on? What's wrong?"

From the far corner of the room, Kyle pointed at his bed. His face was even paler. He looked scared enough that I started to feel kind of bad. "Spiders. In my bed."

Ms. Schirle marched over and threw back the rest of his covers with a fearlessness I almost admired. Then she reached down and picked one of the paper spiders up.

She turned around and dangled it at me like an accusation. "Was this you?"

"They're not real," I said quickly.

Even so, I lost TV and computer privileges for the week, because apparently Kyle is really afraid of spiders.

I even apologized to him, and I meant it. I didn't know he was that scared of spiders! But me getting punished *and* being sorry wasn't enough for Kyle, because now he's started putting my hand in warm water every single night.

Ms. Schirle does the same thing every time I wake up with wet sheets. She takes a deep breath and closes her eyes and says, "It's okay. It's not your fault. But if this keeps happening, you'll have to start doing your own laundry. Either that, or you'll have to start wearing a pull-up to bed."

"I do *not* need a pull-up," I told her. "And this isn't my fault! Kyle's doing it!"

Now it was Kyle's turn to watch from the doorway. He crossed his arms and gave me the smuggest look. "I haven't done anything. You're just a bed wetter."

"Kyle, that's enough" was all Ms. Schirle said. That's it. He didn't even get in the tiniest bit of trouble.

I can't figure out how he's doing it, because before I fall asleep I tuck my hands under my pillow and they're still like that when I wake up. I'll have to think of a new way to get him back.

Last night I stayed up late, to try to catch Kyle in the act. I waited up a long time, but he still got me. He must have come in minutes after I fell asleep. Now I'm so tired I can barely keep my eyes open to write this. It's only two o'clock in the afternoon but I bet I could fall asleep right now and not wake up until tomorrow. Thankfully, I'm alone in the apartment, so at least I have a few hours of peace and quiet. Today Pedro and Kyle are at the dentist. Ms. Schirle had the appointments booked before I came here. I hope Kyle has fifty cavities.

Anyway, I'm cooking right now, too. I'm baking some bread. I don't think it's going to turn out right, though, because the dough was still hard and lumpy when I put it in the oven. It's because I don't have computer rights for the next week. Otherwise, I would have been able to do more research online about kneading and baking bread.

I think

TUESDAY, JULY 18

Dear Nan,

Something terrible happened yesterday.

Did you notice I trailed off in the middle of my last letter? That I didn't say goodbye, or finish my last sentence? It's because I fell asleep while I was writing to you. Deeply asleep.

The only thing that woke me up was the shriek of the smoke alarm.

When I got to the kitchen, it was filled with clouds of black smoke coming from the oven. The door of the oven was so hot I couldn't even touch it to open it. There was one window in the kitchen, but it had this lock on top of it I didn't know how to unlatch. Standing there, I didn't know whether to pour water on the oven, or call someone, or try to find a fire extinguisher somewhere in the apartment.

That's when I got really afraid. I was alone, and I didn't know what to do.

So when the front door opened a few minutes later, and I saw Ms. Schirle, I wanted to rush over and hug her.

But I could tell I was the last person on earth she wanted to hug. I could see it on her face, by the way her eyes went wide and her eyebrows wrinkled.

"Are you okay?" she said. "What happened? Everyone go to the hallway!"

There weren't any flames when she opened the oven, only thick smoke, but the firefighters still came. When they took my bread out of the oven, it looked like a shriveled black brick. Now the whole apartment smells like badly burned popcorn.

Ms. Schirle said this was exactly why I wasn't supposed to cook when an adult wasn't home. Kyle wanted to sleep "in his own room" after the scare, so Ms. Schirle asked me if that was okay. So tonight I'm sleeping on the couch.

That's where I am right now, writing to you. On the lumpy couch with a small fleece blanket that doesn't cover me all the way, and scratchy couch pillows. Ms. Schirle didn't let me have any water after six so I wouldn't wet the couch, even though it's Kyle she should be worried about on that front, not me. I'm thirsty and uncomfortable. But the thing is, I know I deserve it.

I promise this will be the last time I'll cook or bake without an adult home. I never want something like this to happen ever again.

Thanks for watching over me,
Mo

THURSDAY, JULY 20

Dear Nan,

So it looks like I'm moving. Again.

The day after the oven disaster, Ms. Schirle sat me down on the couch. "I'm not sure things are working out so well. I think we can both agree that this isn't an ideal placement for you. For either of us."

Much to my embarrassment, my chin got wobbly and my eyes stung. I'm not all that happy here, so why was I about to cry? Probably because not being wanted—even by someone you don't click with all that much—is the worst feeling in the world.

"Plus," she went on, "after I talked to the agency, they let me know that they'd been working on finding you a more permanent placement, and they might have found a better fit for you. But they want you to meet them first to see how you all get along."

That was a shock to me. It still is. I'm going to that meeting tomorrow. What if it goes horribly? Will I have to stay here? Will I have to go somewhere else?

I wish my phone was still working. I wish I could video-call Crystal, see her face, and tell her everything. Since I lost computer privileges, I can't see if she's been emailing me. I've considered waking up to use the computer in the middle of the night to draft her an email, but I haven't done it yet.

Because what would I even say? "Hi, it's me, your long-lost best friend, my life is totally turned upside down and I don't know what's going to happen to me"? She'll campaign for me to move in with her. I know she will. And this is what worries me: what if she does ask, and her parents say no? How could I ever show my face at their house again? I couldn't. And I can't lose Crystal. I miss her, though. So much. But not as much as I miss you.

Mo

FRIDAY, JULY 21

Dear Nan,

I just got back from that meeting I told you about. It was . . . a lot. I'll start at the beginning.

There was another kid in the waiting area when I got there. It's not that there haven't been other kids there before my meetings—there have been—but usually we just ignore each other. I could tell he was watching me as I sat down, and he kept watching as an adult I'd never met told me to wait right there, that someone would be there to get me shortly.

He got up and slid into the seat next to mine. "You new?"

"New?" I asked.

"New to the system," he said. "You've got that look. That nervous look."

"Oh. Yeah. I guess so," I said.

"Yep." He nodded. "It sucks. I'm Ricky, by the way. Ricky Sanchez."

"My name's Mo."

He didn't say anything after that, so we just kind of sat

there in silence. I had a million questions to ask him, but I wasn't sure if any of them were okay to ask someone you just met.

"What?" he said.

I guess I'd been glancing at him a lot. "How many— how many places have you stayed?"

"Me?" He squinted, and held out his fingers like he was counting. "Five. No, six."

"*Six?*" I repeated. I couldn't imagine it. Trying to settle in at Ms. Schirle's was hard enough. Doing it six times seemed impossible.

"Yeah. The lady I'm with now is all right. Finally. I'm one of three kids with her. One thing I don't like are her two cats. They stink. But it beats the other places I've been."

"Were the other ones . . . bad?"

"Yeah, I'd say so," he said, rolling up his sleeve. On his arm there were two round scars, like he'd been burned by something. "At least she doesn't smoke."

In that moment, I was filled with dread for what was to come. Why hadn't I tried to be better? Ms. Schirle wasn't even mean. She changed my sheets and told Kyle to leave me alone.

That's when a young white couple holding hands walked by us. They both looked like the kind of people you'd see in a magazine, with silky-looking clothes and shiny hair. They seemed totally out of place.

I glanced at Ricky and he widened his eyes at me with a smirk, like he was thinking the exact same thing as me. "Must be donors."

A few minutes later, Moira came to get me, wearing her same old dirty Converse sneakers. "Ready, hon? Your prospectives are here."

Next to me, Ricky snorted. "You gotta be kidding me."

When I glanced at him, he was staring at the floor. "Of course the little white girl gets the rich white family. Of course. Whatever. Have a nice life."

I didn't know what to say. I waved bye before I got up to follow Moira, but he didn't wave back.

"You feeling okay?" she asked as we walked together.

I shook my head no.

"I know. None of this is easy. But, listen. Before we go in . . . it's really looking like your uncle won't be available to you for permanency. We've tried working with him, but—"

"I know that," I said quickly. "You don't have to explain it to me again."

"Right. Of course. Anyway, hopefully this is going to be a permanent placement for you. They've been approved as pre-adoptive foster parents. We're still trying to find more information about your dad or other relatives, but in the meantime, this is a step in the right direction, okay?"

"Okay," I said. I wasn't sure what any of that meant.

More than anything, I was buzzing with nerves as we stepped into the little room.

The couple was waiting at a little conference table, and they stood up when I entered. They had big, nervous smiles, and introduced themselves as June and Tate Townsend. June—she told me to use her first name because anything else would be way too formal—couldn't stop wringing her hands or twisting the wedding ring around on her finger.

"Mo," Moira prodded. "Say hello. Introduce yourself."

"Hi" was all I could manage.

"So you like to be called Mo?" Tate asked. His smile was less nervous than June's. Both of them had extremely white teeth. "Not Maureen?"

I nodded.

"Mo," June repeated. "I love it. What a great nickname."

We talked a little bit more. I was worried I was saying the wrong things, so I kept stopping halfway through my sentences. I could barely pay attention to what they were telling me about themselves. They could have said they were both astronauts or something. All I could think about was Ricky's arm, and why it was me in this meeting instead of him.

It didn't help that a couple more adults joined the meeting at various points, apologizing for being late, and explaining to the Townsends—and me too, since I didn't know, either—who they were and why they were there.

Anyway. I haven't heard from Moira today, so who knows what's going to happen. Ms. Schirle has asked me not to cook after the oven incident, so I don't even have *that* to take my mind off things.

Miss you,
Mo

SUNDAY, JULY 23

Dear Nan,

Well, I did end up hearing back from Moira. Apparently, the Townsends must have liked me okay enough, because they're officially going to be my next placement. Today is moving day.

Moira's out in the living room settling some things with Ms. Schirle before we leave. Any second, Moira could knock on the door, telling me it's time to go, and then I'll probably never see Kyle, Pedro, or Ms. Schirle again. It's a strange thought.

But that's not the only thing I wanted to tell you about.

Moira came early to help me pack, since this is my first time switching placements.

I had some of my stuff spread out on the bed. My phone, which doesn't even work anymore. My school backpack, some clothes, a couple school uniforms, and a few other things I was able to hold on to. It looked like I was packing for a trip, not my whole life.

Moira was helping me get my clothes out from the

dresser when she stopped and pointed. "Mo. Do you want to explain why you have my colleague's family cookbook hidden in your sock drawer?"

Georgie's Family Cookbook. I'd totally forgotten I'd hidden it in there.

Nan, you know what a bad liar I am (at least when I'm not playing poker). My face got hot, and then, I'm sure, so red it was almost purple. A million lies ran through my head, but of course the one thing that came out was the truth.

"I took it from the bookshelf outside of the bathroom."

"Mo." Moira sighed and rubbed her forehead. "This has to go back. Today. She's been looking all over for this."

"It was just on the shelf, forgotten," I said defensively.

"It was not forgotten. And you don't steal. Period. Understand?"

I was angrier with myself than with Moira. Because she was right—I shouldn't have taken it. I stared at the floor and nodded. "Sorry. I was just—it's what I was using to teach myself to cook."

I could feel Moira softening. "You know . . . I have cookbooks you could borrow."

"It's not that. It's the kind of recipes it has." I sat down on the edge of the bed, and Moira waited for me to go on. "They're all her family recipes. They have stories and pictures and stuff."

I didn't mean to sound sappy or sad about it, but I did.

Like . . . I don't even know Georgie. So why was I so sad about having to give back her cookbook? You would have honked my nose and told me to cheer up.

Moira was quiet for a long moment. I could almost see the gears turning in her brain. Then she dug around in her purse until she found her cell phone and said, "Keep packing. I'll be right back."

Then she let herself into the hallway and made a phone call. I couldn't hear what she was saying or who she was talking to. I wanted to eavesdrop, but I didn't. The last thing I need is for her to think I'm a thief *and* a snoop.

When she came back into the room, she had a triumphant look on her face. "You'll never believe it." She brandished a small pad of paper in the air. "But I got my stepdad's mac and cheese recipe. I finally got it. Only took me twenty years to squeeze it out of him. Ha!"

"What?" I was confused. "What about mac and cheese?"

"You said you wanted family recipes, right? Well, this"— she tapped the little notebook—"is about as family as it gets. This is my stepdad's most sacred, most secret, most beloved recipe. We all call it Jim's Ten-Thousand-Dollar Mac and Cheese."

"Ten-thousand-dollar?" I repeated.

Moira nodded. "Peanut butter sandwiches and mac and cheese were the only two things my brother would eat between the ages of four and ten. When I say only, I mean only. The doctor had to put him on nutritional supplements. Dad had so much time to practice it over the years, to perfect it, that he entered it into a competition and won ten thousand dollars." She ripped the top page off the pad and handed it to me. "And here it is. He said it's for you and you alone—but only if you promise to never show it to anyone. Ever. *Especially* the secret ingredient."

I held the piece of paper in my hands like it was a fragile baby bird. Like it was made of spun-sugar gold.

"I promise," I told her.

I'm not even going to show you the recipe, because I promised I wouldn't show *anyone*, not even an angel or a ghost, but I did cut out Jim's instructions for making good mac and cheese, because I thought it would be okay to share that.

Hopefully, the Townsends will let me cook, because I want to make Jim's mac and cheese as soon as possible. Today. This minute.

Oh—Moira just knocked. I guess it's time to go.

I'm so nervous my stomach hurts.

If you have any special good-luck angel (or ghost) powder you can sprinkle on me, now's the time.

Love,
Mo

TOP-SECRET RECIPE NEVER TO BE SHARED
Jim's Ten-Thousand-Dollar Mac and Cheese

Notes from Jim:

- Buy the cheese in blocks and shred it yourself. Get that pre-shredded garbage out of here.
- Do <u>NOT</u> put bread crumbs, cut-up hot dogs, jalapeños, or any other "special" ingredients in this. It will ruin it. This is mac and cheese as God intended it to be—simple and perfect.
- You bake this. I repeat, this goes in the oven, not on the stove top. This is mac and cheese, not soup.
- Even if you leave out the secret ingredient (which he says don't do), this will be the best mac and cheese you'll ever eat. "God bless."

SUNDAY, JULY 23
(LATER)

Dear Nan,

It's late, like *really* late, but I had to write to tell you more about the Townsends.

I already told you that they look like they both stepped off the pages of the glossy magazines we used to flip through in the grocery store. But it's not just them. Their whole apartment feels that way, too.

Like their elevator, for example. Unlike the one in our building, theirs actually works. And it has this plush carpeting in it, and wood-paneled walls, and goes up so smoothly you can't even tell you're moving.

As they were showing me around, they had huge smiles and kept motioning at things with their arms. I could barely talk as I took it all in. It was like someone had stuffed fabric down my throat, like I'd choke if I said anything. I kept my pink duffel bag hugged to my chest.

Then we got to my room. My own room. It was a guest room before this, June said, so I'm not forcing anyone to move out so I can sleep there. I have my own window overlooking a tree-lined street. June put all sorts of nice touches in it. There are lots of pillows and a big furry bean-bag chair. They're even letting me keep one of their old laptops in my room, just for me to use.

But better than all that, there's a signed and framed Joe Namath jersey hanging on the wall. Signed, Nan! Which means he touched it with his own hands. Joe freaking Namath.

I ran over to get a closer look. "Is this . . . *real?*"

Tate nodded and pushed his floppy hair out of his eyes. "Moira mentioned you like the Jets."

"I don't like the Jets," I told him. "I LOVE the Jets."

Because only true love gets you through endless seasons of disappointment, right?

I'm starting to realize what a special thing it is, to have my own bedroom. I'm also starting to understand why you loved telling strangers on the street that we only paid four hundred bucks a month for our two-bedroom Lower East Side apartment. About how you'd been living there since the seventies, and that management, who had been trying to get rid of you for years, could kiss your rent-controlled butt, because you were never leaving.

Only, we did leave.

I wonder who's living there now. It makes my heart ache to think about it.

But back to the Townsends, because I didn't mention the best part of their apartment yet: the kitchen. It's not a galley kitchen without any windows, like ours was. It's big, with windows, and a kitchen island made of white stone.

There's a wooden block of fancy knives, copper pots and pans hanging from the ceiling, and drawers full of every single kitchen tool imaginable. I snuck out to peek in the drawers after everyone went to bed. I don't know what half of them are meant to do.

The only other place I've been that's as nice as this apartment was Rose's brownstone. But it feels different, because you saw Rose everywhere in her house. She was in the piles of junk mail stacked in her kitchen, her slippers kicked off in front of her elevator, in the lipstick-smudged cocktail napkins littered everywhere. Here, there aren't as many personal details. I wish there were. That there was more evidence of who they are, what they're really like. Not that I'm a sleuth. I don't mean to sound creepy. Do I?

Maybe there isn't as much stuff around because they have a housekeeper. June told me that she's here three days a week, which seems like a lot to me because there's barely a fingerprint anywhere.

We ate dinner in their dining room, which is connected to their kitchen by an open doorway. June made salmon with an herby sauce. I felt too shy to tell her I hate the taste of fish with a fiery passion, so I breathed through my mouth and had a sip of water after every bite.

June and Tate each have one sibling. Tate has a brother, who lives in Los Angeles, and June's sister lives in Boston. That's where she grew up.

They asked me a ton of questions, too. Lots more than they did during our first meeting. They wanted to know what I like to do, what my favorite school subject is, and all about you. I tried answering as best I could, but I had that fabric-in-my-throat feeling again, so I didn't say much more than one-word answers.

I kept sneaking glances over my shoulder at their beautiful kitchen. Eventually Tate must have noticed, because he asked if I like to cook.

I nodded. "It's my new hobby."

"I love to cook," June said. "Maybe we can make something together."

"Do you like mac and cheese?" I asked.

Tate grinned. "Who doesn't?"

"I have this recipe," I said. "It's supposed to be good."

"We can go to the store together for the ingredients soon, if you want," June said. "I can add it to our itinerary of get-to-know-each-other activities."

At that, Tate laughed and rolled his eyes, but in a teasing way. "June has lots of activities planned."

June went a little pink as she speared a piece of asparagus. "Not *that* many."

"I'm just joking. You're the boss," Tate said to her, winking at me.

"I like activities," I said.

I feel lucky, because they seem nice, and their apartment is *really* nice. But at the same time I feel bad about it, too. I can't stop thinking about what that kid Ricky said. Because I think he's right. Me ending up in a placement like this isn't random, is it? It's less about luck and more about unfairness. I'm trying to be grateful, but I'm also realizing that there are so many ways that the world is unfair.

Being here also reminds me of that musical we saw together, the one about the orphan Annie who got swept up by the rich Daddy Warbucks. I remember Annie looking so happy and excited. I remember her prancing around the stage in her red dress, her eyes bright.

Even though I'm kind of the real-life version of her, I don't feel anything like that. I just feel sad. Like I said, I know I should be grateful, but a big part of me feels I'm looking at all this nice stuff through a glass wall. Like I'm not actually here at all.

Love,
Mo

THURSDAY, JULY 27

Dear Nan,

Sorry I haven't written since Sunday. I—we—have been busy. Extremely busy. Tate was not kidding when he said that June had a lot of activities planned. Both Tate and June took the entire week off work to spend with me, and it's been a whirlwind. Here are some of the things we've done:

- An escape room on the Upper West Side
- A treasure hunt at the Museum of Natural History
- A watercolor class where we all had to paint the same picture of a lighthouse on the shore. June's was the best by far, maybe even better than the sample watercolor. Mine wasn't good. At the very least, it was better than Tate's. He didn't really try, and he drew a little smiley face on the lighthouse roof. I could tell it annoyed June.
- We've been to Central Park three times. It's only a few blocks from their apartment. For a picnic, a

walk around the Reservoir, and to feed the ducks. (We brought birdseed and lettuce, because June looked it up before we went and found out that bread isn't good for ducks. I had no idea!)

We haven't made the mac and cheese yet, though. There's one more activity on June's list on the shared calendar in the kitchen, so maybe we can do the mac and cheese after that. Hopefully this weekend. I appreciate how much they're doing, but at the end of every day I've been falling into bed, exhausted. Part of me is kind of excited about them going back to work, which they do on Monday.

It's only eight p.m., but I'm zonked. I'll write soon.

Love,
Mo

Dear Nan,

I have something really embarrassing to confess.

This whole time, I thought it was Kyle. I thought he was the problem. But really, it was me. All this time, I was messing with Kyle, thinking I was getting him back, when actually he wasn't doing anything to me.

No wonder Ms. Schirle wanted me gone.

Things were fine this week. I woke up dry every morning, and it felt like everything was back to normal in that department. But then this morning, I woke up with a big damp spot on my sheets—and I knew exactly what had happened. Except this time, there was no Kyle around to blame it on.

There was only me.

Thankfully, it was early, and their laundry closet is in the hallway, right by my room. I stripped my sheets as fast as possible, shoved them into the washer, and pressed a bunch of buttons. All I wanted was for them to be clean and dry before June or Tate woke up.

But when I was getting them out of the dryer, I noticed

they looked all weird and wrinkly, and not at all like they did when they were on the bed. And of course, that's right when June walked into the hallway.

"Oh!" she said. "Did something happen?"

"No," I said quickly. "Nothing happened. I just wanted to clean my sheets."

She came over and took the sheets from my hands. She made a disappointed *click* with her tongue as she looked at them. "Oh, Mo. These are ruined now. They're silk blend, and they can't tolerate high heat. Line-dry or low heat only. Next time you want to launder your bedding, please ask Jessica for help, okay?"

Jessica's their housekeeper, the one that comes three days a week. She was here yesterday and nodded a friendly hello, but that was it. It seems like she wants to get in and out without much conversation. How am I supposed to say what my problem is out loud to anyone, let alone someone I've barely spoken to?

Love,
Your pathetic 11-year-old
bed-wetting granddaughter

SUNDAY, JULY 30

Dear Nan,

When I woke up this morning, my goal was to work up the courage to ask either Tate or June to take me to the grocery store, so I can make Jim's Ten-Thousand-Dollar Mac and Cheese. They haven't brought it up since the first night, and it didn't get added to the shared calendar, so I'm thinking they probably forgot.

I know it's not like I'm asking them for a chest of gold coins or a pony or anything, but I've been doing my best to stay out of everyone's way, especially since the whole bed-wetting thing is such a hassle. (It happened again last night, so I had to tell June the truth. There's a rubber sheet on my bed now. My face got hot just writing that down.)

Tate was on a long run this morning with his running friend—he's training for a marathon—and June had to take an unexpected phone call for work. I don't think I've mentioned this yet, but she has her own handbag company. They make these beautiful leather handbags that are very expensive. She showed me a carousel of little swatches of leathers in different colors and textures. They all felt as soft as butter. She told me she goes to Europe a lot because that's where they make the bags.

When you run your own company, you have to work on Sundays occasionally, which is what June said before she went into her home office for a conference call. So I paced outside the room, waiting for her to get off the phone so I could ask her to take me to the store. But apparently, it was a very long phone call, because I paced and paced and her door stayed shut.

Eventually I felt like I was going to jump out of my skin, so I went down into the lobby. I needed to distract myself, but I also wanted to ride in the carpeted elevator.

There was no one at the desk, which was weird. Usually there's always someone sitting there. So I went outside.

A man with tanned white skin and black hair was leaning against the building, smoking a cigarette. I recognized him (and his dark suit—all the doormen here have to wear the same uniform), and realized I hadn't introduced myself yet. I went over to him and stuck out my hand.

"Hi. I'm Mo. I just moved in with the Townsends."

He pointed at himself instead of taking my hand, so I let mine drop. "Mo? I'm Joe. And I'm actually on my break right now. Is there something I can do for you?"

He's got an accent, too—a New York one. Like he's lived here his whole life. If I had to guess, I'd say he's probably from the Bronx, or somewhere in Brooklyn.

"No. I just wanted to say hello."

He breathed out a puff of smoke. "Well, hello."

"Smoking's really bad for you, you know," I told him. "My grandma used to smoke until she saw an episode of this medical TV show and they showed the insides of the lungs of a dead person and it was so gross, they were all black and slimy."

I didn't add the part about you getting sick in your lungs, though. I don't like to talk about that. I don't even like to write it down.

He closed his eyes and sighed. "I'm not a babysitter, kid. I'm not even supposed to be working today. I'm just trying to have a moment of peace without someone hassling me for something."

My face got hot. "Sorry. I'll leave you alone."

And then I went back inside before I could shove my foot any further down my throat.

I'm back in my room now. June's off the phone and she asked me what I wanted for lunch. I could have said, "Mac and cheese, please," but there's no way I can go to the grocery store now. I can't ever leave this apartment again. At least, not when Joe's working.

Because what if he pulls her aside and I get in trouble for bothering him on his break, and not minding my own business?

I've always been bad at that. I definitely got that from you.

Love,
Mo

TUESDAY, AUGUST 1

Dear Nan,

I have a couple things to report.

First, June and Tate are taking me to the Hamptons this weekend. That's where Tate's mom lives. And guess what? She has five dogs and a swimming pool. I wonder if her cannonballs are half as good as yours. It's a good sign she likes dogs and swimming, like me. I keep checking the weather forecast on my new laptop. I know it might change, but right now it's supposed to be sunny and hot— the perfect swimming weather.

The other piece of news is that last night, I finally worked up the courage to ask June about going to the grocery store.

"Oh, of course," June said, slapping her forehead lightly. "I totally forgot. Yes. I can put an order in right now, and have the ingredients delivered tomorrow morning. What do you need?"

I gave her a list, and with the press of a button, ingredients were on their way. (And I don't have to leave the building and face the doorman who hates me, which is the best part of all.)

I also promised her I wouldn't let anything happen like it did last time.

"What do you mean?" she asked.

Then I realized they must not have told her about the fire at Ms. Schirle's. I immediately got sweaty as I tried to explain.

"It was a tiny fire," I said. "Really small. I don't even think anything was on fire for more than, like, a minute. There was just a ton of smoke."

June said as long as I cook with an adult present, it should be fine. But I did notice a new fire extinguisher in their pantry this morning.

Tate works at an office, but because June's the boss, she was able to tell her team she'd be working from home for a while. I'm guessing that's because of me. We're going to make the mac and cheese to have for lunch today—any minute, actually—as soon as June finishes her morning calls. Her company is doing this big photo shoot all the way in Iceland for their spring advertising campaign. Apparently, they're flying flowers from here—from New York City—to there. Can you imagine, a plane all filled up with flowers instead of people?

Oh, June's calling me—it's mac and cheese o'clock.

I'll report back as soon as I try some.

Love,
Mo

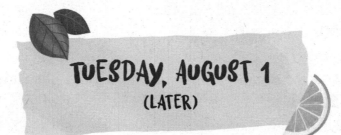
Dear Nan,

I didn't realize that when you die, you go to live in a giant ooey, gooey, cheesy, creamy tray of Jim's Ten-Thousand-Dollar Mac and Cheese. That's where you are, right? Swimming in its cheesy goodness?

Because that

Mac

And

Cheese

Was

HEAVENLY

I don't think I'll need to eat for three days, but I can see why it won ten thousand dollars. It's worth every penny, and more. It was smooth and creamy, but also incredibly cheesy, with a long string of cheese stretching from my fork to the plate every time I took a bite. I ate as much of it as I could cram in before my stomach started sending "warning, overload" signals.

When we sat down for lunch, June only ate a tiny little bit of it.

"Don't you like it?" I asked.

"Oh," she said, laughing. "Believe me, I love it. But I have to watch my figure or else—" She puffed out her cheeks and held her arms in front of her in a silly way.

But I didn't laugh. She's skinny as a pole. It made me feel self-conscious, like maybe she thought I shouldn't be eating as much, either, since I'm way . . . I don't know. Rounder than she is? More squishable through my middle? I bet she can't make a donut with her belly like I can. Definitely not a double donut like you could.

With you, I never thought about this stuff.

Anyway, I decided in a post-mac-and-cheese-induced haze that I had to make peace with Joe the doorman. So I fixed a plate and brought it down to the lobby with a fork and a paper towel.

"I'm sorry about the other day," I said as soon as the elevator doors dinged open. "I didn't mean to bother you on your break and talk about black lungs." I put the plate down on his desk. "A peace offering. This is the best mac and cheese you'll ever eat."

"Aw, man. This looks incredible." He leaned over to breathe in the steam, and then he looked up at me. "And listen, kid, I'm the one who should apologize. I've been hoping you'd come down ever since I snapped at you so I could say sorry. It's no excuse, but Sunday was a tough day for me." He laughed a little. "In fact, it's pretty much been a tough year."

I nodded. Because that I understood. "Yeah. Mine, too."

"Can we try this again?" he asked, sticking out his hand. "Joe Bianco, at your service."

I gripped his hand firmly and pumped it up and down, the way you taught me. "I'm Mo. Mo Gallagher."

When we let go, he rubbed his hand. "Quite the handshake you've got there."

"I know," I told him proudly. "My grandma taught me."

While he ate (he agreed it was the best mac and cheese he'd ever tasted), we talked.

His hair isn't black, like I thought, but dark brown. He said his family's originally from Sicily. He looks a bit older than the Townsends, but it's hard to tell. Maybe he's younger? I don't know. Sometimes I feel like all adults look like they're the exact same age.

Anyway, I learned five interesting facts about him.

1. Joe has three brothers and a wife named Carlota. She was born in Mexico and her parents still live there. Joe said she's an only child, so in a weird way, I already feel connected to her. He showed me a picture. She has dark hair and tan skin, like Joe, but different.

2. They live in Brooklyn (but Joe said he grew up in the Bronx, so I was right about that), and have two dogs, one cat, and zero children.

3. His favorite food is lasagna. "Like Garfield," he said.
4. He's a Giants fan. I know, I know. But don't worry too much about it, Nan. I'll work on him.
5. Carlota works in a *bakery*. As her job.

I asked what her favorite thing was to bake.

"Everything under the sun," Joe said. "She's got magic in her fingers when it comes to baking. Chamucos, cannoli, hot cross buns, biscotti, conchas, you name it."

I didn't recognize half those words, but I made a mental note to look them up. I told him about how I was teaching myself to cook. How it had all started with *Georgie's Family Cookbook*. How it was my new hobby, for at least the next year.

"Do you have any family recipes?" I asked. "Or does Carlota?"

"From a baker and a guy with a huge Italian family? Oh, yeah," said Joe.

"Shoot," I said, glancing at the clock over his shoulder. Somehow, we'd been talking for more than an hour, and I hadn't told June where I was going. "I should go."

He handed me the empty plate. "Thanks for lunch. And the company."

When I got back upstairs, June was working—thankfully. I don't think she even noticed I was gone. I snuck back in, no problem.

Oh—someone's knocking on my bedroom door. Maybe it's June, wanting to see if I want to do something with her. It's a beautiful day. Maybe she'll want to go to Central Park or get a Mister Softee with me.

Love,
Mo

PS Jets rule. Giants drool.

WEDNESDAY, AUGUST 2

Dear Nan,

Wow, wow, wow—I have so much to tell you, I have this new idea, this new amazing plan, and—

Phew. Okay. Deep breaths, Mo. Relax.

It started with me bringing another microwaved plate of mac and cheese down to the lobby a couple hours ago.

Joe was there, at the desk, just like I hoped.

"Hungry?" I asked, lifting the plate in the air.

"Always," he said. "Oh," he said after taking his first bite. "Oh, yeah. That's the stuff."

I grinned. "Still good the next day, right?"

"No. Not good. Incredible. *Ambrosia*." He forked himself a bigger mouthful. "You really made this yourself?"

I nodded. "Yep."

(Okay, fine, June helped, but not that much.)

"Wow. Seriously, wow. Genius." He took another bite and chewed thoughtfully. "You know, I was thinking about yesterday, about how you said cooking was your new hobby. My niece has a hobby, too. She buys old, crusty furniture and refinishes it, and she makes posts and videos about it on her website, or whatever. On her socials, I guess, I don't know what you kids are calling it these days. Point is, people go nuts for it. I don't know if you're looking to share *your* hobby, but"—he pointed his fork at his plate, which was already almost empty—"recipes as good as this should be out in the world."

"What?" I said, going very still.

"It's just an idea," Joe said.

A website. A food website.

And right then, it was like a million flowers bloomed inside me. A parade with fireworks, lighting up the sky of my mind.

Because yes.

Yes, yes, YES.

I've been reading food websites and watching videos on TikTok and YouTube for the past month or so, learning what different cooking words mean, like "separate," "blanch," and "deglaze." Some of the websites and accounts are popular, with thousands if not millions of followers.

Joe's right: I should start my own.

I have my own laptop now, don't I? And there's still another month left of summer, which means I have the time, too. It's the exact distraction I need.

"Joe," I said. I'd bet a hundred bucks my face was as serious as Pedro's right then. "That's not just *an* idea, it's the *perfect* idea. That's exactly what I'm going to do."

I spun on my heel to go back to the elevator, so I could go upstairs and start planning.

"Wait, Mo, before you go—"

Joe reached under the desk and took out a pink box, tied up with baker's twine.

"This is for you," he said, almost apologetically. "Carlota made them for you last night. I was telling her about you, and about how you're teaching yourself to cook. I'd barely finished talking, and she was already dusting the countertops with flour and putting on her apron." He laughed. "This isn't her regular bakery fare. I told her you liked family recipes." He flicked the little piece of paper, folded on top, stuck beneath the twine. "These are biscuits like her abuela used to make. She wrote the recipe down for you on this."

I took the box and held it to my chest. The top was shut tight, but I could still get whiffs of buttery dough rising up from whatever was inside. "Thanks, Joe. Really. And thank Carlota for me, too."

"Yeah, don't mention it." He put his now-empty plate gently on top of the box. "Thanks for lunch."

I pressed the elevator button with my elbow.

As I waited, I realized: Joe was right, again. About me liking family recipes. And that's exactly what I can write and make videos about. Family recipes. Other people's, I mean. With their stories and pictures and smudged recipe cards. Not Jim's mac and cheese, because I'm sworn to secrecy, but still. I could be the gatherer, the collector of people's beloved recipes. I could be the one to share them with the world, to show people how special they are. Maybe I could write about or show my experience making them.

I got into the elevator, thinking about it. And then right as the doors were about to close, I called out, "Can I share it online? Carlota's recipe?"

Joe laughed. "I'll ask her, but I have a feeling she'll say yes."

As soon as I was back in the apartment, I marched right to June's office door and knocked, even though it was closed, which meant she was on a call. A few seconds later, she pulled it open, her eyes wide and worried.

"Mo? Are you okay? Is something wrong?"

"I'm sorry to bother you," I said. "But it's important."

"Manon," June said into the phone. "Can I call you back?"

Then June hung up and fully turned to me in her swivel chair. "I'm ready. What's up?"

So I explained the idea. About sharing videos and writing posts about beloved family recipes.

"Oh, Mo," she said. "I think that's a fabulous idea. Nothing teaches you about perseverance as much as starting and running something yourself. I'll have to talk to Moira about it, just to make sure it's okay. As long as you don't post too much personal information, I'm sure it will be fine."

"I won't. And I'm glad you like the idea." I could feel

my cheeks getting warm. "I just need a way to take pictures. Of the food, I mean. Would it be okay if I borrowed your phone to take them? Or Tate's?"

"Of course. I'm so sorry. Tate and I have been meaning to get you a phone. I'll go tomorrow." She smiled. "Now I'll just make sure we get you one with a great camera."

Without thinking, I threw my arms around her. She seemed startled at first, but then she wrapped her arms around me and hugged me back.

I forgot how good it feels to be hugged.

And get this—I've been brainstorming, and I already came up with a name.

I'm going to call it the Family Cookbook.

It's not my own, obviously, because if I had one of those, I wouldn't have needed Georgie's. But I want the recipes I post to feel like a shared family cookbook. Like a scrapbook of stories and memories and food that mean a lot to people.

What do you think? Do you like it? I hope you do.

Love,
Mo

Dear Mo,

Joe told me a spark plug of a girl moved into his building, and was teaching herself to cook. I couldn't help myself from sharing these with you. They are called bisquets chinos, just like my abuela used to make. When I was a girl, we used to eat them for breakfast with lots of butter and strawberry jam, and my father always let me have a small cup of coffee alongside them. I hold this recipe dear to my heart, and I hope you will like it, too.

I'm so grateful you're there to keep an eye on Joe for me. Especially his smoking. I'm trying to get him to quit.

Abrazos,

Carlota Rivera Bianco

Abuela Tati's Bisquets Chinos

Makes 10–12 bisquets

Ingredients

3 cups flour

¼ cup sugar

1 tablespoon baking powder

1 teaspoon salt

1.5 sticks of butter or 1 cup lard

1.5 cups milk

2 egg yolks

Directions

Preheat oven to 350 degrees F.

Mix all the dry ingredients together. I like to do this on a large wooden cutting board, but you can do it in a bowl, too.

Add butter and mix with your hands until you reach a sand-like consistency.

Create a well and add one egg yolk, mixing it into your dry ingredients.

Gradually add milk until the dough is tacky and supple. (You may not need all the milk!) Make sure not to overmix your batter.

Flour a countertop and roll out the dough until it's about 1 inch thick.

Using a mold—the sharper the edges the better, because it will help your biscuits rise—cut out rounds.

Using a smaller mold, like the mouth of a plastic water bottle, cut a smaller circle in the center of the rounds, but don't push all the way through.

Brush tops with the second egg yolk.

Bake for 15–20 minutes or until golden brown. Enjoy!

THURSDAY, AUGUST 3

Dear Nan,

The Family Cookbook is a go! A yes! June called Moira, and she said it was okay, as long as I'm careful about what I post. Tate and June are going to be involved in approving comments and stuff like that, but I don't mind at all. Tate helped me buy a domain name after dinner last night. Cool, right? We ate Carlota's biscuits as an after-dinner snack while we worked. I wanted to hold off until tomorrow to have them for breakfast, but I couldn't wait that long. And I'm glad I didn't, because they're like little biscuit-y pillows of doughy happiness. We slathered them with jam and butter, just like Carlota said. I can't wait to try making them myself.

Tate's good with computers. Maybe he's got to be, for his job in finance? But I'm not really sure what "finance" means. Anyway, he spent more than two hours showing me how to use what's called a "hosting" site. He showed me how to put up posts, how to change the font and insert pictures, and how to see how many people have visited my website.

He nudged me in the side. "Now it's up to you. I can't wait to see what you come up with."

June went out this morning and got me a new phone. It's an iPhone, way nicer than our old ones. I couldn't believe it. I've snapped a few pictures around the apartment. I even took out a plate of salad greens from the fridge just to test the camera, but all my pictures came out blah. Like, oh look, there's a pile of lettuce on a counter. How exciting. The phone is amazing, so I know it can probably take knock-your-socks-off pictures. The problem is me.

"June?" I tapped on her office door. "Do you know how to take good pictures with the phone camera?"

She opened the door as she was sliding on a pair of pink heels. "Shoot, I'm sorry, Mo. I have a meeting out. Later?"

"Okay," I said. "Later."

Jessica is here. Maybe she's good with cameras. She doesn't seem to be big on small talk, though, so I guess I shouldn't distract her from her job too much.

By far the most artistic person I know is Crystal. Do you remember how she won first place in the Wallace photo contest last year? It was the first year a fifth grader has ever won. And she didn't even use a real camera. She just used her mom's phone. I bet she'd know how to make my photos look amazing.

Hopefully, June can show me some camera tricks when she gets home.

If she isn't back by the time I finish writing you this letter, I'm going to work on my first post. I don't think

I'll need any photos of food for that. Maybe just a photo of me. I like the one you took last September, when we played hooky and went to Coney Island and got ice cream sundaes. Yours with extra maraschino cherries, mine with double fudge sauce.

Even though there's ice cream dripping all over my fingers and shirt, and my hair's blowing in my face, I'd still like to use it. That was a good day, wasn't it? No—the best day. We didn't know you were sick yet. I think we found out a few weeks later.

I wish I could rewind time and spend that whole day with you again. If I could, I'd know to hold on to every single moment.

I miss you,
Mo

Dear Readers,

Thanks for stopping by, and welcome to the Family Cook-book!

My name is Mo Gallagher. I am eleven years old, I live in New York City, and I am teaching myself how to cook.

But I am not learning with just any recipes. I am learning from family recipes. The thing I like about family recipes is that they usually come with history, with an interesting story, and most importantly, with lots of love attached. And because of that, they're much better than just any old recipe you can find lying around on the internet.

If you have any family recipes of your own, I hope you'll send them to me, so I can write about them here. It's even better if you send them with pictures, or with a story about why it's important to your family. Because that's what will make it important to me, too.

My grandma always said I should never post my information on the internet, because that's how people steal your identity, so I made a new email.

It's momolovesfamilyfood@gmail.com.

MoMoLovesFamilyFood is also my name for all my social media channels. I plan to make videos and post pictures, too.

Anyway, I hope this will make you want to learn how to cook, like me. That way we can learn together. If you already know how to cook, that's fine, too. I hope you'll stay anyway, for the family recipes and the stories. I'm just glad you're here.

Thanks for reading,
Mo Gallagher

FRIDAY, AUGUST 4

Dear Nan,

My first post is up! It took me all yesterday afternoon to get it right. I must have written seventeen drafts. I've checked my new email a bunch, but no one's sent me any family recipes yet.

June didn't get back until right before dinner, so we weren't able to play around with the camera. It worked out fine, though, because I needed the time to work on my first post. She said we could practice taking cool pictures tomorrow, since it will be Saturday, and she doesn't have anything on her work calendar this weekend.

Oh, that reminds me—we're not going to the Hamptons anymore. Tate has a business dinner tomorrow he couldn't get out of, and now the forecast says there's a chance of thunderstorms. We took a rain check—literally. Ha ha.

Tate's mom is busy next weekend, but hopefully we'll be able to go the weekend after. I can't wait to meet those dogs and swim in her pool.

Over dinner tonight, I finally got up the guts to say two things. First, I admitted I don't like fish.

Tate's eyes lit up when I said so. He turned to June. "Finally, an ally! Two against one." He glanced at me. "I am also not wild for fish."

June pressed her lips together. "Fish has lots of omega-3s. It's very good for you."

I felt a little bad, because June is the one who makes dinner. It's a lot of work—cooking, cleaning up, putting all your tools away. She should be able to make what she likes if she's the one doing it all.

"Maybe I can help," I offered. "I could cook a meal or two. Or help you in the kitchen more."

"Cooking dinner is sort of my time to unwind," June said. "My alone time, after work. I'll figure out some new recipes that we all like."

"Oh, right," I said. "Of course."

As for the second thing, I also asked about whether I'd be going back to Wallace in September. Summer's not forever, so I figured I would have to ask sooner or later.

But as soon as the question was out of my mouth, my heart started pounding. Because what if the Townsends hadn't planned to keep me until the fall? Was I making an assumption? Was I—

But my worrying was interrupted by Tate. "Is that what you would want in an ideal world? It'll be a long commute. Upper East Side all the way to Brooklyn every day would be . . ." He whistled. "Far."

I hadn't really thought about that, honestly. Before, it

was only a fifteen-minute subway ride from our old apartment, but now . . . I'd have to calculate it.

Then again, Rebecca Hufstedler (remember her?) commutes all the way from Harlem. And if she can do it, so can I. In fact, I'd walk to Wallace if it meant I could still go. So I nodded and wiped my sweaty palms on my thighs. You know what a nervous sweater I am. Ugh.

"Yeah," I said. "I have friends. I know the teachers. I'd . . . I'd like that."

"Mo, we actually already put a deposit down for you at Chapin," June said, "which is an excellent school, much closer to us. It's a miracle they had an open spot."

"Wow. Thank you. But if it's okay with you, I'd really like to go back to my old school."

June opened her mouth to say something else, but Tate reached across the table and took her hand. "Remember what Moira said? We should keep it as normal as possible for Mo. And I think that includes her going back to her old school. We can make it work."

June bit her lip, but after a minute she nodded. Then she smiled, but it seemed like she was forcing herself to. "Then Wallace Charter it is. I'll make some calls tomorrow."

Oh, Nan, as soon as I got back to my room after dinner, it was like a big, heavy, terrible weight was lifted.

I get to go back. Crystal and I get to wear our matching first-day-of-school outfits, like we've done since first grade. This year could be our silliest yet. I bet even the teachers are looking forward to it.

That is, I thought, if Crystal still *wants* to do it with me.

With a start, I realized the date. August fourth. I hurried to the computer, to check the Google calendar we share (or *used* to share, at least . . .)—it said she was getting back August second.

Which means she's been back for two entire days and I haven't texted, written, or anything.

I paced around my room. How long had it been since I'd responded to any of her emails? A long time. She doesn't know where I am, or that I have a new phone number. That Uncle Billy left. She doesn't even know that I'm safe and okay. How could she? I haven't told her anything. All this time I've been telling myself I haven't wanted to ruin her trip, but I think I've just been scared to tell her the truth. I should never have let it go this long. She's probably been worried sick. Or thinks I hate her.

I've been a terrible friend.

I picked up my new phone and texted her.

ME: Hi. It's Mo. 👋 I have a new phone

Text bubbles popped up, letting me know she was typing. They popped up and disappeared, then popped up and disappeared again.

Finally, a text came through.

CRYSTAL: Hi. I thought u didn't want to be my friend anymore

I swallowed. Whatever I texted next had to be exactly right. My fingers hesitated over the buttons.

ME: I do want to be your friend. So badly. I'm so sorry. I have a lot to tell you. Do you want to come over tomorrow? Or I can come to you. Whatever you want.

CRYSTAL: K. I'll come to ur place

ME: Actually, I live somewhere new

Then I texted her the Townsends' address.

CRYSTAL: What??? U moved? And u didn't tell me??

ME: Yeah it's kinda a long story. Im really sorry

There was another long pause that nearly killed me. More of those stupid bubbles. Eventually I tossed my phone onto the carpeted floor, screen down, so I wouldn't have to watch them pop up and disappear again.

Finally, my phone buzzed. I scrambled to grab it.

CRYSTAL: K. I guess I'll see u tomorrow

Then I went to go talk to June and Tate.

They were watching something in the den. That's the name for their TV room, because they have a formal living room different from where the TV is. Can you imagine? Anyway, I like the den—it's small and cozy, with a big plush couch and soft white blankets draped everywhere, and big black-and-white photographs on the wall.

Tate pressed pause as soon as I came in. "What's up, Mo?"

"Want to join us?" June asked, patting a spot on the couch next to her.

"Thanks, but . . . I was actually wondering . . . is it okay if my friend Crystal comes over tomorrow?"

June and Tate glanced at each other like they were checking to see what the other person thought about it.

"Sure," June said. "I don't see why not. I'd love to meet a friend of yours."

"Thanks. She's my best friend. Or at least . . . I hope she still is. It's been a while since we talked."

June smiled. "I'm sure all will be well as soon as you see each other."

I was about to leave the room when I had an idea. "Do either of you have any recipes that would be good for saying sorry?"

"Hmm," June said. "Maybe a cake?"

Tate motioned to June with his chin. "The only acceptable way to say sorry in this household is with roses. Expensive ones."

June elbowed him. "Shush, you. And oh! What about your friend? Gosh, what's his name. The one from college? Who always made those lemon bars?" She snapped her fingers. "Beau Carlson."

"Oh, yeah!" Tate sat up and turned to me. "Of course. My buddy Beau used to make lemon bars whenever anyone was mad at him. Said the tradition started with his dad, who would make them whenever Beau's mom was upset with him. And man, they were good. Beau got engaged because of those lemon bars."

"To Beth, right?" June asked. "I never liked her."

Tate rolled his eyes. "Oh, come on. She's fine."

"Do you have the recipe?" I asked Tate hopefully. "Crystal loves anything tart."

"I don't, but I could text him."

Tate pulled his cell out of his pocket, and as he typed, I crossed my fingers and went to sit on the couch next to June.

"Here we go," Tate said a few moments later. "Got it. I'll forward the text to you."

Once I had it, I asked, "Is it okay if I go down to the bodega around the corner? To buy the ingredients?"

"It's almost eight." June looked at the delicate gold watch she always wears. "How about we go tomorrow morning?"

"It's fine, Junie. It's Friday night." Tate stood up. "I'll take her."

"We can go to the Safeway a few blocks down," Tate said as soon as we were outside. I waved at the doorman. (It wasn't Joe. He goes home for the day around six.)

As we made our way down the block, we passed a woman walking a tiny black poodle. I asked if I could pet him, and when I bent down, he was so excited he jumped onto my knee and got all wiggly. It made me think about Tate's mom in the Hamptons, with all those dogs.

"So, did you grow up with a lot of dogs?" I asked Tate.

"I did. After my parents got divorced, my mom became an amateur breeder for a while. Golden retrievers." He glanced at me with a half smile. "It's how she coped."

"I always wanted a dog, but our old building didn't allow them."

"Hmm," Tate said. "I'm not sure if you've noticed, but our building is dog-friendly. Maybe such a thing could be arranged."

"My birthday's in April," I said hopefully.

He laughed. "Well, Christmas is even sooner."

And then he winked at me.

This totally means we're getting a dog, right? I looked up pictures of cuddly golden retrievers online. I like the ones that are round and fat and fluffy. They look the most huggable.

But I would still take a single day with you back in our old building over a lifetime with a cuddly golden retriever. If you were wondering.

Oh! My oven timer is going off—got to go. I made a triple batch to make sure there will be enough lemon bars to enact my plan. I'll write again tomorrow to let you know how it goes.

Cross your ghost (or angel) fingers for me, Nan. Maybe you could visit Crystal in her dreams tonight and remind her how much she loves me. But don't scare her or do other spooky ghost things. It would be better if you were nice about it.

Love,
Mo

Beau Carlson's "I'm Sorry" Lemon Bars
Makes 1 apologetic batch

Base

1 cup (2 sticks) butter

½ cup powdered sugar

2 cups flour

Cream sugar and butter.

Add flour; mixture will be crumbly.

Press into 9 x 13 glass baking dish. Bake for 15–20
minutes at 350°F.

Filling

Beat 4 eggs and add:

2 cups sugar

7 T lemon juice

4 T flour

1 t baking powder

¼ t salt

Pour filling over hot crust.

Bake for 25–30 minutes at 350°F.

Let cool and sprinkle with more lemon juice and
powdered sugar.

SATURDAY, AUGUST 5

Dear Nan,

Crystal just left. It was a *day*.

I spent the whole morning in the lobby with Joe, waiting for Crystal to arrive. He usually doesn't work Saturdays, but he was covering someone's shift, and I'm glad he was there. I stayed awake until past midnight fussing over the lemon bars, but I still woke up early. And there was no way I could wait around upstairs.

"Stop pacing," Joe told me. "You're making me nervous."

He tried going out for a cigarette at one point, but I stopped him. "What if someone comes in and tries to abduct me? It'll be on you. Plus, Carlota said in her note to tell you to stop smoking."

Joe leaned back in his chair. "Oh, great, she's got you on my case now, too, huh?"

I kept pacing. "Yep."

"All right, all right. You got me. I'll stay put."

After a few minutes, I stopped. "Does my outfit look weird?"

I'm pretty sure I tried on every piece of clothing I

have this morning. I decided on my bright-yellow-and-blue-striped shirt, plus the purple shorts Crystal got for me—the ones she embroidered the rainbow flowers onto. Remember those? Anyway, all of a sudden I wasn't sure if the outfit was exactly right, or if I just looked stupid.

"Not weird at all." He considered me. "In fact, you look like a bouquet of tulips."

I tugged on my ponytail. "Is that a good thing?"

"The best thing. Tulips are a big hit in the Bianco household. Carlota likes them because they're cheerful and sunny. She says they're happiness in flower form."

My cheeks flushed a little. "Thanks, Joe."

Then the building doors chimed.

It was Crystal. Well, Crystal and her older cousin, Rachel, who must have taken the subway uptown with her. Rachel waved and put her earbuds in. "I'll be back in a few hours to get you."

"Bye," Crystal said. "Thanks."

She was wearing her long black hair in a way I've never seen before: braided around her head into a crown. She'd even woven sparkly strands of tinsel into it. She had on a sundress I've never seen before, plus lip gloss. *Lip gloss*, Nan. Bright pink and shiny.

She looked so . . . different. Older.

I guess things—and people—are always changing, even when you don't expect them to. Even when you hope things will stay exactly the same, forever. My heart gave a painful thump.

"Hi," I said.

"Hi," she said back as she looked all around the lobby.

There was a long, awkward silence.

Then a scraping sound, as Joe stood up from his chair behind the desk. "Hi. I'm Joe. You have no idea how much Mo's talked about you. She waited down here all morning for you. She couldn't stop pacing."

I widened my eyes at him. "*Joe.*"

But it made Crystal crack the tiniest, almost invisible smile. She turned to me. "So are you going to show me you and your uncle's new mansion or whatever?"

"I'm, um, actually not living with my uncle right now," I told her. "But I'll explain everything." I pointed to the elevator. "It's this way."

"Good luck," Joe mouthed, right as the elevator doors were closing.

Crystal looked down as the elevator went up.

"Weird, right?" I said. "Carpeting in an elevator?"

She shrugged a little but didn't say anything else.

"This is it," I said as we walked into the foyer. Because the Townsends have one of those. A *foyer.* Not a nub of a hallway where you keep your shoes and jackets in a messy pile, like we had in our old apartment. It's a big entry room that's mostly empty except for a polished wooden table and a vase of fresh flowers.

June appeared, with one of her big leather purses slung over her shoulder. "Mo, I have to—oh. Hi there! You must be Crystal." She smiled her glittering, white-toothed smile.

"I'm June. It's so nice to meet you. I absolutely love your hair."

Crystal touched her braid crown. "Thanks."

"Mo," June said, turning to me. "I've got to run out for a bit. Tate's at the gym, but should be back within the hour. Will the two of you be okay by yourselves until then?"

"Yep," I said.

I was actually relieved Tate and June wouldn't be around. Because what if Crystal didn't want to forgive me? What if I cried? I didn't want them to see any of that. I only want them to see cheerful, happy, and out-of-the-way Mo.

"Great," June said. "Have fun, girls!"

"What's going on?" Crystal asked as soon as June had left. "Who was that? Where's your uncle?"

"I have a lot to tell you," I admitted. "I—"

"I thought you didn't want to be my friend anymore," Crystal said quietly. "I spent most of the trip staring at my phone, hoping you'd talk to me. But you never did."

I'd never heard her voice so quiet or trembly before.

All this time I've been so focused on the bad things that happened to me. I haven't thought how these things might have affected my best friend.

I'd planned to show her around the apartment and save my surprise for last, but I realized I needed to start with the big guns.

"I need to show you something. This way." I led her down the short hallway to the kitchen. She let out a small little gasp as soon as we stepped through the swinging door.

93

I'd spent a while last night cutting the lemon bars into the shapes I needed. Then this morning, I arranged them on the wide kitchen island so they spelled out, in delicious lemony pieces:

I'M

SORRY

Crystal went and touched the edge of one of the bars. "Did you make these?"

"Yes. You like lemons," I said stupidly.

When she turned back to face me, we both started talking at the exact same time.

"I'm so sorry I disappeared—"

"I've been *so* worried about you—"

And then we both stepped toward each other and suddenly we were hugging, both of us crying and laughing at the same time.

"I don't think it's even possible to miss another human being as much as I've missed you, Mo Gallagher, you dummy. Never do that to me again."

"I won't. Not ever."

"And I need to know everything," she added. She glanced at the lemon bars sitting on the counter. "Specifically while eating one of those."

We both took two.

"I'm glad you decided to bribe me with sugar," Crystal said in between bites. "Because it's working."

I nodded, wiping powdered sugar off my lips. They were

good. So good. Perfectly tart and sweet with a dense, buttery base.

"But since when can *you* cook?" she asked. "No offense."

"It's the new hobby Nan wanted me to start. I even have a website and everything."

"A what? Website?" She put her bar down and looked at me. "Okay. Time to spill."

We sat there and talked. And talked. First I made her tell me about her trip to China, and then I told her about Billy leaving, about all the meetings and strangers and Moira, about Ms. Schirle, about how I ended up here. I left out the part about the bed-wetting, though. There are some secrets you should keep to yourself.

"I'm so sorry about your uncle," she said, grabbing my hand and squeezing it. "What a jerk. He doesn't know what he's missing."

"He's not a jerk," I said, even though I wasn't sure—I'm still not sure—how I feel about Billy. "And who knows what's going to happen. Maybe he'll change his mind."

"Okay," Crystal said, but she didn't seem convinced. "What about these people? The Townsends? Are they nice?"

"Yeah," I said.

"But . . . ," she added, waiting for me to say more.

"No but. They're nice. Really nice."

But there was a but. There *is* a but. They're nice, *but*

I wish I was still living in our old apartment, with Uncle Billy.

They're nice, but in a perfect world, I never would have met them at all. Because to live in this nice apartment, in this nice building with its carpeted elevator, I had to lose everything.

Plus, I haven't been able to shake that funny feeling of being behind glass with June and Tate. Like there's an invisible wall making it hard for me to connect to them. At least Tate's easygoing. He doesn't care if I put plates in the top part of the dishwasher and mugs in the bottom. June is a little more structured. She likes things exactly the way she likes them. I still feel like I don't know all the rules, so I'm always afraid I'm going to mess something up.

But I didn't want to get into all that. I just wanted to be with my best friend. I dusted powdered sugar off my hands and said, "Is there any way you can show me how to take artsy pictures on my phone? For my website?"

She stared straight at me. "Oh, so you invited me over to use me?"

"No!" I cried. "I was—I wanted to—"

I was still sputtering when she grinned. "Kidding. I just wanted to see you squirm."

I knocked into her with my shoulder, and she pretended to go flying off the stool so dramatically that we both couldn't stop cracking up.

Oh, Nan. I've missed this.

The leftover mac and cheese was crusty, so we decided

to practice taking pictures of the lemon bars. Crystal chose three of the squarest-looking pieces, and we set them up on one of June's nice porcelain plates.

"We should put a strawberry on the side," Crystal said.

"But there are no strawberries in the recipe."

"It's for the aesthetic, Mo."

"The what?"

She patted the top of my head. "You have much to learn."

So I plopped a strawberry on the plate.

"No. You have to *arrange* it."

I wanted to roll my eyes, but then again, she's the artist, not me. I watched as she cut tiny slices into it and fanned it out.

And I have to admit, it did look a lot better.

"Perfect," Crystal said. "Now we have to find the best light."

We checked every corner of the apartment, including the bathroom, but Crystal decided the best light came from the corner window in the living room with the sheer white shades.

"You don't want bright light shining directly on it," she explained. "Otherwise, you'll get shadows."

"Are shadows bad?" I asked.

"Yes," she said gravely. "The worst."

We took a bunch, and then she said, "Now we have to upload them to see which ones are best. The secret is to get them on a big screen."

We put all the pictures on my laptop, and Crystal downloaded some free picture-editing software she uses, and showed me how to sort through them at the kitchen table. She elbowed me. "Mo. Pay attention. We should delete this one. Can you see why?"

The whole taking-pictures-and-editing-them process makes my head spin, but some of the photos came out looking professional. Like something you'd see in a magazine.

Crystal left a few hours ago. Tate said Beau Carlson told him it was okay for me to post the recipe for the lemon bars, and the story behind them. He texted the story about how he used them to get engaged to his wife (but I'm going to leave out the part about June not liking her). It's going to be the very first recipe I share.

If you were wondering, Crystal and I have already texted back and forth like a million times—and there hasn't been one single period in any of her texts. Just hearts and !!!!! and links to funny TikToks.

Underneath the braid crown and the lip gloss, it's the same old Crystal. Still there, still willing to be my best friend. And I know I probably don't deserve it, but I'm thankful for it all the same.

I felt happy today. But then I felt guilty for feeling happy, because you aren't here, and then I felt sad remembering that. But I also know you want me to be happy, just happy, because you told me so, so, so (so) many times. I don't know. It's confusing.

So I'm trying to let myself feel it. The sour, and the sweet. At the same time. But mostly the sweet.

Love,
Mo

PS Wow, this was a long letter. My hand is all cramped up. It might be a record, my longest letter to you yet. Time for more frozen peas. I hope you didn't get bored and nod off, snoring loud enough to wake your ghost (or angel) neighbors.

PPS I love you. And I miss you.

FRIDAY, AUGUST 18

Dear Nan,

It's been two weeks since I posted my first recipe on my website. I've posted more since then—Georgie's grandma's egg-lemon soup (Moira asked for permission after returning the cookbook to her), Carlota's biscuits, and I posted a bunch of pictures Moira gave me of her stepdad holding a giant foam check made out for ten thousand dollars. Not his secret recipe, though. I'll never share that. Only the pictures, the story, and all of Jim's tips for making great mac and cheese. I've posted some videos on TikTok, too. Crystal's much better at editing and transitions than I am, so we've been doing those together.

But I have to admit something: a secret hope is growing inside of me, more and more, every day.

We still have relatives out there somewhere, right?

We must. Maybe a second or third or even a fourth cousin. Because that's how families work, right?

And maybe if my website or videos get popular enough . . . maybe they'll find me. And they'll have a family recipe or two to share.

That way, I could have a family recipe of my own.

Or pictures of you as a little girl, in the kitchen. Maybe you liked to cook at my age and then got bad at it. Or maybe there was a fire and you got scared or something. Uncle Bill doesn't know *why* you were such a horrible cook, after all. No offense.

I want a family recipe that tells more of your story. I want there to be an epilogue. An undiscovered recipe box filled with memories of you. Even just one recipe—with one story—would be enough.

My videos are getting some views, but not my website. Even with all these posts, which, between the writing and the picture-taking, took *hours* to make, I've only gotten one visitor. One.

How am I supposed to find a family recipe if I can't get anyone to look at what I'm doing?

I FaceTimed Crystal to complain about it. I could hear Charlie screaming in the background.

She sighed. "Hold on. Let me go into the closet."

That's Crystal's private place. Her whole family knows not to bother her when she's in there. It was hard to see her face in the dark closet, but at least Charlie's crying was muffled. "Okay. Go ahead."

So I told her again. "Only one visitor, Crystal. One!"

"Oops. I think that was me. I was showing it to Lao Lao."

"Everyone hates it. This whole thing was a stupid idea."

"No one hates it. How could they? No one's *seen* it," she said back. "You need to get out on the streets. Pound the pavement. Interview people, like the guy does with his camera, the one who interviews strangers for their stories. The Humans of New York guy. You need to be like him, but for recipes. You need to grow your audience."

Pounding the pavement. I thought about it. "That's not such a bad idea."

Because if people aren't going to come to me with their family recipes, then maybe Crystal's right—maybe I have to go to them. "But we're going to visit Tate's mom in the Hamptons. We leave this afternoon. I'll start when I get back."

"This afternoon? It's only ten. You've got time. In fact, why are you still on the phone?"

Then she hung up on me. Classic Crystal. I could imagine her smiling to herself in her dark closet. And if I texted her, she'd ignore me until I told her I'd gone out and talked to people.

So that's what I did. I wanted to go to Central Park, but June and Tate were both busy packing for the weekend, so instead I stood outside on the street. Joe keeps saying he's not a babysitter, but he also told me to stand where he could keep an eye on me.

"Hello, excuse me!" I cried.

But the man in the suit whizzed by me without stopping.

"Hello, ma'am—"

The elderly woman glanced at me quickly before picking up her pace.

Person after person ignored me. Finally, I spotted a woman with a baby stroller and a dog.

She's the one, I told myself.

As soon as she was about ten feet away, I took a giant breath and stepped into the middle of the sidewalk so she couldn't get past me without veering far off course.

"HELLO," I bellowed, waving my arms at her. "I AM NOT TRYING TO SELL YOU ANYTHING. DO YOU HAVE A MINUTE TO TALK ABOUT FAMILY RECIPES?"

There's a chance I shocked her into slowing down, but the important thing is that she did.

"Sorry, what?" she said. "Honey, are you okay?"

"More than okay." I put on my most charming smile. Then I took another big breath and told her about my family recipe project, and that I was looking for new recipes and stories to post, as quickly as I could get the words out.

"Oh . . . wow," she said once I'd finished. "You know, my grandma actually grew up on a farm in Minnesota. She still lives there. She has recipes she'd probably love to share with you." Her baby started to cry, and the woman made hushing noises and rocked the stroller. "I have to get moving, but do you have a card? With your email address and website?"

Cards. Business cards. That's exactly what I need. I remembered the kind you splurged for when you were trying to get your Etsy shop for handmade pet sweaters off the ground. The hot-pink ones with the leopard print on the back. *I need to make something like that.*

"I don't," I told the woman. "But I will. Soon. I can write it down for you, though, on your phone if you want—"

Somehow, she had managed to maneuver past me without me noticing. "It's okay," she interrupted. "Just tell me and I'll remember."

"My website is called the Family Cookbook!" I called after her. She was already halfway down the block. Wow, she was quick. "Mo Mo loves family food dot com! My name is Mo Gallagher! The Family Cookbook!"

I called out my email address, too, and the woman nodded and gave me a thumbs-up before she disappeared around the corner.

Nan, I'm not stupid—I know she won't remember, but that's okay. At least she gave me the idea for the business cards. I already know how I'm going to make them, too. All I need is glitter, some craft paper, and those really nice markers with silvery ink that Crystal loves. Growth, here I come.

Oof—I'm getting carsick. I should probably stop writing. We should be getting to Tate's mom's house any minute now. The roads are lined with beautiful green trees, and the sky is robin's-egg blue with puffy white clouds flitting here and there. And it's hot. I can't wait to swim.

Love,
Mo

TUESDAY, AUGUST 22

Dear Nan,

We're back in the city. We've been back for a few days. I don't know where to start telling you about this weekend. So I guess I'll just . . . start.

To say Tate's mom's house is beautiful is a huge understatement. Everything in June and Tate's life is beautiful. The car they rented didn't bounce or jolt like taxis do, their clothes barely wrinkle, and their flowers never look sad or droopy or get that weird-smelling cloudy water, when you've kept them for maybe a few days too long.

The gravel driveway was the length of a city block, and the grass on either side was so freshly cut you could see the patterns from where the lawn mower had gone back and forth. And the house—it was like a mini castle. I think it had fifty windows. I'm not exaggerating. Okay—well, maybe a little. But not much.

Four of her five golden retrievers came bounding out to bark at the car as we crunched to a stop in front of the house.

Tate's mom came out next. She was wearing a white

linen shirt with matching white linen shorts, and diamonds the size of marbles hanging from her earlobes. She
definitely falls into that whole beautiful and unwrinkled
category Tate and June belong in. Literally—I didn't see
one wrinkle on her face. It was like a smooth, freshly
ironed sheet. Her forehead didn't crease when she smiled.
Nothing moved at all.

As Tate parked, June took a deep breath, almost like
she was at the dentist, about to get a cavity filled. When
she noticed me looking, she smiled. "Here we are. You
ready to swim?"

"Sure am," I said. Then I hopped out of the car.

"*Hello,*" Mrs. Townsend said. "You must be *Mo.* It's so
nice to meet you."

"Nice to meet you, too, Mrs. Townsend," I said. And then,
because I was nervous, I did something dumb. I curtsied.

Tate laughed and put a hand on my shoulder. "You
don't have to be so formal, Mo."

"Yes, I *agree.* And call me *Bitsy,* for heaven's sake," Mrs.
Townsend said. She has a funny way of emphasizing every
other word in a weird, breathy way. She pointed at the
dogs. "That's Nixon; Ford's there, with the *bandanna;* the
pale blond one is Ike, and that's Reagan. But where H.W.
is, I don't know," she added, looking around.

"Aren't those the names of presidents?" I asked.

Mrs. Townsend looked delighted. "Why, yes, they are."

"Bitsy's a Republican," June explained.

"Yes, yes, dear, I know how you disapprove," Mrs. Townsend said, patting June on the cheek. "Now, everyone, come in! Lunch is *just* about ready. Then we can have a swim. How does that sound?"

"Good," I said, nodding. Because it did.

And it was good. The food was amazing. Mrs. Townsend said she has a chef come twice a week to make food and leave it in her fridge. Her own chef. No wonder it was so good. I wish the chef had been there over lunch, so I could have asked them all kinds of questions and if they had any cooking tips to share.

"Do you have any family recipes?" I asked Mrs. Townsend over lunch. I'd asked both Tate and June a couple weeks ago, but they both said they wanted to think about it. I thought maybe going straight to the source would be a better strategy. "I need more content. You know. So I can get more visitors."

She swirled her drink. "I have an incredible recipe for a gin gimlet."

"A what?" I asked.

"Mo isn't looking for cocktail recipes, Mom," Tate cut in. He glanced at me. "Sorry. Mom was never big on the cooking front."

I forked a green bean. "Don't worry. Neither was my grandma."

"Oh?" Mrs. Townsend leaned forward. "That's who you grew up with, yes?"

I nodded. "My mom died when I was little, so it was always just me and Nan."

I wanted to say more about you, because you were never *just* my grandma. But, like, if someone didn't know you before, how could they possibly understand you just from a couple things I said? They couldn't. No one could. You're impossible to distill.

Mrs. Townsend pressed a hand against her heart. "How *awful*. I am *so* sorry. Losing one's mother at such a young age is simply heartbreaking. What about your father?"

"Mom." Tate put his lemonade down hard on the table and turned to me. "Mo, we don't have to talk about any of this right now, if you don't want."

"It's okay," I said. Tate and June haven't asked many questions about Mom. It's kind of felt like they've danced around it. More than anything, I want them all to understand. Because like you always said, addiction is a disease, like cancer. And getting sick isn't something to be ashamed about, not something to hide. It's something to get help for. It's something to be sad about, definitely, and maybe a tiny bit mad. And so I explained about Mom's addiction and her overdose.

"And I don't have a father," I added when I was done. "Not really."

Mrs. Townsend stared at me. "Well, I'm very sorry to hear about your mother. That's terrible, terrible business. But surely you *do* have a father. It's a simple fact of *biology*."

I thought about the year after Johnny stopped coming

to see me, when I was six. I was still sad about it then, but I had you. You'd wrap your arms around me and hug me and snuffle my neck like a pig until I started to laugh, and everything would be okay. But you aren't there to do that for me anymore. And I was starting to feel done answering her questions.

"No," I snapped. "It isn't simple. And I don't."

Mrs. Townsend pressed her hand to her chest. "Well."

June pushed back from the table. "I think it's time for a swim, don't you?"

After lunch, I swam and swam and swam. I wanted June to swim with me, but she was sitting in the shade reading a book, and she kept telling me, "One more page. One more page, and then I'll get in."

But then she fell asleep. It was fine, though. Nixon and Ike (the dogs, not the presidents) love to swim, and every time I cannonballed into the pool, they jumped in after me.

After a while, I had to pee. Drinking four enormous glasses of chef-prepared mint lemonade will do that to you, I guess. And I didn't want to do it in the pool, ever since you told me the water would turn bright purple and stain my bathing suit. So I went inside, trying not to drip too much water on the polished wooden floors.

I heard Tate and his mom talking in the kitchen. I was about to go in, to ask which way the bathroom was, when I stopped. Mrs. Townsend was talking.

". . . rubber sheets, though, Tatey? Isn't she a little old to be wetting the bed?"

"It's part of the readjustment. She's been through a lot. Her caseworker said it happens."

I wanted to melt into the floor from the embarrassment. Or burst into flames. Just imagining Tate telling his mom about my problem was bad enough.

But then it got worse.

"Mom, what?" Tate said. "You're giving me that look."

Mrs. Townsend sighed. "She seems sweet enough. But she's a bit . . . rough around the edges, isn't she?"

"She's a good kid, Mom," Tate said. "Stop."

I couldn't see into the kitchen, but Mrs. Townsend must have stirred her drink, because I could hear the ice cubes clinking in her glass. "But are you *sure* you wouldn't rather start with a baby? Babies you can mold. No baggage, no history."

"June didn't want a baby."

"Why? Didn't want to deal with all the diapers and sleepless nights?"

"No," Tate said. "Because of her experience. Because of Terry Duclair."

"Ah. That's right," Tate's mom said. "I'd forgotten about all that. But, honey, listen. All that addiction business is not good news. That's in her genes. It could be something you have to deal with. I just feel like—"

"Mom, seriously," Tate said. "Stop."

"All right, all right," Mrs. Townsend said. I heard the smack of the fridge shutting. "But don't say I didn't warn

110

you, when she turns into an odd teenager with serious *problems*, and things start to go south."

I waited for Tate to respond. To say something, anything. But he didn't. He stayed completely silent.

After I found the bathroom, I tiptoed out of the house.

Once I was back outside, I didn't feel like swimming anymore. I didn't feel much like sunshine anymore, either.

Because she's right, isn't she? I don't belong in a place like this. Maybe there's a reason I've been feeling like I'm behind glass when I'm with Tate and June. A good reason.

The rest of the weekend went . . . fine. I swam with the dogs, we ate the chef's delicious food, we went to the beach to collect shells. I was there, but I wasn't really *there*, if that makes sense.

I emailed Billy yesterday. I told him I just needed to talk. But really, I want to see his face, because his face reminds me of you.

Oh, Nan. I wish you were here. Sometimes I wish for it so hard it seems almost impossible you don't puff into existence in a cloud of pink sparkles, ready to pack me up and take me back to the home where I belong.

Please come back. I know it's impossible, but please.

Please, please, please.
Mo

THURSDAY, AUGUST 24

Dear Nan,

I talked to Billy earlier today.

We used Signal, like we did last time. But today his connection was bad, so he kept freezing with these weird expressions on his face.

I only meant to check in with him. I really did. But I got a little carried away, and ended up saying the things I've been wanting to say since he left earlier this summer.

I guess you could say the conversation didn't go so well.

It started because he asked me about the Townsends, how I liked being there with them. And before I knew it, I was telling him all about what Tate's mom said about me. I even cried. I didn't do it on purpose—the tears just started falling. But I don't know if he even noticed, because he didn't seem sorry for me at all.

"Sounds like you hit the jackpot, Mo," he said. "I mean, a house in the Hamptons? Doesn't get much ritzier than that. Okay, so you have to deal with a mean old lady. So what? You're lucky."

"I know," I said, nodding. "I know I got lucky in a lot

of ways. But . . . I'd much rather be with you. I belong with you, not with them. I wouldn't ask if I didn't need it. Please, Billy."

"Mo . . ."

"Please. I need you," I said. "I need you more than the United States of America needs you."

He let out a long breath. But he didn't look sad or sorry. He looked . . . mad.

"Mo, there's something you need to understand," he finally said. "Everything in my life growing up was always about your mom. It was Molly this, Molly that. 'Molly's struggling, Molly needs help,' Ma always said. It was never 'Billy needs help, Billy's struggling.' I barely graduated high school because Ma was so focused on Molly. Ma's whole life was spent cleaning up her messes. And when Molly had you, the whole process started over again. It became 'Let's protect Mo,' and 'Let's make sure to give Mo the world.' It was all about you. Never me. She never even *asked* if I was okay with the idea of taking you after she was gone. You know that? Not once. She just assumed I'd be willing to give up everything that was important to me. So, Mo, I'm sorry, but for once in my life, I need to prioritize myself."

It came out in a burst, like all this had been roiling and storming inside of him for a long time. I felt like I'd been slapped.

"So, does that mean"—I swallowed—"does that mean you won't move back?"

113

"Yeah, Mo. That's exactly what that means," he said firmly. "I thought I've been clear about this. I thought you understood."

I pressed my teeth together so hard I thought they might break. He'd felt this way for all this time and never said anything? "Well, I lied. Because I don't need you. In fact, I *hate* you!"

And then I slammed the computer screen shut.

But the thing is, I don't hate him. I'm mad at him. And I'm mad at Mom. And I'm even a little bit mad at you.

Mo

FRIDAY, AUGUST 25

Dear Nan,

Something bad happened this morning.

Something worse than the black clouds of smoke at Ms. Schirle's apartment. Because this time, the thing that went haywire wasn't the oven—it was *me*.

I was sitting at the kitchen counter, eating a piece of toast with grape jelly, when June came in. "Hey, Mo, does this dress look okay? I've got a meeting with a clothing brand for a potential partnership, and . . ." She laughed a little. "I guess I'm nervous."

I looked at her. Her blond hair was swept back into a low bun, and she was wearing dangly blue earrings that complemented her crisp white dress. Her lipstick was so perfectly applied it was like a makeup artist had put it on for her. She looked beautiful.

Then I caught a glimpse of my own reflection in the black of the oven door, which Jessica had polished until it sparkled, like a mirror. My hair was in a bunch of puffy knots—because you know how it gets in the mornings. My saggy pajama top was slouched off my shoulder, and I'm pretty sure I had a smear of something—jelly, probably—on my cheek.

I wanted to smudge out my reflection until I wasn't just rough around the edges, like Tate's mom had said. I wanted to smudge it out until I disappeared.

"You look perfect," I told June, my eyes on the counter. I couldn't bear to look back at her.

"Okay, good. Thanks, Mo. Wish me luck."

She squeezed my shoulder on her way out. I sat there, staring at my fingerprint-smudged water glass and sticky, half-eaten toast, until I heard the front door click shut.

I went to take a drink of water, to help get rid of the lump in my throat. But instead of picking it up, I slowly, slowly pushed my glass off the counter.

And this glass didn't *thunk* like the one at Ms. Schirle's did. This one shattered. Bits of glass sprayed across the kitchen floor. And it felt just as good as I hoped it would.

Next, I picked up my plate. I didn't even bother to take off the toast, and I didn't slowly push it off the countertop, either. I threw it. The plate shattered, too.

It was like an alien parasite had taken over my brain. I don't think I could have stopped even if I'd wanted to. I reached out and grabbed the pretty glass fruit bowl next, letting the bananas fall out and the apples roll off the counter. I'd just heaved it when I saw June standing in the doorway between the kitchen and the entryway.

"I—forgot my phone," she sputtered. "Mo, what are you doing?"

I finally snapped out of it and burst into tears. "I'm sorry. I don't know why I did that. I'll clean it up. I'll pay for it all—"

"I don't have time to handle this right now." June pressed her hand to her forehead. "I really don't."

"I'm sorry," I said again. I slid off the stool, and I could hear the glass crunch beneath my rubber-soled slippers. "I'll clean it up, I'll—"

"No, Mo, don't. I don't want you to hurt yourself."

But I already have, haven't I? I hurt June, and I hurt myself. I'm not just growing up to be a kid with problems. I already *am* a kid with problems.

"Mo, please." June's voice was strained. "Just go to your room."

And so I did. I walked there slowly, replaying what I'd done in my head again and again. Replaying the horrified look on June's face.

I expected her to come barging into my room after she finished cleaning up my mess, like you would have, to chew me out, to ground me for a million years, to make me apologize, right this instant.

But she didn't. No one did.

I'm still here, sitting fully under my blanket. Head and everything. What is wrong with me? What have I done?

Oh—someone's knocking.

It's . . . Moira.

Why is *she* here?

Oh, Nan. Truly: what have I done?

FRIDAY, AUGUST 25
(LATER)

Dear Nan,

Sorry for that cliff-hanger.

So anyway, when I opened the door, Moira was standing there.

"Hi," I said, staring at her feet. She had on her old Converse sneakers, as always. I didn't want to look her in the face, to see how disappointed she was in me.

"June called. She said—"

I nodded and swallowed, trying to keep myself from crying. "Is she—are they—"

"Why don't you get changed, and we can go for a walk."

My hands shook as I pulled on a pair of shorts and my rainbow tank top. It would have taken too long to brush the knots out of my hair, so I put on my lucky Jets hat instead.

I knew I could use all the luck I could get.

When we got down to the lobby, Joe put his hand up for a high five, but lowered it when he saw my puffy red eyes. "Hey, kid, you good?"

I wasn't, not at all. I sort of shrugged.

"Hey, lady, what's up? Everything okay with our girl?" he called out to Moira.

The words "our girl" stabbed me, right in the heart. Because who knew if that's what I would still be once Moira and I were back from our walk?

"It's fine," Moira said, a little bristly. I don't think she liked being called lady. But when she glanced over her shoulder, she must have seen how concerned Joe looked, because when she spoke again, the bristle was gone. "My name's Moira, by the way."

"Joe." His eyes didn't leave us, even after we went out the door.

Moira and I went to Central Park. It's only a few blocks from June and Tate's apartment. Have I told you that? And the only thing I could think was, I'm going to miss being so close to the park.

Once we'd walked for a bit, we sat together on a green bench. A man was playing the guitar a few benches away, its melody drifting on the air. A jogger ran by with her dog. The sun was warm on my skin.

"So," Moira said. "Talk to me. What happened?"

I still couldn't look at her. "I don't know. I sort of . . . lost control."

I told her that I didn't like Tate's mom, and also about how I got in a big fight with my uncle. And I told her how in the moment, smashing stuff seemed like the only thing that could possibly make me feel better.

"I know you're still hurting. I know things are hard. But that's completely unacceptable behavior," Moira said. "And there are better ways to deal with your feelings when they get this big. I think we should consider getting you into therapy."

"My grandma didn't believe in therapy," I told her.

"Well, I do, and I think it would help you."

I thought it over for a minute. Would therapy help fix whatever is inside me that's making me do such stupid, weird things? Like smashing glasses and wetting the bed? Doubtful. But I didn't feel like I had much choice.

"Okay," I said, even though I didn't love the idea.

She told me she was going to get it set up, and in the meantime, we talked about better ways to deal with it when your insides feel like bubbly lava. Drawing, journaling, taking deep breaths, going for a walk, calling a friend. Things like that.

They were all good ideas, but the dread was still there, icy and cold in my stomach. So finally, I came out with it.

"Moira . . . I . . . I don't really belong with the Townsends, do I?"

"What?"

"I'm not a good fit."

Moira stared at me. "What are you talking about? I thought you were doing well with them. Missteps like this aren't unusual, Mo. It happens."

"I . . . I don't know." I scuffed the ground with the toe of my shoe. "They probably don't want to keep me, after what I did, right? Isn't that why you're here? To tell me I have to move again?"

Moira had an odd look on her face. "I thought you understood. June and Tate are a pre-adoptive placement."

"Wait," I said. "What do you mean?"

"Remember? We talked about it before you met them in the office. When it became clear to us that your uncle wasn't going to be available to you for permanency, we changed the classification of your case. Pre-adoptive means they're fostering with the intent to adopt you."

Her words washed over me. Now that I was thinking about it, Moira had said something along those lines to me, hadn't she? I don't know how that didn't click in my brain until now.

"They want to adopt me?"

"I'm sorry. I thought this was clear," Moira said again. "There's obviously still a lot of hoops we have to jump through. We're still trying to figure out if we can reach your father, though we've been unsuccessful thus far, which usually isn't a good sign. They understand that things can change if we find family for you in the meantime. That's what it means to be a pre-adoptive placement. I'm sorry, clearly I didn't explain this to you well enough. Do you have any questions?"

Did I have any questions? I had a million. But I shook my head. I needed time to digest all of this.

"Okay." She patted my leg. "But now, it's time to make some apologies."

When I got back to the apartment, Tate still wasn't home from work. June was there, though, which means she must have canceled her meeting.

"I'll leave you to it," Moira said before letting herself out.

"I'm so sorry for what I did." I looked up at June. "For ruining your beautiful things. For making a mess. I don't know what's wrong with me, but I can promise you it won't happen again. I'll stop messing up your perfect lives."

"Oh, Mo. We're not even close to perfect. Some days I feel like I couldn't be further from perfect." For a second, she looked like she wanted to cry, but instead, she started to laugh. She slid to the floor, right there in the entryway. She patted the spot next to her. "Sit with me."

So I did.

"I owe you an apology, too," June said, which is the last thing I expected her to say. "I'm sorry I wasn't calmer or more understanding in my response. I know being in care can be incredibly stressful. I of all people should know that. I should have handled my reaction better."

"What do you mean, you of all people?" I asked.

"I probably should have told you this before now. I don't know why I haven't. But I've also been in the system. I spent eight months in foster care as a teenager."

I stared at her. At her clear skin, her nice clothes, her soft blond hair. "You did? *You?*"

She nodded. "It was only a temporary thing. My parents

had to get themselves ironed out. My childhood wasn't exactly stable, and I was starting to act out."

Again, I couldn't help but shake my head in disbelief. It was hard to imagine June acting anything but put-together.

"The point is, my sister and I were placed with an older woman. She was single. She'd moved to Boston from Haiti when she was a little girl, and didn't have any family or kids around. But she had the biggest heart, and so much love to give, so she became a foster parent." She smiled a little. "Her name was Terry Duclair."

Terry Duclair. That was the name Tate had mentioned to his mom when we'd been in the Hamptons. He'd said she'd been the reason June wanted to foster a kid like me instead of adopting a baby.

"Even though my sister and I only lived with her for a little while, I never lost touch with her," June went on. "Terry became a better mom to me than my actual mom, even after I went home. She was there for everything. She was the one I asked to walk me down the aisle when Tate and I got married. She died two years ago."

"Oh. I'm so sorry," I said, and I meant it.

"Thanks, Mo. It was so hard for me to lose her." She looked at me. "I'm sure you understand better than anyone. Once she was gone, I realized I wanted—no, I needed—that relationship in my life. But I also knew I wasn't a kid anymore." She put her arm around my shoulder and squeezed me closer to her. "Which meant if I wanted a relationship like the one I had with her, it was my turn to be the Terry for someone else."

We sat like that for another moment, and then at the exact same time, we leaned more into each other and hugged right there, on the entryway floor.

That's when the front door opened, and Tate stepped in. He looked frazzled, like he'd jumped over trash cans and bumped into people to get home fast, but when he saw us like that, he gave us a tentative, hopeful smile. "We all good here?"

June and I both nodded at the same time.

And, Nan—it's the strangest thing.

You know those summer storms, when it's so hot and humid you almost feel like you're walking around in a steamy bathroom after a shower? But then the sky breaks open with thunder and lightning and rain, and the next morning the air is perfectly clear and crisp?

It feels like that. The air between the three of us feels cleaner, clearer, and maybe I'm imagining it, but I almost feel . . . closer to them.

Like maybe I belong here more than I thought I did.

I guess sometimes a storm can be a good thing.

I love you, Nan. Thanks for watching over me.

Mo

SATURDAY, AUGUST 26

Dear Nan,

You'll never guess who emailed me.

Remember that woman I ran into on the street, with the little dog and the baby in the stroller? Her *grandma* emailed me. From Minnesota. I never thought I would hear from either of them. But instead of telling you what she said, I printed out her email and I'm going to staple it on the next page.

She may be a grandma all the way in Minnesota, but the Family Cookbook has its first fan! Exciting, right?

Love you,
Mo

From: martha.c.walker.674@hotmail.com
To: momolovesfamilyfood@gmail.com
Subject: "The Family Cookbook"

Dear "Mo,"

What a charming nickname. Is it short for Maureen, or for Mona? Whatever the case, it most certainly made me smile.

My granddaughter mentioned your website to me when we spoke on the phone last week. She said you told her about it quite exuberantly on the streets of New York City.

I live on a farm in Kellogg, Minnesota, and I'm sure it is very different from where you live. We have cows, chickens who peck and scratch at the dirt, and a huge vegetable garden. In the summer, we grow a whole field of watermelons for our town's annual watermelon festival.

I've lived on the same farm since I was a little girl, back when the only heat we had came from the woodstove, and we used to have to heat up wooden buckets of water from the well to take baths.

But as I looked through the recipes you've posted on your marvelous website, I realized that while times have certainly changed, many of my favorite family recipes have not.

Particularly one for buttermilk pie. My family lived on the farm through the Great Depression, and much of what one cooked depended on what ingredients were available at one's fingertips. Many of our family recipes had lots of eggs, because they could be gathered every day from our laying hens. We churned our own butter, which meant we often had leftover buttermilk needing to be used. The result was a delicious buttermilk pie.

Even though the Great Depression is long in our country's past, this pie is still my granddaughter's favorite dessert to this day. And I hope my great-grandchildren will enjoy it, too, once they're old enough to eat solid food. It brings me great comfort to know a small piece of our family's Minnesota history will continue on, all the way in bright and bustling New York City.

I've scanned a copy of the recipe here, along with some old photographs of how things used to look on the farm, back when this recipe was first dreamt up by my own grandmother. It was my first time using the scanner setting on my printer, so I hope everything looks all right. I had to have my grandson talk me through it over the phone. So if you have trouble reading the recipe card, take issue with him. (And email me back, and I will try to scan it again.)

Keep up the wonderful work, Mo. I've already told my church group about your project, as well as my neighbors. We can't wait to see what recipes and stories you post next.

With warm wishes,
Martha C. Walker

Buttermilk Pie (Mom's recipe)

Use any kind of pastry shell in a 9" pie
pan. Pie filling goes into an unbaked
shell.

1 cup sugar
1/2 cup butter
3 eggs
3 Tbsp. flour
1 cup buttermilk
1/4 tsp. salt
1 Tbsp. lemon juice
1 tsp. lemon zest

For the buttermilk pie filling, cream
butter and sugar. Add eggs one by one,
mix. Add flour, lemon zest, lemon juice,
buttermilk, and salt.

Pour into unbaked pie shell. Bake at
350°F for 60 minutes. Cool before slicing.
Best served with whipped cream.

TUESDAY, AUGUST 29

Dear Nan,

I made the buttermilk pie this weekend. No—I made butter-milk *pies*, plural. This recipe was way harder than I was ex-pecting, since the instructions were so simple. And I even used a frozen pie crust to make things easier on myself. Even so, the first pie I made got way too dark on top, and when I sliced into it, water pooled in the pie tin. I thought maybe I hadn't cooked it long enough, so I made a second one and baked it longer. But the filling got all lumpy! I really wanted to get it right, so I spent an hour on Google reading about pie-baking. After doing a ton of research, I decided to make a third pie. This time, I used buttermilk with more fat in it, and mixed it in last. Halfway through baking, I covered it with aluminum foil to keep it from getting too dark. Then I used a food thermometer to test when the center of the pie was 180 degrees, because the internet said that's how I would know it was done.

I guess the third time really is the charm, because this pie came out golden brown on top, and the filling was creamy and tangy and totally different from anything I've ever tasted. It wasn't lumpy or weeping water. I still feel proud of myself for sticking with it. I guess getting better at something means being willing to try again and again.

As I ate it, I tried to imagine myself on a farm nearly one hundred years ago, during the Great Depression, surrounded by a big family and some chickens and cows, too. Tate had a slice, but June didn't. She's taking a break from gluten and sugar this month.

The photos I took of the pie turned out great, thanks to Crystal's coaching. Probably my best round of photos yet.

I called Crystal over video chat yesterday to tell her all about it. She had her phone propped against a pillow on her bed, so my view of her was crooked.

"Guess what?" I asked the top of her head.

"What?" she said, not looking up from her summer math packet.

(Which reminds me, I better get started on that. . . .)

"I've got a fan in Minnesota," I told her.

"Cool." Crystal put her pencil down and straightened her phone. "You've got a fan in Brooklyn, too. Lao Lao goes to your website every morning. She likes when you post lots of pictures. Oh, and I forgot to tell you—she wants you to come over so she can show you how to make dumplings."

"Really?" I said. "For real?"

I've told you how important dumpling-making is in the

Wang household, right? Especially around Chinese New Year, which usually happens in January or February. I've never been invited before, and I assumed it was because it was Wang family only.

Crystal laughed. "Yep. You'll be the first non-family attendee."

"Tell her I'm honored."

"You can tell her yourself," Crystal said. "Does this weekend work? Sunday?"

"Perfectly."

"Good. We also have to figure out what to wear for our first day."

"We have time," I said.

"Not really. School starts next week."

She's right. It snuck up on me, Nan. How can summer be almost over already?

I'm getting better and better at stopping people on the streets. I've started walking Joe to his subway stop after his shift is over at six o'clock. Partly because he's nice to walk with, and June and Tate say I'm allowed to walk the few blocks back to the apartment alone, as long as I always bring my phone with me.

But mainly, I go to make sure he doesn't smoke. He showed me his nicotine patch today. He told me it's been thirteen days since he had a cigarette, so I gave him thirteen high fives.

On our walks to the subway station, I stop to talk with

people about the Family Cookbook so I can collect more recipes. And I'm getting a lot better at it. I've practiced my speech—or my *spiel*, as you would say. The secret is to not approach people who are walking, because they're usually in a hurry to get somewhere, but people who are standing still, sitting, or thinking. A captive audience, Joe joked.

Often I'll ask if I can sit down next to them, and then I'll introduce myself. Sometimes I use my phone to pull up my website or my TikTok, depending on how old the person is. I'll tell them about the kinds of stories and recipes I'm looking for—Georgie's egg-lemon soup, the Great Depression buttermilk pie, the "I'm sorry" lemon bars that worked not only for Beau but for me, too.

The stories often interest people more than the recipes. It gets them thinking about their own families.

Today I had a nice talk with a gray-haired man from Iran, who was sitting outside of a coffee shop, drinking a tiny cup of espresso. His name was Asad, and he was quiet for a long time after I asked about a family recipe.

"When my wife and I first came to this country," he finally said, "she wanted to do everything American. American this, American that. Instead of making things that tasted like home, she wanted to make new things. One night, she made chicken potpie. She was so proud. Her first completely American recipe, she said. But she put walnut paste in it. And saffron. It came out bright yellow, and she sprinkled the whole thing with pomegranate seeds. But it was also delicious. It became our joke. A little Iran in America. And for us, it was perfect."

"Oh," I said. I loved his story. "Do you remember the ingredients?"

"It—it's hard to remember, exactly," he said. He cleared his throat. "It's been a long time since I tasted her cooking. She passed away ten years ago."

I know exactly how much it can hurt when someone brings you up, right when I'm not expecting it. I walk around every day with the weight of knowing you're gone, but sometimes a stranger asking about you can still feel like a lightning bolt of sadness from a clear blue sky. "I'm sorry."

"No—I'm glad to think of it. To think of her."

And I know that feeling, too.

He used the heel of his hand to dab the corner of his eye. "I could send you a letter, once I find a copy of it. And maybe some pictures, too."

"Here," I said, passing him one of the glittery cards I'd made with all my info on it. "You can email me. I'd love to write about it. About her."

"I am not very good with email, but I can try," he said. He smiled at my card and then put it in his shirt pocket carefully, like he was afraid to bend it even the tiniest bit.

I waved goodbye.

"Ready?" Joe asked. I nodded.

Joe never interrupts my conversations, even when they last for a while. Whenever I ask if he wants me to hurry,

134

if he's worried he'll miss his train, he always says the same thing.

"Nah. There'll be another one. There always is."

I like that he says that. But what I like even more is it seems like he actually means it.

Love,
Mo

SATURDAY, SEPTEMBER 2

Dear Nan,

Today was a good day. A big day. A few things happened I want to tell you about.

First is something I've been dreading: I had my first therapy appointment. My palms were sweating as I sat in the waiting room with Tate, because I could almost see you up in the sky, angel arms crossed, tongue clucking, saying something like "my granddaughter doesn't need to be there."

But it wasn't at all like I thought it would be. Neither was my doctor. Her name is Dr. Barbara Nielson. She's tall and big and warm like you. She said, "You can call me Dr. Nielson, or Barbara, or Dr. Barb. Or even just Doc. Whatever you like most." I like Dr. Barb, so that's what I'll be calling her.

I didn't have to lie back on a couch and talk about my feelings or my deepest fears. Mostly, we played some games and drew things together, which sounds babyish, but wasn't. First, she wanted me to draw a picture of a person, so I drew you. After that, Dr. Barb gave me this zenlike sandbox to play around with. I used one of the tiny rakes and combed the sand into neat patterns for a little while. Then we talked. About you, mostly. We also talked a little about what happened that day with the glass smashing in the kitchen, but we didn't get into any of the bed-wetting stuff.

The hour went by like (imagine me snapping my fingers) *that*. I don't feel different, but I think you might have the wrong opinion about therapy. We'll see.

After, I got to go out to lunch with Tate and his dad, Ed, because he was in town for work. Ed lives in Santa Barbara now, close to Tate's brother, Andrew, who lives in LA.

Ed dresses like a college professor and still has all his hair. He told me about how he goes surfing most mornings. When I told him that I didn't know old people could still go surfing, he threw his head back and let out a big, booming laugh. If you met him, you'd probably have a crush on him.

After we finished lunch, he gave me a big hug. "You've got to come to California soon, Mo! I know Andrew and my grandsons would love to meet you."

"Yeah, that would be fun, wouldn't it? I can check with Junie. You know her work schedule," Tate said to his dad.

"Ah, yes. Busy as a bee, that one."

Ed brought me back to the apartment in a taxi, because Tate had to get back to the office. It was just as easy to be with him as it is to be around Tate. Maybe this isn't a nice thing to say, but I can see why Tate's parents got divorced.

I can't picture him and Tate's mom together at all. And I can also see where Tate gets his Tate-ness from. I hope we get to see his dad again soon.

And then the third good thing that happened today is that once Ed dropped me back at the apartment, June took the afternoon off work so we could go school shopping together. It was kind of incredible.

She'd made a list of things she thought I'd need, and we went through each store, aisle by aisle, checking things off her list. No offense, but I've never felt so organized and ready for a new school year in my entire life.

After we got back from the store, she helped me label all my binders for different subjects, and organized my pens and pencils in a new rainbow pencil case. She even put little labels that said "Mo Gallagher" on everything so if I lost anything, it could be returned to me.

"I live for this kind of stuff," she told me. "My childhood home was incredibly disorganized. My parents never got rid of anything, and it would pile up in boxes in the hallways, the living room. Everywhere. It makes me feel centered when everything has its place."

And I can see what she means. I feel ready, prepared, and excited for Tuesday. Maybe I'll even get on the honor roll this year. A girl can dream, right?

Love,
Mo

SUNDAY, SEPTEMBER 3

Dear Nan,

It's been a couple days, but I haven't gotten an email from that man I met. Asad. I want to make his wife's recipe. A bright-yellow chicken potpie with pomegranate seeds would look great in pictures. I love colorful food almost as much as I love colorful clothes.

I'd also like to hear more about Asad's wife. I wonder if she came up with that recipe by herself. If she passed it along to friends or family. If she has any special tricks for making potpie that I wouldn't learn online or in a cookbook. I bet she does. I also wonder if Asad has ever made it for himself, so he can think about her while he eats it. That's what I would do, if I had a recipe that connected me to you.

But maybe . . . would it make me sad instead of happy? I don't know. If I had a recipe of yours, then at least I would find out.

I couldn't stop thinking that maybe, if Asad had been able to send me a real letter instead of an email, he would have written to me.

"June," I said after dinner last night. "Can I put the address for the apartment on my website?"

By the look on her face, I realized it was a stupid question.

"That's not safe, Mo," June said. "You should never share your address on the internet. Why would you want to do that?"

"Sorry," I said. "Never mind. It's stupid. I wanted people to be able to send me letters, not just emails."

"We could open you a PO box," she offered.

Apparently, there are mailboxes at the post office you can sign up for, so you don't have to give out your personal address. The post office is closed tomorrow for the holiday, so she promised we'd go later this week to sign me up. As soon as I get one, people will be able to send not only emails, but real paper letters. I updated the information on my website that a PO box was coming soon.

Maybe Asad will visit my website, and see that he can send me a letter now instead of an email. I hope he does.

Oh—I should go. Today is the day I'm going over to Crystal's to learn how to make dumplings with her family. I've doubled-checked three or four times to make sure my phone is charged to one hundred percent. I want to take a lot of pictures.

I'll make sure to save you a dumpling or two.

Love,
Mo

SUNDAY, SEPTEMBER 3
(LATER)

Dear Nan,

It's official: I'm a dumpling.

Or maybe it's that I'm so full of dumplings I feel like I'm turning into one.

It took a lot of persuading, but I convinced June and Tate it was okay for me to take the subway to Brooklyn by myself.

"I promise. I've been doing it since I was eight," I said. "I know all the lines backward and forward. It's the only way me and Nan got around the city."

"To Brooklyn, though? That's a long trip. There will be transfers. I don't know." Tate turned to June. "We should probably ask Moira."

"We can make *some* decisions by ourselves, Tate," June responded. "I say it's okay. As long as you call us as soon as you get to Crystal's."

And it did take a long time. A little more than an hour, and I didn't just have to transfer lines, I had to transfer stations, too. I didn't realize how far away I live now. Before, all I had to do was take the M, no transfers, nothing.

Sure, there was some walking involved, but nothing too bad.

That's when it dawned on me: school is in Brooklyn. Which means getting there every day is going to take about this long now, too.

I tried to push it out of my mind—because maybe I can do my homework in the mornings on my commute, instead of the night before—as I walked up the steps to Crystal's narrow white house.

One of the windows was open, and I could hear a mix of music, English, and Mandarin coming from inside. I stopped for a minute to savor it. Crystal hates it, but I love that her house is like this. Always loud and full of people and sounds.

Both front doors banged open—the metal-barred one, and the wood one behind it. Crystal stood there, bouncing baby Charlie on her hip. He already looked so much bigger than when I saw him last.

"There you are. Mom!" she cried over her shoulder. "Can you take Charlie now? Mo's here!"

I stepped inside right as Crystal's mom appeared. "Hi, Mo!"

As soon as I saw how happy she was to see me—how uncomplicated her smile was—it made me feel like it was the right decision not asking Moira to check if the Wangs would take me in. The best decision. Because I can come here and be the old me.

"Thanks for having me over. I'm really excited."

"No one more than my mother," Crystal's mom said, taking Charlie from Crystal. Then she called out, "Ma, Crystal's friend Mo is here!"

Crystal's grandma called something back in Mandarin.

"She wants us in the kitchen," Crystal said. "Come on."

"Is your dad here?" I asked.

"No." She rolled her eyes. "Band practice."

I don't know why Crystal is always so embarrassed. It's cool he plays bass in a punk band and wears ripped-up T-shirts. Software engineer by day, rock star by night. But whenever I say that, she rolls her eyes even harder.

"Rock stars don't play at dive bars for a hundred bucks a gig," she's said to me before. But at the same time, I know Crystal has more of their song lyrics memorized than anyone in the world.

Crystal's grandma was sitting at their kitchen table, a spread of ingredients all around her. One of Crystal's cousins was sitting on the stool across from her, on her phone, texting so fast her thumbs were a blur.

Crystal's grandma smiled at me and patted the seat next to her. I went and sat down, and then we got started.

"Squash." She pointed at a big pile of long green vegetables that looked a lot like zucchini. She moved on. "Pork. Dried shrimp. Chives. Green onion. White pepper, soy sauce, sesame oil, eggs, and this is dumpling wrapper. I used to make from scratch, but much faster with these."

Even though Crystal's told me that her grandma speaks

Mandarin ninety-nine percent of the time, she always makes an effort to switch to English whenever I come over. Wallace offers Mandarin starting in seventh grade, and I'm thinking I'll take it. It would be nice to be able to return the favor.

First we grated the squash and added salt to draw out the water. We let it sit out while we made the meat and egg mixtures.

"Sometimes we use other kinds of vegetables instead," Crystal whispered to me. "I actually like it with cabbage better. But don't tell Lao Lao."

Once we squeezed the water out of the squash, we mixed it together with everything else. Then came the hardest part: filling and folding the dumplings.

Everyone was at the table now to help—Crystal's aunt, two of Crystal's cousins, and Crystal's mom, with Charlie bouncing on her lap. Crystal's grandpa was sitting in a folding chair in the corner of the kitchen, reading a Chinese newspaper and drinking tea.

Everyone had a slightly different style, but Crystal's grandma was the fastest by far.

"This is how you fold," she instructed me. "Look."

But I could hardly figure out the steps as I watched her fold dumpling after dumpling, each one coming out perfectly. It was like a dance her fingers knew how to do without trying.

When it was my turn, I kept using too much water or putting in too much filling, or too little. So after I'd folded about five good ones (which took a long time), I started taking pictures.

Crystal's mom laughing as Charlie tried to grab the dumplings off the table. Crystal concentrating hard on folding the edges of her batch, the tip of her tongue between her teeth. Her grandpa drinking tea, leaning back in his chair.

Crystal's grandma waved me over to look at something on the countertop. There were photographs spread out. "So much history. Here. Look. This is me." She pointed at one picture in particular. "In China."

One of the photos, which was a little faded, showed a family around a table, making dumplings. But even though the hair and clothing styles were different, it looked a lot like the scene in the Wangs' kitchen right now. The same smiles, the same concentration, the same focused postures, shoulders sloped and necks bent. Except now she's not the little girl learning how to do it, but the grandma passing the tradition down.

I saw it then: their family like a strong chain—generation after generation, connected through the years by food. Suddenly the ingredients didn't just feel like dumpling wrappers and vegetables and pork filling anymore.

They felt like something precious.

I made another silent wish that I would get an email from a Gallagher. Someone who knew you, Nan. And then maybe I'd feel that same connection to our family that I was seeing here today.

"Oh," Crystal's mom said, coming over. She looked at the photos. "I'd forgotten about these. Look how young you were!"

"Ha!" Crystal's grandma said, shaking her head. She patted her gray hair. "Feels impossible."

Crystal's mom laughed. She handed the photos back to me, and I took videos and pictures of it all with my phone. I found the good lighting, just like Crystal had instructed me. And then I arranged the old photographs on the table, so there were dumpling wrappers and leftover squash in the corners, framing it. It looked pretty artsy. I've gotta say, I'm getting good at this whole picture-taking thing.

Later, once we'd pan-fried the dumplings, we each got a plate of them with sauce to dip them into.

Crystal and I ate ours sitting on the front stoop.

While we ate, I decided to tell Crystal about my secret hope. About how I hoped the Family Cookbook might help me find a family recipe of my own.

"Well, you can't expect it just to happen, can you?" Crystal said as soon as I was done talking. "You have to put it out there. Write about it as your next post. Tell people that's what you're looking for."

"Really? You think?"

"Yep. I do. Manifest your destiny. That's what Mr. Gregory always used to say, remember?"

Then she reached over with her chopsticks to grab the last dumpling off my plate, but I fought her off, speared it with a single chopstick, and stuffed it in my mouth.

146

"Is too goo," I said, my mouth full.

We both laughed.

A minute later, Crystal stood up. "I'm still hungry. Will you come get chicken nuggets with me?"

"Sure." And so we did.

After, Crystal copied down the dumpling recipe for me, as dictated by her grandma in a mix of English and Mandarin.

You would have loved it, Nan. Not the dumpling-making part—you're too impatient for that—but the to-getherness, the chatting, the eating.

I miss you.

Mo

PS Football season is kicking into full gear soon. If you have any of that angel (or ghost) good-luck dust left over, please give the Jets a hefty sprinkle. Because boy, do they need it.

NEW YEAR'S DUMPLINGS

Makes a lot of dumplings. I don't know how many exactly. Neither does Lao Lao.

Lao Lao says it's easiest to think about making the filling in three steps. This is always how she does it.

<u>For the meat:</u>
10 ounces ground pork
10 dried shrimp (Lao Lao says you can use fresh shrimp, too, just add a little extra salt), diced into tiny pieces
3 tablespoons soy sauce
½ teaspoon grated ginger
¼ teaspoon white pepper
1 tablespoon cooking wine (Lao Lao used Michiu Tou rice wine for this batch)
½ cup unsalted chicken broth
2 green onions, sliced very thin

1. Mix the pork, shrimp, soy sauce, ginger, and white pepper together. Lao Lao says it's important to stir it in one direction only.
2. Next, slowly mix in the wine and chicken broth. She says it's okay if the mixture looks a tiny bit more liquidy than you would think. It's good for it to be soft.
3. Sprinkle your sliced green onions on top of the mixture.

For the eggs:

2 eggs

⅛ teaspoon salt

1–2 tablespoons of cooking oil

1 tablespoon sesame oil

1. Beat the eggs together with the salt.
2. Add 1–2 tablespoons of cooking oil to a hot pan. Scramble the eggs, using a wooden spoon to break up the eggs into the smallest pieces possible. If they still look too big, Lao Lao says chop them up with a knife or use a food processor.
3. Add the eggs and the hot cooking oil on top of the meat mixture.
4. Add 1 tablespoon of sesame oil and mix it all together. Lao Lao says always stir in one direction!

For the vegetable:

2 small zucchini squash (or 1 big one)

Salt

1. Grate the squash and add ⅛ tsp. salt over the top, letting it sit for 10 minutes.
2. Squeeze out as much water as possible and then add the grated squash to the filling mixture.

For the dumplings:

1. Add a little spoonful of your filling to a dumpling wrapper. I don't exactly know how much. You just made a bunch, so you understand. Enough so when you go to pinch it, the filling doesn't spill out the sides.

2. Use water around the edges of the wrapper and press the dumpling together into a half-moon. I'm sure there are videos on YouTube you can watch if you can't remember from today.

3. Cook the dumplings in batches. We like to pan-fry them. Add some cooking oil in a pan over medium-high heat. Pan-fry one side of your dumplings until they start to brown, which can take about 30 seconds. Then add water, about ½ cup, and cover. Cook for 3 minutes. Take the cover off and cook until the water evaporates, which usually takes about 2 minutes.

4. Eat as many as Lao Lao will let you as she makes the batches. I love them hot out of the pan.

Hello,

I hope you are enjoying these family recipes, stories, and photographs. Every time I get a new submission, I do a little happy dance! So keep them coming, and tell all your friends and family about the Family Cookbook.

I wanted to write a special post today about something personal. And that is: I would really like to find a family recipe of my own.

The only problem is, other than my uncle and grandma, who both have never cooked, I've never known any other members of my family.

Here's my question: are *you* a Gallagher who might be related to Maureen Gallagher (me), William Gallagher (my uncle), or Kathleen "Kath" Gallagher (my grandma)? We are all from New York City. Well, my grandma moved here from Kansas in the 1970s. She worked in telemarketing and sold handmade pet sweaters on the internet. Even if you don't know them, do you know *any* Gallaghers who might be related to me? If so, please send me an email or a message. And especially send me an email if you have a recipe that belongs to my—our—family.

I would really like to find one soon.

Thanks for reading and watching!

Mo

From: timgall1974@aol.com
To: momolovesfamilyfood@gmail.com
Subject: Hello from a Gallagher!

Mo:

I'm not a relation of yours (at least I don't think so), but I *am* a Gallagher. Just wanted to say, keep up the great work. My daughter found you on TikTok and shared your website with us. My wife loves it, and our daughter most of all. She's already made that "I'm sorry" lemon bars recipe twice.

Good luck finding folks who are related to you. But for now, I wanted you to know you've got a family of us Gallaghers here in Ellsworth, Maine, who love what you're doing with this project!

Tim Gallagher

MONDAY, SEPTEMBER 4

Dear Nan,

I'm in bed but I couldn't sleep, so I turned my lamp on to write to you. Somehow, it's already Labor Day. How did this happen? It's September, but the air still feels like summer. My math packet is done, I read four books for summer reading, and Crystal and I have our first-day outfits ready to go—tie-dye jumpsuits we made ourselves in the bathtub. I'm so glad Wallace lets us have our first day back be uniform-free.

I wanted to use temporary spray-on hair dye to match the tie-dye, but Crystal said she didn't want to deal with the mess of it.

You would have loved it, though, right? The hair, I mean. If I came out of the bathroom with a head that looked like it had gotten stuck in a cotton-candy machine? You would have cackled and clapped and said, "You look like a troll doll!"

I'm not sure if June and Tate would like it, though, so I didn't push for it too hard.

Over dinner, I thought about our last-day-of-summer

tradition: walking to the corner for a giant Mister Softee cone. I almost suggested doing it with Tate and June, but it didn't feel quite right to do it without you.

"You seem far away. Thinking about school tomorrow?" June asked. We were eating dinner in the den. "You excited?"

"Yes," I said. I was. Nervous, too, but I didn't say that.

"Any more emails from any Gallaghers yet?" Tate asked.

"Not yet." I spun my fork in my zucchini noodles, more playing with them than eating. When I got that email from Tim Gallagher, my heart nearly pounded out of my chest. I've been checking my email at least once every twenty minutes ever since, but nothing else has come through. I don't think I have enough people who even know about Family Cookbook for it to reach the right people, but I'm going to keep hoping.

"I might have something that will cheer you up," Tate said, putting his fork down. "Hold on. Let me go get them."

Tate ran out of the room and was back just as fast. Fanned out in his hands were three little stubs.

Three little stubs that looked suspiciously like tickets. June was looking at them curiously, too.

"What are those?" I asked.

Tate grinned and passed them to me.

I stared at them, almost not believing it. Not believing it could be real.

"Are these . . . ," I started to say.

"Three tickets in a suite to see the Jets at their first home game?" He grinned wider. "Why, yes. Yes, they are."

"Oh. My. God!" I yelled. Then I got up and started hopping up and down. "Jets, Jets, Jets!"

Because a JETS GAME, NAN. Fancy seats! At a Jets game!

"Thank you," I cried. "Thank you, thank you, thank you! My grandma and I never actually went into the stadium. We always stayed in the parking lot."

"You're very welcome. I thought it would be a fun outing. Usually the suites are for way more people, but I found a couple of guys online who wanted to go in on one together. Maybe we can turn June into a sports fan."

"Doubtful," June said. "What weekend is it?"

"September seventeeth." I didn't need to look at the tickets. I already knew. "They're playing the Broncos. They're probably going to get slaughtered. The Jets, I mean. But hopefully, they'll go down with pride."

"Tate." June stared at him. "Kiera's wedding is that weekend. In Arizona, remember?"

Tate swore under his breath. "It's the same weekend? I totally forgot. The tickets are nonrefundable."

"We can't miss the wedding for a football game," June said. "I'm a bridesmaid."

"It's okay." I put the tickets on the coffee table. I didn't want them to see how disappointed I was. After I smashed the stuff in the kitchen, I made a promise to myself I was only ever going to be on the best behavior. No outbursts. No water after five p.m. so I don't wet the bed. (It's been working, although I wake up so thirsty I could drink an entire lake.) "I don't have to go."

"Don't be silly," Tate said. "You should definitely still go."

"With who?" I asked. This was the first I'd heard about their trip.

"I meant to mention it last week," June said. "It must have slipped my mind. Bitsy is coming to watch you for the weekend."

"Oh. Okay." That, I was not looking forward to. "Can't I just ask if I can have a double sleepover at Crystal's?"

"We already asked Tate's mom to come," June said. "But maybe Crystal can go to the football game with you."

"What about your dad?" I asked Tate hopefully. "Is he still in the city?"

"Oh, come on," Tate said playfully. "My mom's not that bad, is she?"

"No," I said quickly. I felt bad, because here he'd given me the best gift ever, and I was kind of insulting his mom. "You're right. Sorry. I'm sure we're going to have a really good time. Does she like football?"

June made a skeptical face, but Tate said, "I'm sure she'd love to take you to the game, Mo. I'll make sure of it. How does that sound?"

Mrs. Townsend is definitely not my first-choice companion, but maybe Crystal can sit between us. And honestly, I would go to a Jets game with absolutely anybody. I mean. A suite at their first home game!

"It sounds great," I said. And I meant it. Though part of me wishes I could share this experience with June and Tate. Oh well.

My clock says 10:17—I should get to sleep. Have to be up first thing.

Wish me luck on my first day!

Love,
Mo

TUESDAY, SEPTEMBER 5

Dear Nan,

I'm writing to you from the backseat of a fancy black car, on my way back from school.

I feel weird about it. The car, I mean. Both June and Tate don't want me taking the subway all the way down to school alone every day, so June had her assistant, Olivia, arrange a car service for me. It's going to drop me off and pick me up every day.

I wanted to tell them it would be faster if I took the subway, but I didn't want them to think I wasn't grateful. Because I am. But I did tell the driver—his name is Mario—to drop me off two blocks from school this morning. I already feel funny about going back to Wallace, after everything that's happened, and I feel like showing up in a fancy car on the first day would only make me stick out even more.

Crystal was waiting for me out front when I rounded the corner. Part of me had been anxious she wasn't going to be wearing her tie-dye jumpsuit. That she'd tell me she forgot, or she woke up not in the mood to do this anymore. But thankfully, she was wearing it.

"Here," she said in greeting, handing me a rainbow headband with butterfly antennae. It matched the one she had on. "I made these last night."

I took it from her and put it on. I could feel the butterflies boinging around. "How do I look?"

Crystal grinned. "Ridiculous."

"Perfect," I said, looping my arm through hers.

I was worried school was going to feel bad. Weird. Like I was stepping back into my old life, a life that doesn't exist anymore. But with Crystal by my side, and that silly thing on my head, it felt okay.

I have Ms. Potts as my homeroom teacher. She said she'll miss seeing you at the PTA meetings. That you were always the one who brought the most color and flair. She said one time you brought a huge thermos of frozen mango margaritas to a meeting. Her eyes got all crinkly as she laughed about it. I like Ms. Potts.

And guess who else is in my class?

Travis Ortiz. *The* Travis Ortiz.

He's cuter than last year. If that's possible.

He's got a walking cast on his left leg. I'm dying to know what happened to him. I hope he's okay. He definitely looked okay—better than okay. He was wearing a crisp white T-shirt that set off his golden brown skin, and I think his dimples have gotten deeper. And he's taller. And he's got a new haircut that shows off his ears. He's got nice ears, Nan. Probably the nicest pair I've ever seen. And when I walked by him he smelled like clean laundry and lemons. And—

Ugh. I thought I got rid of my crush on him over the summer. Apparently not.

For your information, I'm blushing so bad even my fingers are getting all red and sweaty. It's embarrassing to write this down, to you of all people, but I figure you can probably use all the entertainment you can get, especially if you can't watch the Jets or read your stack of romance novels wherever you are. So you're welcome.

Anyway. After school, I was waiting outside for the car to pick me up, and I was responding to a TikTok comment on my phone.

Then I felt a tap on my shoulder.

I looked up. It was Travis.

"Hey!" I shouted. Too loud. Way too loud.

"What are you doing?" he asked, nodding at my phone. "You're so focused."

"Uh . . ."

He waited.

"I have a . . . thing. A cookbook-y kind of project. Family food recipes?"

He raised his eyebrows at me, like he was waiting for me to continue.

But instead of telling him more, what came out of my stupid mouth was: "Your leg. What happened to it?"

It was for sure the wrong thing to say, because the expression on his face totally changed.

"We went to the DR to visit family last month. I was

playing soccer on the beach with my cousins and tore my ACL. It pretty much ruined the whole trip."

"So does that mean you can't play soccer this fall?"

I'm not sure if you remember, but Travis is Mr. Soccer King. He's the reason Wallace stands a chance against the other schools.

"Yup. That's exactly what it means. But I don't really want to talk about it. Tell me about this project you're working on."

"Oh. Yeah. Just—here," I sputtered, digging a business card out of my jumpsuit pocket. I shoved it at him. "A website project thing. Cooking, food. You know. You can look. At it. On a computer. Or on your phone!"

Travis grinned. I stared at his dimples. Then I made myself stop staring at his dimples, because WHAT IS WRONG WITH ME?!

"Cool," he said, slipping the card into his pocket. "I'll check it out. See you, Mo."

Once he disappeared around the corner, limping a little because of his cast, I sagged against the wall, equally sad and happy he was gone.

There's no way he'll look at it. I'll bet that card's going to stay in his pocket until one of his parents puts his jeans in the washing machine, and then it will be nothing but a fuzz ball. And he'll completely forget we had this conversation, and then he'll forget I exist. Again.

And—oh my gosh. Mario dropped me off, and after I

got back to my room to finish writing to you, I had an email on my phone.

I . . . can't believe it. It's from Travis.

Listen to this! It says:

> The Family Cookbook is cool. Did I ever tell you my brother is in culinary school? I sent him one of your TikToks so he can check it out.
>
> See you at school.
>
> T

Is this your doing? Do you have this power in the after-life? If you could see me now, you'd see my cheeks are flaming red. I'm red all the way up to the roots of my hair, which I should probably start brushing more. Or maybe Crystal can do one of those complicated braid crowns for me every morning, for the rest of my life.

Do you think Travis likes braid crowns?

How do people walk around, feeling like this? I can't focus on anything.

Love STINKS.

Mo

PS Don't you dare laugh. I can almost hear your witch's cackle from all the way down here.

THURSDAY, SEPTEMBER 7

Dear Nan,

It's the middle of the night, and I'm wide awake.

Why I woke up, I don't know. But I lay there, thinking of you, and I realized I couldn't remember your face. Not perfectly. Not exactly.

I couldn't breathe until I scrolled through pictures on your Instagram and found one of us together. I zoomed in and studied every little freckle, every wrinkle, every strand of your red-mixed-with-silver hair. It hit me that these are all the pictures I'll ever have of us. Every photo of us together—every photo of *you*—that will ever be taken already exists. I cried into my pillow until it was wet and soggy.

I wish I had something to say about how maybe it will feel okay tomorrow morning (like you'd tell me it would), but I don't think it will.

Sometimes I don't think it ever will.

I miss you,
Mo

SUNDAY, SEPTEMBER 10

Dear Nan,

Okay, I am pleased to tell you I *am* feeling a tiny bit better after my last letter to you. I must have had a swampy sleep brain, because there's no way I could ever forget you. Not ever. You're unforgettable. I guess you were right again—things do feel better in the mornings. Sunnier. Less scary.

But I'm also writing because I wanted to tell you something exciting. Not only have I gotten through the first week of school without managing to completely embarrass myself in front of Travis (or anyone else, for that matter), but I also got my first piece of mail in my PO box.

A woman with shaky cursive handwriting sent me a recipe for Filipino chicken adobo, along with a collection of old photographs. I hope she has copies, because she didn't send me a return address, so I can't send anything back. I'm going to tape what she sent me to the next page.

I read her letter so many times. I don't think I quite got it before, but I'm now starting to understand the weight of what I'm gathering, Nan.

Because food isn't just food. It's tradition. Heritage. A way to celebrate your culture and your roots. It's love.

Do you see now why finding a family recipe matters so much to me? I hope you do. I bet you do.

Love you,
Mo

PS The Jets play their first game later today. Away, in Atlanta. I've tried not to talk or think about it all week. I don't want to jinx them. Maybe you can get the Jets to win one game. Give them extra luck. Or curse the Falcons. Either one works. (Please? Pretty please?)

Dear Mo Gallagher,

My daughter showed me your website. I like it very much. I took extra Advil so I could write to you this morning, despite the arthritis in my hands that makes my knuckles swell up to the size of acorns. Getting older is somehow a blessing and a trial at the same time.

My mother and father moved to the United States from the Philippines when she was twenty-five years old, and he thirty. I was one of seven children. We didn't have the money to travel back to visit our extended family when we were little, but my mother made sure to keep the Philippines close—with food.

We had pancit, which are stir-fried noodles that my mother always made with shrimp, snow peas, and cabbage, at least once a week.

She made us sinigang, a sour soup with tamarind, salty chunks of pork, lime juice, and creamy coconut milk, whenever one of us was sick.

When there was a good report card, she made us turon—slices of banana rolled in brown sugar, wrapped in a spring roll wrapper, and deep-fried. I liked mine drizzled with chocolate syrup, and for years I got good grades to get this treat.

I could go on and on.

My mother worked two jobs, and so did my father, but

my mother took care of us children and cooked on top of that. My father was a good man, but times were different back then. I like to think that if they were both alive today, he would have helped more. I'm glad things are changing.

As the oldest, I helped her the most in the kitchen.

My favorite recipe was her chicken adobo. I liked it best because we were allowed to eat it with our fingers, so it always felt special and fun.

I wasn't able to go to the Philippines until I was a young woman. But because of my mother, because of her food—of the smell of pork sizzling in its fat, rice steaming, and the tangy, fruity smell of tamarind that always filled the small kitchen of our house in Virginia—as soon as I stepped off the plane, it already felt like home.

Along with the recipe, I've included some photos of me and my mother cooking together.

Warmly,

April Manahan Shriver

Manahan Chicken Adobo

Chicken adobo is my family's favorite comfort food. It's a classic Filipino dish, with as many versions as there are families! That's one wonderful thing about it—you can make it your own. From my family to yours . . . masarap! Delicious!

INGREDIENTS

3 tablespoons of canola or vegetable oil

2–2 ½ pounds of skin-on, bone-in chicken thighs

2 teaspoons kosher salt

8 cloves of garlic, crushed

3 bay leaves

1 ½ teaspoons whole black peppercorns

½ cup water

½ cup of all-purpose or light soy sauce

½ cup of vinegar (we use Filipino cane vinegar but can be substituted with any vinegar, including white distilled vinegar or non-seasoned rice vinegar)

Steamed white rice for serving

INSTRUCTIONS

1. Heat oil in a heavy-bottomed pan over medium-high heat. Lightly salt and pepper the chicken and add it to the pan, skin side down. Cook for a few minutes on each side until the skin is a beautiful golden brown. Set the chicken aside.

2. Using the same pan, add a bit more oil and sauté the garlic until fragrant.
3. Add water to deglaze the pan (scrape off and leave the good bits!). Add chicken, skin side up. Add the vinegar, soy sauce, peppercorns, and bay leaves.
4. Reduce heat to medium low. Cover and simmer for 30 minutes. Uncover and simmer for another 10–15 minutes until the sauce reduces and thickens. Taste and adjust acidity to your liking with a little more vinegar, or by diluting with a little water.
5. Serve with steamed white rice. Next-day leftovers are wonderful, too, because the flavors have time to intensify.

THURSDAY, SEPTEMBER 14

Dear Nan,

It's been a little while since I've written.

Here are some updates:

#1: The Jets lost to the Falcons. Badly. Big surprise (not). Huge shocker (not).

June was traveling for work this week—she was in Paris—so it was just me and Tate. We watched the game together in the den. He winced when there was a particularly pathetic interception in the third quarter.

I only shrugged. "I'm used to it by now."

June is back now, but it was kind of nice spending extra time with Tate. We got takeout most nights and watched TV, and I didn't feel like I had to be as careful about making sure every little crumb was cleaned off the counters. Things can be more stressful with June. No—that's not fair. With June, things are more ordered.

#2: I've been busy with school. There's so much more homework in sixth grade. And it's only the second week of school! I've started getting carsick, so I can't even use my long commute to do it.

#3: I made the chicken adobo. Like the recipe said, the sauce got all syrupy when the chicken was done cooking. The kitchen smelled garlicky and rich. I made a big batch of steamed rice, which has its own special smell when it cooks. Sort of like steamy bread dough, but different. I got three comments on my chicken adobo post—a new record. Still no other emails from any Gallaghers, though.

#4: During my second therapy appointment, Dr. Barb and I talked about the bed-wetting issue. It was embarrassing, but not nearly as bad as I thought it was going to be. Probably because it's not happening nearly as much anymore. She said other kids my age sometimes have this problem, too, especially if they've gone through something stressful or bad. Knowing that made me feel a lot better. Like it wasn't only me.

But these updates aren't the only reason why I'm writing. Something else sort of strange happened a few hours ago. I'm still not exactly sure how I feel about it.

I was with Tate and June in the elevator. We were going out for a super-early dinner, even though we don't usually go out on weeknights because June likes to cook. But they're leaving for Arizona tomorrow for their friend's wedding, and they wanted to do something special with me before they left.

Once we were in the lobby, Tate's phone started ringing.

"It's Mom," he said. "Give me one sec. I bet she wants to know what time to get here tomorrow."

While he went over to the corner to talk to her, I went to give Joe a high five. We've been working on a secret handshake. It starts with a high five, then a finger blast, but that's all we have so far. Like I said, we're working on it.

When Tate got off the phone, he walked back toward us with a funny look on his face.

"What is it?" June asked.

"Bad news," Tate said. "My mom broke her wrist. She got tangled up with one of the dogs' leashes and had a bad fall."

"Is she going to be okay?" I asked. As you know, I've never broken a bone. It makes me woozy to think about it.

"She'll be fine. It's a hairline fracture, the doctor said, so she doesn't need surgery. Just a cast and lots of rest."

"But she'll still be able to come and watch Mo this weekend, right?" June asked.

"No, Junie. That's why she was calling. To cancel."

June swore.

"It's too far a trip for Dad, but maybe we could try your parents? Or your sister? Boston isn't such a far drive."

"How many times do I have to tell you that we can't rely on them?" June snapped. "They'd probably say yes and then cancel minutes before they were supposed to get here. We have to figure out something else." June turned to me. "What about your friend Crystal? Do you think you *could* have a weekend sleepover with her? You suggested that before."

I shook my head. "No. She's busy. She can't even come to the football game with me. She's visiting her great-aunt in New Jersey."

"Can you go with her?"

"June, come on," Tate said. "Don't make Mo ask that. I can miss the wedding. I'll stay here. It's no big deal."

"It's a big deal to me," June said. "You know that. Kiera's one of my best friends."

At that, Tate buckled. "All right. Then what?"

I watched as June's eyes landed on Joe. I could almost see the gears turning in her head. Her eyes got all bright, and she had that look she gets whenever she's determined about something. "Joe, you two are close, aren't you? Would you consider babysitting Mo for the weekend?"

"Oh," Joe said, running his hand through his hair. "I don't know—"

"You spend a lot of time together as it is, don't you?" She turned to Tate. "You have to get a bunch of background checks to work for the building."

"June, stop," Tate said. "I don't want to put Joe—or anyone, for that matter—in a weird situation."

I could have melted into the floor. I was *this close* to exiting the building. I really like Joe, but, like—we're not *friend* friends, you know? I walk him to the subway station and we hang out in the lobby. I've only ever seen him in his work uniform.

But June was determined. "We'd pay. A lot. Joe, please. We're desperate."

Joe hesitated, which only made it worse. "Well . . . she'd need to come stay with me and my wife in Brooklyn. It wouldn't feel right staying"—he motioned around the lobby—"here."

"No," Tate said. "June, it's against the rules. You said it yourself. Family or resource families only."

June threw up her hands. "Moira said she's allowed to have sleepovers with her friends. This isn't all that different, is it? And it's better to ask forgiveness than permission, in my experience. It's two nights. Moira doesn't have to know."

"Okay," Tate said uncertainly. He glanced at Joe. "Like June said, we'll pay you well."

Joe's eyes flashed to me. "Okay, then. It's a deal."

Tate and Joe arranged a few more details between them. I'm going to Crystal's place tomorrow after school, before she leaves for New Jersey in the late afternoon. We've had that planned all week. Joe said he'll ask to get off early and come pick me up as soon as his shift is done.

I feel awkward about it. A little sick to my stomach, too. Like . . . I'm happy I don't have to spend an entire weekend with Tate's mom, and also I want to meet Carlota, but—let's face it, I was forced on them. Joe didn't have much choice but to say yes.

Maybe the wedding will be canceled. Maybe Tate and June will miss their flight and have to stay home. I don't even know what I hope will happen.

I guess I'll find out tomorrow.

Love,
Mo

FRIDAY, SEPTEMBER 15

Dear Nan,

I'm writing from last period at school. I'm supposed to be spending the last ten minutes of class writing a short story for language arts, but I figure writing to you counts, too.

Tate and June's flight didn't get canceled, the bride didn't get cold feet, and Crystal still has to go to New Jersey tonight, so I can't double-sleepover with her. Which means I'm definitely staying with Joe and Carlota.

I could tell Tate and June felt bad about everything, because they laid out a special breakfast this morning before school. There were donuts, scrambled eggs, bagels, and bacon, and they let me have half a cup of coffee, which I doused with sugar and cream.

Oh—the bell's ringing. Wow, those ten minutes went quick.

Wish me luck so I don't screw this weekend up. Because if I do, and Joe decides I'm annoying and he doesn't like me anymore, then it's going to be weird for the rest of my life going in and out of Tate and June's building.

I will play it cool. As a cucumber. As a cool, not-annoying, non-bed-wetting cucumber who everyone likes.

Okay, Crystal is tugging on my arm, gotta go—

Mo

Dear Nan,

Yep, it's a double-letter day. I couldn't help myself. I had to tell you about the rest of my day.

Crystal and I didn't do much at her house—we made paper bead necklaces and I listened to her complain about her loud new roommate (Charlie). But I was having trouble focusing. Because I kept thinking, what if I couldn't be as cool as a cucumber, and Joe started thinking I was annoying, and Carlota flat out didn't like me at all? What if I wet the bed this weekend? What if their two dogs and one cat hated me?

All I wanted was for this weekend to go better than my trip to the Hamptons.

When the doorbell rang, I nearly threw up.

"Hey." Crystal nudged me with her toe. I was on my knees with my face pressed against her carpet. "Stop being a weirdo. Come on."

When I got downstairs, Joe was waiting at the front door, wearing jean cargo shorts and a black T-shirt. It was weird seeing him without his doorman suit on. I spied the edges of a big tattoo peeking out from beneath his sleeve. He's supposed to work until six, but he asked to get off early specifically for me, because Crystal and her family are leaving at four.

"You look different," I blurted out.

He looked down. "Schlubbier than usual, huh?"

"No. I didn't mean—"

"I know, kid, I'm only teasing. You ready?"

After saying goodbye to Crystal and thanking her mom for having me, Joe and I took the subway to his apartment. It only took fifteen minutes.

"This is it," Joe said, once we'd reached a narrow brownstone with colorful flowers spilling out of window boxes.

I looked up at it. "You live *here*?"

Joe laughed. "Not quite." He pointed down the narrow steps leading to a door with black metal bars on it. "We rent the basement apartment. Nice family lives upstairs, though."

I felt another wash of anxiety as I followed him down the stairs. Had I insulted him somehow, by assuming he lived in the brownstone? Or by sounding surprised if he did? Was I making things weird already?

The moment I stepped into their apartment, their two dogs went berserk. But worse, their cat actually *hissed* at me. Fur raised, claws out, like in a Halloween movie.

It was as I feared: the animals hated me already. My stomachache got worse.

Joe motioned at the cat. "Don't mind Mrs. Business. She's a jerk."

"Oh," I said weakly. "Okay."

And then Carlota appeared, from what I guessed was their bedroom. She's short and round, with wavy black hair that falls halfway down her back. She was wearing a thick-knit cropped sweater over a long skirt, and she was barefoot, with a silver bracelet around her left ankle.

She smiled wide and held her arms out. "Mo! I'm so happy to finally—"

"I'm going to be sick," I said suddenly.

Her eyes went wide. "Oh—the bathroom's right—"

She pointed and I hurtled forward, not even stopping to take my backpack off. And then I did it. I threw up.

When I'd finished, I wanted to disappear. I'd been afraid all day of doing something stupid and here I was, a weird vomiting girl who their pets hated.

"You okay, Mo?" Joe asked when I came out of the bathroom.

I nodded and kept my eyes on the floor. "I'm really sorry."

I felt a warm hand on my shoulder. I looked up; it was Carlota. "Don't be silly. I'm so sorry you don't feel well." She led me over to their couch. "Sit here and I'll get you all fixed up."

I sat, and the couch was so squashy I nearly sank halfway into it.

Carlota walked ten paces from the living room into their kitchen. It was all a part of the same room. "Joe, can you help me reach the lemons?"

As Carlota pointed out to Joe what she needed from the higher cabinets, I looked around. Purple and white crystals and candles in short and colorful glass jars were arranged on the windowsills. Long green plant tendrils hung down from over the kitchen cabinets and from on top of the TV, and sheer scarves had been thrown over the lamps to soften the light.

As I sat there, one of the dogs—the bigger one, who I could now see had only one eye—leapt onto my lap and started licking my face.

"I thought you hated me," I whispered. I started petting him and his little tail flew back and forth.

"That's Nacho," Carlota said as she squeezed the juice out of a lemon. "He loves to bark. And Toast—he's the Chihuahua—is sulking. It takes him an hour or two to warm up to people."

"And your cat?" I asked nervously.

Joe laughed. "You won't see Mrs. Business for the rest of the weekend. She hates everyone. Even me. The only one she likes is Carlota."

"Oh, shush." Carlota came over to me, a blue glass in her hand. "Drink this. It will make you feel better."

I took a sip. It was fizzy and lemony.

"Mmm." I took a bigger sip. "This is good. What is it?"

"A secret concoction of mine for sour stomachs. When you work at a bakery and love to eat, you get a lot of those." She winked. Then she turned to Joe. "We should cancel dinner with your brothers if Mo isn't feeling well."

"She's fine! You're fine, right? Look at that recovery." He knocked me gently on the arm. "You don't mind if my brothers come by for dinner, do you, Mo?"

Carlota stared at him. "Joe. No. She was just sick. What is wrong with you? Cancel, right now."

Joe rubbed the back of his neck. "It's—we were gonna make her the thing."

"What thing?" Carlota said.

Joe threw up his hands. "For her website, all right? Ma's lasagna." He turned to me. That's when I noticed his face was all red. "We want you to try it. Me and my brothers. Maybe you might want to write about it."

"Joe, if she isn't feeling well . . ."

"No," I said. "I'm fine. Really—I—it was just nerves. I'd like to meet your brothers and eat lasagna."

Carlota looked at me. "Are you sure?"

I nodded. Nacho licked my chin.

Half an hour later, the small apartment was filled with the sounds of four loud Italian men. Because Joe has three brothers: Vinny, Don, and Tony. When Joe told me their names, he added, "Yeah, yeah. I know. Central-casting New York Italians."

They arrived laughing and bickering, with shopping bags from the grocery store slung around their arms.

They all cried "hello" and "what's up" and "hey, Mo!" like we'd already known each other for a long time.

Apparently, his brothers were as excited as Joe to have

me try their mom's lasagna. Or as Vinny said, "Ma's la-sawn."

"Bianco brothers only," Don said when Carlota and I offered to help. "The ladies should kick up their feet and relax."

"Can I watch?" I asked. "Take pictures?"

Don frowned. "I'm not very photogenic."

"It's for her project, Donny," Joe said.

"Oh. Well, in that case . . ." He wet his hands beneath the faucet and ran them through his hair until it was slicked back and shiny. "How do I look?"

When Tony pretended to choke at the sight of him, Don went over to grab him playfully around the neck.

Vinny explained that the most important ingredient in this recipe was time, which is why they came over so early. "The sauce takes a little while, but it's worth it."

"Probably too much time," Don said under his breath.

"We'll be lucky to eat at nine," Carlota called from the couch as she flipped through a magazine.

Vinny pointed a wooden spoon at Don and then at Carlota. "Hey. You two. Respect the sauce."

Vinny was right—the sauce did take forever to come together. At least two hours, and even then, Joe said it would have been better if it had simmered even longer. But the rich, tomatoey smell that filled the apartment—Oh, Nan, I wish you could have experienced it.

When it came time to assemble the lasagna, the four

of them crowded around the stove, pushing and heckling and disagreeing with each other.

"No, she layered the cheese in first," Don said.

Vinny shook his head. "No, the pasta first, Donny."

"I think Vinny's right," Tony said.

Joe elbowed them out of the way to smear a spoonful of bright red tomato sauce on the bottom of a large glass dish. "Get outta here, all of you. Sauce is first."

I couldn't help but laugh as I took pictures. They were more entertaining than a reality show. I also tried to write down the recipe as best I could, but since they couldn't agree on most of the steps, I just wrote it down as they made it.

A few hours after Joe's brothers had arrived, the six of us were crammed around Joe and Carlota's tiny table. The candles stuck into wine bottles flickered, and the hot lasagna bubbled in its dish on the table in front of us.

"First piece for our food critic," Joe said, serving me a large cheesy square.

Vinny, Joe, Tony, and Don all leaned forward over their own plates and watched as I took my first bite. Carlota shook her head, an amused smile on her face.

"Is good," I said. I took another bite. "Wow. Really good!"

The table erupted in cheers and chatter.

"See? Maybe she is Italian! You got Italian blood, Mo?"

"She's smart. You're a smart kid, you know that?"

"Glad to see you've got good taste."

"So much talk," Carlota said. "Talk, talk, talk, all the time."

Joe slung an arm around her shoulders and kissed her loudly on the cheek. "Yeah, but you love it."

I snapped picture after picture.

After dinner, Carlota sat down on the couch with a book and both dogs in her lap, and the Bianco brothers cleared the plates and did the dishes. Then they sat back down at the table with a rack of poker chips and two decks of cards. I recognized what they were playing immediately.

It was my moment, Nan.

I stepped forward. "Can I play?"

"Sorry, Charlie," Tony said, counting his chips. "It's not a kids' game."

"I know." I motioned at the cards on the table. "It's Texas hold'em poker."

One of them whistled. Joe turned to his brothers. "Well?"

"If she knows the game, I say let her play," Don said.

And then, an hour later, I had the biggest stack of chips at the table. I looked down at my own cards, then at the cards that were displayed. I made sure to keep my face as blank as possible. I pushed forward my stack of chips. "All in."

The guys all burst out laughing.

"I can't believe it," Vinny cried, elbowing Joe. "She's a shark!"

And I am, Nan. Thanks to you and all those lessons. I cleaned house, exactly like you taught me.

When his brothers left, they gave me high fives, Carlota kisses on the cheek, and very loud, backslappy hugs to Joe.

"Lasagna, bro," Joe said to each of them as he hugged them, one after another.

"Lasagna!" his brothers yelled back as they filed out of the apartment.

"Lasagna?" I asked.

Joe grinned as he closed the door after them. " 'Lasagna' means I love you," he explained. "Our mother made it so much growing up, it sort of became shorthand in our family."

"Oh. I like that," I said.

"Yeah. Me too."

Now I'm snuggled on their couch for the night, but it isn't anything like sleeping on Ms. Schirle's couch. Carlota put down fresh sheets and gave me a feather bed pillow, plus one of those cozy-soft blankets from Target. It still smells like lasagna in here, but in a nice way, and the glow of the lamp is lighting everything a soft yellow.

And—oh. You won't believe it.

Mrs. Business just jumped up on top of me. She's— kneading my stomach. And purring. I'm barely moving my arm as I write so I don't disturb her.

What should I do?

Okay. Hold on. I'm going to put my pen down and try to pet her.

Wow. She liked it. And I think all that petting made her fall asleep. She was purring like a car engine before, and now I can feel the rise and fall of her breath as I write this.

So much happened, right? I told you so. And this was only the first day. Tomorrow is Saturday, or I guess *today* is Saturday, and then on Sunday we're GOING TO THE JETS GAME.

Mrs. Business's warm weight is making me sleepy.

I hope you're up in heaven, hustling the other angels in poker and emptying their pockets.

Lasagna, Nan. Lasagn-ya so much. Good night.

Mo

"Ma" Bianco's Lasagna

Makes 1 large tray, enough for four growing boys

Ingredients

1 lb ground beef ("It doesn't have to be the extra lean
stuff, fat is flavor" —Tony)

2 yellow onions, diced

3–4 carrots, diced

2–3 stalks of celery, diced

2 cups mozzarella, shredded or cut into small cubes

1½ cups grated parmesan cheese

2 lb good Italian tomato sauce, "passata" in Italian ("You
want sauce, not whole tomatoes, and not tomato
paste" —Vinny)

A handful of fresh herbs (parsley, thyme, Italian oregano,
sage), finely chopped

A glass of red wine

Lasagna sheets, preferably the ones you need to boil
and aren't "ready to cook" in the oven

Don said you should have enough to make 3 layers in
a medium sheet pan. Tony agreed, and said "two
layers is a little sad, and four layers is over the top."

Steps

1. Vinny says, "Clear your afternoon. Duck out of work early so you can start the sauce." In a large pot, heat a generous amount of olive oil (a couple swings around the bottom) at medium-low heat.

2. Throw in your onions, carrots, and celery and let them soften to form a nice "soffritto." Do this slowly to avoid burning the onions—that'll kill the sauce.

3. Add half a glass of red wine and let the soffritto soak it up. Now add the beef and mix it into the soffritto. Let it absorb the flavor slowly, then after 5 minutes, add the second half of the glass of wine and the herbs and turn up the heat for a minute.

4. Season with salt and pepper and mix in the tomato sauce.

5. Turn the heat to extremely low and cover the pot with a lid, leaving a small opening for the smell of the sauce to fill the apartment. Now wait, but don't leave. The sauce can cook anywhere from 2–4 hours, the longer the better. Periodically check on the sauce, stirring and making sure it's not burning, sticking to the bottom of the pan, or reducing too much. If it's reducing too much, put the lid fully on and make sure the heat is ultra-low.

6. After you're happy with the sauce (taste it for seasoning), you can assemble the lasagna. Put a generous amount of sauce on the bottom of your baking dish. ("Always sauce first" —Joe)

7. Check how many sheets you need for each layer. Boil the first layer of sheets in a pot of salted water for 2–4 mins, leave them al dente, they will finish cooking in the oven. Lay the sheets on top of the sauce and add a new layer of sauce.

8. Add a handful of mozzarella and grated parmesan on top of the sauce. Boil your next layer of sheets, lay them on the cheese and repeat. On the top layer of sheets add the remainder of the sauce and a bit of parmesan (not as much as in between the layers).

9. Preheat oven to 375°F and cook for 30 mins. You want the top layer of pasta to be slightly crispy but definitely not dry. If anything, pull the lasagna out a few minutes before, if it looks like it's drying out.

10. Serve immediately and eat as fast as you can, because it's so good that your brothers will finish it off before you have a chance for seconds.

MONDAY, SEPTEMBER 18

Dear Nan,

I'm back on the Upper East Side with Tate and June, and even though it's Monday (and you know I hate Mondays like you hate Tuesdays), I'm in a good mood. I think it's because the rest of the weekend with Joe and Carlota went great. At least, most of it did.

It rained all day on Saturday, so after Carlota got back from the bakery in the early afternoon, we made biscotti together. As it baked, we all watched a movie.

Halfway through the movie, Joe got up to use the bathroom. That's when Mrs. Business appeared from beneath a chair and came to sit on my lap. Carlota froze and then slowly took the phone from her pocket.

"Don't move," she whispered. "I need evidence. To show Joe. In case she moves."

I stayed perfectly still while Carlota snapped a photo of Mrs. Business on my lap.

"Amazing," she said. "I've never seen her do this with someone so quickly. It means you have good energy."

"Really? I do?"

Carlota nodded sagely. "Yes. I could tell the minute you walked in the door."

"Are you having a baby?" I blurted.

The question slipped out. I asked because after I finished writing my last letter to you on Friday night, I got up to use the bathroom in the middle of the night (I didn't have to go, but I've been making a point to force myself if I so much as stir). Except I was so sleepy and fuzzy-brained I opened the wrong door. It was to a small bedroom, which was filled with baby stuff. A crib, a changing table, a rocking chair, and a bunch of boxes.

Carlota stiffened, and the look on her face changed, in a not-so-good way. I immediately wished I could take the question back. "What makes you ask that?"

"I accidentally went into the other room last night," I said. "You have a lot of baby stuff."

"We're not having a baby. We had a baby. A daughter. Her name is Isabella."

That surprised me. "Where . . . is she?"

Carlota was quiet for a long minute. "She died. Last July. She wasn't sick. She was perfect. The doctors said it was something called SIDS, and that sometimes, it just happens. She was a month old."

My heart squeezed for her. For Joe, too. "I'm so sorry. I shouldn't have said anything."

"It's okay, honey. It's just been a difficult year."

"I know all about that," I said.

"I know you do."

Then the toilet flushed, and Mrs. Business slunk off my lap, thumped to the ground, and prowled to hide beneath the TV stand like she didn't want Joe to see her cozying up to me.

When he came out of the bathroom, Joe looked between Carlota and me. "What is it?"

Carlota patted my hand and then smiled. "Mrs. Business sat on Mo's lap."

Joe stared. "No. I don't believe it."

Carlota wiggled her phone in the air. "I've got proof."

I still feel bad about bringing up their baby. Carlota was quiet for the rest of the afternoon.

But oh, Sunday. The game. THE GAME.

The rain from Saturday was gone, and we had a perfectly bright and sunny crisp September day.

The suite was . . . I don't even know how to explain it. It must be what it feels like to fly first-class on an airplane. We had a great view, and all the snacks were free. Joe piled up three plates' worth of food, and not even a glare from Carlota could keep him from putting candy in his pockets.

"What?" Joe said. "It's free!"

I wore every piece of Jets clothes I own: my Jets pants, jacket, lucky hat, and my jersey.

It was such a good day, I didn't even care they lost. I'm a Jets fan, after all. I was expecting it.

When we were back at Joe and Carlota's after the game was over, my phone pinged. It was a text from June.

JUNE: Did you have fun? Just left JFK. Arizona was great! We should be there to pick you up in 45 <3 <3

As I gathered my stuff, Carlota put together a Tupperware of the cranberry–white chocolate biscotti we'd made together.

"Thanks for a great weekend," I told them. Then I knelt down to scratch the dogs. "Bye, Toast. Bye, Nacho."

And then, right as I was about to walk out the door, I called out, "Bye, Mrs. Business!"

There was a loud meow, and then Mrs. Business appeared from behind the couch. She trotted over to me and started twirling her body through my legs.

"See?" Carlota turned to Joe, her eyes sparkling triumphantly. "I told you."

"A miracle," Joe said. "You got the touch, kid."

So . . . yeah. The weekend started rough, but it ended okay. I think. I hope.

I spent the rest of Sunday night finishing my homework and editing the lasagna pictures. The candlelight was warm and glowy, but still bright enough to see all the details. But what I liked the best was that in every picture someone was laughing.

I posted the recipe and the photos earlier today. The TikTok video I made is already getting more views than I usually do. I think it's because the Bianco brothers are pretty entertaining. I'm happy with how it all turned out, but . . .

Keeping up the Family Cookbook is a lot of work. Be-

194

tween the videos I've been making, and the posts and pictures on the website. And I still don't have a lot of readers. And besides that one email, I haven't heard a peep from any other Gallaghers.

Sometimes it feels like it's too much work to be worth it. Or maybe the work *was* worth it, but I don't need it as badly anymore. Things have been feeling okay recently. Like, when I got back from Joe and Carlota's, it felt good to sleep in my own bed. Because it is my own bed now. Or at least, it feels that way.

I'm getting hungry, so I'm going to go see what's for dinner.

I'll write more later,
Mo

Dear Nan,

I bet you weren't expecting to hear from me again today, but I needed to write to you about what happened.

While June and I were talking about what we should order for dinner, her phone rang. It was Moira.

"Hello?" June said.

I could hear the murmur of Moira talking, but not what she was saying. The look on June's face changed. "Yes, but, we wouldn't have, unless—" Then Moira must have cut her off. June turned her back to me and walked into her bedroom, shutting the door behind her. "I know, but—"

I waited right where I was, as if my legs had rooted to the ground. Finally, after ten minutes, June came back out. "Well, we're certainly in trouble."

"Why? What happened?"

"She knows you didn't stay with Tate's mom this weekend."

"Really? How?"

"Maybe next time don't post about your weekend on the internet, Mo."

Horrible icy-cold dread came over me. Of *course* that's how she found out. I guess I didn't think Moira would be checking up on the Family Cookbook.

"It's fine," June said distractedly, after I'd apologized. She rubbed her forehead with two of her fingers. "I just need to talk to Tate."

When June went to find him, I went back into my room. Sweaty and red-faced and angry with myself. Why was I so dumb?

I made this mess, I figured, so it was up to me to fix it.

I called Moira back myself.

"Mo?" she answered. "What is it?"

"Please don't get them in trouble," I said. "I'm happy here. With them, I mean. I want to stay."

And only when I'd said it out loud did I realize how much I meant it.

"Of course you're going to stay." She sighed. "Listen, everyone makes mistakes. But the truth is important, okay? The rules are the rules for a reason. It's the way I can make sure you're safe and properly taken care of. Only the truth from now on."

"Only the truth from now on," I repeated. "I promise."

I opened my bedroom door to go tell June and Tate I'd called Moira, but June was already standing there, her fist raised like she was about to knock. "Oh," she said, stepping back in surprise.

"I was just coming to find you," I said. "I called Moira. She said you won't get in trouble."

"Thank you, Mo. You shouldn't have had to do that."
She sighed. "Can I come in?"

I nodded.

She sat lightly on my bed. "I wanted to say sorry for snapping earlier. It's just . . . there have been so many hoops throughout this whole process. So many meetings and forms, so many 'what-if's. All I wanted was for us to be able to feel settled together without having to answer to anyone, without having to constantly ask, 'May we please do this with Mo, may we please do that.' My usual way of existing—especially with my business—is that it's better to apologize than to ask permission. But that approach doesn't work in this system. I didn't really see that side when I was a kid. I guess Terry hid it from me. It's been harder than I expected." She smoothed a wrinkled spot on my comforter. "So much harder."

I just kind of stood there, because I wasn't sure what she wanted me to say. I wasn't sure if I should say sorry again, or if she was the one who was trying to apologize to me.

"Hey," she said suddenly. "Do you want to come see the line of purses we're doing for next season? I want to show you something."

We went into her office, and she pulled up a file and scrolled down through pages of different purse styles. Each page had photos and a description of the purse. All the different styles have their own names. Like the Jackson, the Helena, the Margaux.

She stopped when she got to a bright-pink purse with a shimmery, almost-rainbow-colored handle. "We're calling this one the Mo."

"'The Mo'? Like, me Mo?" My cheeks went hot with pleasure. "You named it after me?"

She nodded. "It's the most colorful purse we're releasing next season. What do you think?"

It looked a little out of place among the others—all muted browns, with golds and silvers. But even so, June made a place for it. A place for me.

"I love it," I told her.

And I meant it.

Love,
Mo

SUNDAY, OCTOBER 1

Dear Nan,

After almost getting June and Tate in trouble because of the Family Cookbook last week, I've decided the best thing to do is to stop the whole thing. Not only is my plan to find a Gallagher with a recipe not working, but it's getting people in trouble, too. And making the TikTok videos takes forever, and each one only gets a couple thousand views.

So today we're going to Central Park so I can find my fiftieth and final recipe. Fifty is a nice round number, don't you think? A good stopping point.

(And before you widen your eyes and call me a liar, that there's no way I've made forty-nine different recipes since this summer, you should know I haven't made *all* the recipes myself. Just a handful. Lots of them I just post the recipe with the story and the family photographs people give to me. I might even like those ones the most. Especially when the stories are good.)

Oh—Tate's yelling to say he's ready. We're bringing a

blanket and some food, and after I find my recipe, we're going to have a picnic celebration.

Don't worry. I'm not upset. And neither should you be. I don't need a hobby anymore. Writing to you is enough of a hobby, don't you think? Because I'm totally, totally fine.

Mo

SUNDAY, OCTOBER 1
(LATER)

Dear Nan,

We just got back from Central Park. It was the first day that felt like fall. October in New York City really is the best, isn't it? A few of the trees are beginning to change colors, and there's a whisper of winter in the air, but you only need a heavy sweater instead of a coat.

Lots of other people must have felt the same way, because we weren't the only ones who had the idea for a picnic in Sheep Meadow. June packed a thermos of hot apple cider. She put cinnamon sticks in it and simmered it low on the stove. I wish you could have smelled the kitchen this morning.

After about ten minutes in the park, June had to get up to take a work call, so I decided it was the right time to find my final recipe.

First I went to two women drinking a bottle of light-pink wine. I didn't notice that one of them had a mascara-streaked face until I'd already started my pitch and handed them a business card.

Once I'd finished, the woman who'd been crying took

a huge sip of her wine. "I'm sorry to be the one to tell you this, honey, but family's a sham."

"Oh, okay," I said.

Her friend winced and then looked up at me. "Now's not the best time for this." She lowered her voice. "She's going through a pretty messy divorce."

I approached a little family next, because I figured *they* wouldn't think family's a sham. Two dads were lying on a plaid blanket, leaning over two of the cutest babies I've ever seen.

"They're so cute," I said, approaching them. "Are they twins?"

The man in the blue sweater nodded. "Yep. Fraternal. This little lady is Ophelia, and this is Kacen."

"Hi, babies," I cooed.

I introduced myself, and they told me their names were David and Gabriel.

Whenever I see babies, I think about the time we took the bus to Atlantic City. Remember that trip? I always think about the look on the woman's face when you offered to hold her screaming baby. She looked like you'd offered her a million dollars. And then you held that baby for the rest of the ride while her mom slept.

I told them that story about you.

"She sounds like a wonderful person," Gabriel said.

"She is. She was." I cleared my throat. "But talking about babies isn't why I'm here today."

And then I told them about my project and asked if

either of them would be willing to share a family recipe for my fiftieth and final post.

"One with a funny story from when you were a kid? Like, my age?" I asked hopefully. I like those stories the best.

Both of them were quiet.

"It's okay if you don't have anything," I said quickly. "I don't need to take up any more of your time."

"No," said Gabriel. "It's not that." He glanced at David. "We both come from food-loving families. But they weren't as accepting of our family as we'd hoped. It's hard—at least for me—to think about."

"I'm sorry," I said.

"Thank you, honey," he said. "But I have just the thing for you, actually." He reached into the pocket of his jeans and took out his phone. "Let me pull up the recipe."

"Oh," David said, sitting up. "Are you thinking of the chard pasta?"

"Yes. Exactly." Gabriel held out his phone for me. "Here. You can copy this down."

"It looks really good," I said, although I had no idea what chard was. (I've looked it up since then. It's a green leafy vegetable with colorful, rainbow-bright stems.) "Can you tell me why it's special to you?"

"We served this at our wedding, seven years ago. It was small, just our closest friends at our apartment for dinner. Our families didn't come. It was casual; we just threw the pasta together with what we had. But it came out per-fectly balanced—a little bitter, the right amount of salt and sweet. And it's become our go-to dinner for special occasions ever since."

"It's *our* family recipe," added David, reaching out to take his husband's hand.

Something about that made me want to cry. I think it made me realize that if you were still here, now, we would've had a chance to come up with a family recipe together. Something special that shouted *us*. It wouldn't have been something I had to try to hunt down across the internet.

But I didn't say that to them. I wiggled my phone in the air. "Can I take your picture?"

After I took a few photos and said goodbye, I had the strangest conversation. I was sitting down on a bench to finish writing some notes. I waved at Tate to let him know I'd be back over soon.

A woman sitting to my left with a dark-red scarf and a paper cup of coffee leaned over and smiled. "Are you writing down a recipe?"

"Yep," I said. Then I closed my journal with a snap, because most of what I write in here is private.

"Sorry. I write about food. As my job. I notice it wherever I go." She nodded at my journal. "I didn't mean to snoop."

"Really? I'm a food writer, too," I told her. "Well, sort of. Do you come up with your own recipes?"

"No. I'm a journalist," the woman said. "But back to you. What kind of food writing do you do?"

She actually seemed interested, so I told her about the Family Cookbook. She didn't get that glazed-over look some adults get when I talk to them about what I like to do.

"Oh?" she said, suddenly interested. "May I see it?"

I showed her on my phone.

"Wow," she said, scrolling through the entries. "This is great. How'd you get started?"

I told her about your letter to me, and how you wanted me to find a hobby. Georgie's cookbook. Joe's suggestion I start a website.

"Do you have any of your own family recipes on there?" she asked.

I shook my head and told her that had kind of become the point of it all. How I was looking to find a family member who might have a recipe to share with me, but that I'd been unsuccessful.

She asked a lot more questions.

"And your grandmother," she said. "Was she Kath as in Kathleen?"

I nodded. "And this is me," I said, handing her my card. "Mo Gallagher."

"I love the glitter." She slipped my card in her pocket and stood up. "It's been a pleasure to chat with you, Mo. I'll be in touch."

"But after today, I'm stopping," I called to her as she started to walk away.

She turned around and smiled. "You know, I don't think you should give it up. At least, not yet."

Then she was on her way.

Kind of funny, right?

Anyway, I'm going to go post the recipe from Gabriel and David now. The pictures came out so nice. The babies are gurgling with chubby-cheeked smiles, and the October sun is shining all around them, filtering in through the trees. Maybe this year I'll even enter the Wallace photography contest.

Look out, Crystal, because here I come!

Love,
Mo

Gabriel and David's Chard Pasta

Serves 2–4

Ingredients

½ pound orecchiette pasta

1 butternut squash, peeled and diced into 1-inch cubes

4–5 shallots, diced into large pieces

1 bunch rainbow chard, chopped, with stems and leaves
separated

2–3 garlic cloves, minced

1½ cups chicken or vegetable broth

½ cup half-and-half

2 tablespoons grated parmesan cheese

1 tablespoon white wine vinegar

1 tablespoon fresh sage, chopped

Olive oil

Salt and pepper, to taste

Red pepper flakes (optional but encouraged)

Directions

1. Preheat oven to 400°F.

2. Toss shallots and butternut squash with olive oil,
salt, pepper, and red pepper flakes, if you like spice,

and bake for 30–35 minutes. Once golden brown and caramelized, set aside.

3. In a large saucepan, heat olive oil and sauté your rainbow chard stems first over medium-high heat. Once tender, add greens and minced garlic. Sauté for 2–3 minutes and then add the broth and white wine vinegar and simmer for an additional 2–3 minutes. Turn heat on lowest setting and then add sage, half-and-half, and parmesan. If you want the sauce to be thicker, you can mash up some of the roasted butternut squash and mix it in.

4. Meanwhile, bring a large pot of salted water to a boil. (David says the water should be salted so it tastes like the sea.) Then cook pasta according to the instructions on the box.

5. Drain and combine the pasta, sauce, and roasted squash and shallots. Serve with lots of parmesan and cracked pepper.

SUNDAY, OCTOBER 8

Dear Nan,

Oh man. Oh man, oh man. Where to start? How do I even—aah, I don't know!

Something happened, and things have gotten totally out of control! (In the best way possible.)

Okay. So remember how in my letter from last week I told you about that funny conversation I had with that woman in Central Park? Who said she was a food writer? And a journalist?

Her name is Fiona Crenshaw, and do you know who she writes for?

The *New York Times*. The New–York–Freaking–Times.

And guess who she wrote an article about? Yeah, that's right. ME.

Right now there's an article in the food section of the *New York Times* about me, Mo Gallagher.

The *New York Times*!

It's about my project. She emailed me this past week with a bunch more questions because she wanted to write an article about me. I didn't want to tell you about it because I didn't want to get my hopes up. It almost didn't happen because of all these rules and regulations having to do with me being in foster care, but Moira worked extra hard to get special approval for it. The article is about me, and about you, about how I started cooking, and the Family Cookbook. It's about how I'm using it to try to find family—and a family recipe—of my own.

Nan, you know what this means, right?

I'm famous!
Mo

FRIDAY, OCTOBER 13

Dear Nan,

Sorry I haven't been writing as much. I can't keep up with everything that's happening.

Emails are pouring in. So are letters. A few people have sent me food! June said I shouldn't eat it because you never know what someone might put in it, though I've been tempted. Especially by a container of toffee-white-chocolate-chip cookies. Tate and I had to go down to the post office to expand the size of my PO box to keep up with it all.

I haven't had time to read all the emails, but along with the recipes, there's story after story. Some are sad, some are funny, and some are just . . . weird. Like the guy who emailed me about his bearded dragons, saying his favorite family recipe was "raw crickets." He said he lived with over twenty bearded dragons. He sent a picture. He really does have that many. Twenty-three, actually. I counted.

Yesterday, the traffic to my website got so big it crashed. I'll admit . . . I didn't handle it well. Tate came back from work early to help me figure out a new hosting situation.

That basically means finding a new place to put my website on the internet so it can handle a lot more visitors. It was really nice of him to do that.

I'm getting way more comments now, too. Even on the earlier posts. Tate and June used to sit down and go through them with me, to approve them, but they stopped doing that a little while ago. I'm kind of glad, because I can go through them much faster this way.

There's one more thing I want to tell you. I've been saving the best for last.

I got this email.

And . . . I guess I'll let that speak for itself, too.

I love you,
Mo

From: annie.hauser49400@gmail.com
To: momolovesfamilyfood@gmail.com
Subject: Hi darlin! We might be related

Hi Mo,

I read about you and your project in the New York Times. It was a great piece, and I'm so sorry about the loss of your grandmother.

I'm writing because there's a chance you and I are related. My mom's maiden name is Gallagher, and she's originally from Kansas. She's around the same age as your grandmother and I'm pretty sure she has (or had) a favorite cousin by the name of Kathleen, who moved to the East Coast in the '70s. Which would make us some variety of cousins twice removed? I'm not sure. But in my opinion, family is family.

My mom's on a cruise in Ecuador right now (she's very adventurous), but as soon as she's back online I'm going to ask her.

Fingers crossed we'll be able to confirm this. We've got some great recipes to share. My family and I now live in the Maryland area, so a trip to New York City to meet you (and maybe even cook together!) wouldn't be too difficult, if you'd be interested in something like that.

Hugs to you,
Annie Hauser

THURSDAY, OCTOBER 19

Dear Nan,

I haven't been able to stop thinking about Annie Hauser's email. Doesn't she seem nice? It makes sense you would have a favorite cousin who's adventurous and goes on cruises in Ecuador. I bet she *got* you. I bet she understood why you moved to New York City and never looked back.

After I got home from school this afternoon, I found June in the kitchen, working on her laptop. She was wearing a white turtleneck sweater that looked so soft and cozy I wanted to wrap my arms around her and put my face against the fabric. But I still feel a little weird about hugging June and Tate, so I didn't.

"June?" I asked as I unwound my scarf. "Can we go down to my PO box? Just in case Annie sent me a letter instead of an email?"

June didn't look up from her laptop. "I'm sure she'll email as soon as her mom gets back from her vacation. Don't worry. Oh, also, I wanted to check in with you about Halloween. Do you know what you want to be? Things are light for me this week, and if you wanted me to make you a costume, I could." She looked up from her screen and smiled at me. "I had to sew almost every stitch on every handbag when I was first launching my company."

I thought about all the nights leading up to Halloween that you and I spent bent over paper-mache zombie heads, glow-in-the-dark paint for skeleton bones, or gluing pink feathers onto a jumpsuit that one year I wanted to go as a flamingo. Making a Halloween costume wasn't something I wanted to do without you.

"I'm a little too old for Halloween," I told her.

"Oh. Okay. Right."

For a split second, her expression made me think I hurt her feelings. But then she was typing on her laptop again like nothing had happened, so maybe I imagined it.

I wiggled my scarf and coat in the air. "I'm going to go hang these up."

"Mo, wait—one more thing. Tate and I are going on a date tomorrow night. It's been a long time since we've gone out just the two of us. Would you rather Tate's mom come here, to New York, or do you want to go to the Hamptons? For the weekend, if Moira says it's okay?"

I twisted my scarf in my hands. Crystal has a family party thing tomorrow, so I couldn't sleep over there, but maybe . . .

"Can't Joe watch me? Moira said I'm allowed to have a babysitter for a night. Wouldn't that be easier? Isn't Tate's mom still recovering?"

"Listen," June said. "I get it. She's tough. But she's also

family. And Joe's our doorman. The last time, it was our only option. It's a little . . . awkward for us, to be totally honest. And I don't want things to be awkward for him, too."

I understood. I mean, I threw up because I was worried about it being awkward between all of us. But I really didn't want to spend Friday night with Tate's mom.

"But it's so much easier if he watches me. He's already in the building, and he gets off at six."

June hesitated.

"I'll go down and ask him right now," I said. "I'll tell him it was my idea."

"Okay," June finally said. "But only if he's truly okay with it."

So now I'm going to ask Joe to babysit. Maybe Carlota can come over too and we can cook something together.

Cross your fingers he's free so Tate's mom can stay in the Hamptons where she belongs. (Sorry, but not that sorry.)

Mo

FRIDAY, OCTOBER 20

Dear Nan,

It's Friday night, late. But I can't sleep, because I have a couple important updates for you.

I'll start where I left off. Ready?

When I asked Joe if he could babysit after work, he said, "Shoot, Mo. I wish I had known. I'm helping Tony and his girlfriend move apartments."

"Oh," I said. "Of course. Never mind. Sorry."

Joe pretended to knock me on the arm. "You don't need to apologize all the time, Mo. Plus, Carlota's free. Let me talk to her. I'll let you know what she says."

We all traded phone numbers the weekend I stayed with them, in case we got separated at the Jets game. "Okay. Cool. Thanks, Joe." I started back to the elevator when I stopped and turned around. "It isn't weird for you, right? Hanging out with me?"

"Weird?" he repeated. "No. Get outta here. It's the highlight of my week."

And guess what? Carlota could do it. She came over at

six p.m. on the dot so she had a chance to give Joe a kiss on her way up.

"Thank you *so* much," June said. She was rushing around the apartment in black heels and a black dress, leaving a trail of her soft floral perfume in her wake. "There's food in the fridge you can heat up for dinner. Tate's already at the bar and he's always on me about being late. We should be back by ten at the latest."

"Of course," Carlota said. "It's my pleasure."

June patted me on the cheek. "Have fun!"

The silence felt loud when the door clicked shut. Would it be the same as the other time I stayed with them, I wondered? Would it feel as easy to be around each other, or would it feel different with just the two of us?

But then Carlota took off her shoes and spun in a circle in the foyer, just in her socks. "How nice is this?" Then she stopped spinning and grinned at me. "Can I have a tour?"

"Sure. Do you want to see my room first?"

She came over and slipped her hand into mine. "I'd love that. Lead the way."

I showed her everything, room by room. When we got to the kitchen, she had the same reaction I did when I first saw it. Her eyes went wide and she said something under her breath in Spanish.

"Nice, right?"

"Better than nice." She went over to the fridge and

pulled it open. "Let's make dinner. I can't have a kitchen like this at my fingertips and not cook."

Carlota took one of the glass containers and opened it. "What is this?"

"That's cauliflower rice," I said. She opened another one. "And that's steamed chicken breast."

"Hmm." Carlota sniffed the chicken. "No seasoning?"

"We're trying to be healthier," I said. Though honestly, all this healthy food started showing up after I'd been living here for a while. I suspect June wants *me* to be healthier. Maybe she thinks I'm too pudgy or round or something. I don't really like it. The food, I mean. It's bland when things are steamed and don't have much butter or spice. But I don't want to be a complainer, and it makes June happy, so I go with it.

"You know," Carlota said. "There are different kinds of healthy. There's healthy for the body, the mind, and the soul. And healthy for the body doesn't always mean healthy for the soul, or the mind. And vice versa."

"You think so?" I asked quietly.

"Yes. I know so." She grinned. "And tonight, we should make food that's healthy for the body *and* the soul. Let's go to the store. My treat."

Nan, have you ever had mole? It's a savory sauce that has, get this: both tomatoes *and* chocolate in it. I thought it would be too weird of a combination for me to like, but the smell filling the kitchen as the chicken cooked was rich and delicious.

Carlota lit candles and set two spots at the kitchen island. She also made rice with lots of lime and cilantro mixed in to go with the chicken.

"Close your eyes and savor it," Carlota said.

She was right. I could taste the flavors better when I shut my eyes and chewed slowly. The chocolate and the spices melded with the tomatoes better than I could have ever imagined. It was so good we both had two servings.

After we loaded the dishes in the dishwasher and the kitchen was sparkling, I said, "I think my soul needs Mister Softee."

Carlota laughed. "You know, I think mine does, too."

When we got back from our ice cream run, Carlota connected her phone to the apartment's sound system so we could turn on music and dance. She started to teach me how to salsa.

Well, at least she *tried*. Because I was bad. Worse than bad. I've got two left feet. Carlota just laughed and kept trying to teach me.

But about ten minutes into my salsa lesson, my phone pinged. It was the special alert I set up for when I get an email.

"One sec," I told Carlota. (Well, I panted it to her, because I was so out of breath from all the dancing.) I took my phone out of my pocket and my heart nearly stopped beating.

It was from Annie Hauser.

I read it twice. I kept hoping the words would rearrange themselves and say something different—but they didn't.

Apparently, her mom's favorite cousin was named *Katherine*, not Kathleen, and she'd moved to Boston, not New York. She apologized if she'd given me any false hope, and wished me all the best.

As I read her email, my face must have changed, because Carlota turned down the music.

"Mo?" she said. "Is everything okay?"

"It's . . ." I swallowed. "I thought . . ."

And then I burst into tears.

Carlota came over and put a hand on my shoulder. "What is it? Do you want to talk about it?"

"Sorry." I wiped my eyes and tried to get ahold of myself. I told her about the email, about how I had gotten my hopes way, way up that Annie's family was my family, too. "It's stupid. Can we keep dancing?"

"You sure? We can stop."

I shook my head. "No. It feels good."

"Okay, then I have a suggestion. Let's change up the music."

Carlota shuffled around on her phone until she found what she was looking for. A loud, fast-paced pop song came on. She turned it up until it was so loud the cabinets were shaking.

She started jumping up and down, moving her arms this way and that.

"Dance with me!" she shouted over the music. "Close your eyes and move however you like! As wild as you can!"

I took a breath. I tossed my phone on the counter. And then I squeezed my eyes shut and started jumping up and down and yelling. I moved my arms. I grooved. I spun and I stomped and I didn't hold anything back.

And, Nan, it felt good. No—great. I didn't need to break a glass or punch a pillow when I could fill myself up with music and *dance*.

But then, about a minute into the song, I opened my eyes, and noticed June and Tate were standing in the doorway, looking a little bit shocked.

"Sorry!" Carlota shouted, fumbling for her phone to turn the music off.

The quiet that filled the apartment was sudden and sharp.

"Wow." June smiled. "You were pushing the limits of those speakers, huh? Mo, you should have been in bed an hour ago."

"Carlota was teaching me to salsa."

Tate laughed. "That didn't look like salsa to me."

"We were dancing out some bad news," Carlota said. She came and squeezed my hand. "But I should go. Thanks for a great night, Mo. Let me know if you need anything, okay?"

"I'll walk you out," Tate said, reaching into his pocket for his wallet.

"It certainly looks like you guys had a nice night," June

said once Carlota and Tate were out of the room. "What was the bad news?"

I hesitated. Part of me wanted to tell her about Annie Hauser's email, but the other part of me didn't want to have to talk about it. To explain it out loud, again. "It's nothing. I'm pretty tired. I should go to bed."

"Okay. Sleep tight."

There was an almost invisible flash of hurt across her face again, the same as when I told her I was too old for a Halloween costume. Like maybe she was wondering why I would tell Carlota my bad news, but not her. I felt bad, but we'd already said goodnight, so it would have been awkward to start talking again.

Once I was back in my bedroom, I read Annie's email over and over again, to double-check there hadn't been a mistake. I even tried to convince myself your name was actually Katherine instead of Kathleen. (I know it isn't. Don't worry.)

But then I had an idea. It must have shaken into existence when I was dancing.

I pulled up Fiona Crenshaw's email and wrote to her. And only half an hour later, I heard back from her. I'll print and add our emails to the journal. So what do you think, Nan? Do you have any ideas?

Love,
Mo

From: momolovesfamilyfood@gmail.com
To: fcrenshaw@nytimes.com
Subject: One More Article?

Hi Fiona,

It's Mo. Mo Gallagher (the kid you wrote about). Sorry for emailing on a Friday night but it's important. I wanted to tell you I got an email from someone who thought they were related to me, but it was a false alarm. We're not actually related after all. Her name was Annie and she was really nice, so you can probably guess how disappointed I am.

Here is what I'm wondering. Could you write about me in the New York Times one more time? Maybe more Gallaghers who I'm actually related to who didn't see your first article will see your second article, and then they'll write me, too.

What do you think?

Mo (Gallagher)

From: fcrenshaw@nytimes.com
To: momolovesfamilyfood@gmail.com
Subject: re: One More Article?

Mo,

That's not how this works.

The news demands exactly that: something new.

So. You got anything new for me to write about? Any
exciting updates? Any big changes?

FC

(for exciting updates or big changes)

Fiona Crenshaw will <u>definitely</u> write another article if Mo:

—Posts 100 more recipes??

— ~~Publishes a cookbook~~ (too hard)

— ~~Opens a "the family cookbook" truck~~ (WAY too hard)

—Guest stars on a TV cooking show → but who would we call about this?

—Starts an organized food fight in Times Square

—Gets celebrities involved (OLIVIA RODRIGO!! Or maybe LIL NAS X)

—Starts a YouTube cooking channel

—Goes super viral & gets TikTok famous

— ~~Streaks naked down Park Avenue playing a French horn~~

Crystal, come on. Be serious! THIS IS IMPORTANT

I know but I'm thirsty. Let's go get some bubble tea

SUNDAY, OCTOBER 22

Dear Nan,

We found it.

Not just an idea.

We found THE idea. The idea that's going to get me a second article in the *New York Times*.

Because it's new. And it's big. And it's definitely exciting.

I'm grateful Crystal made us leave her house for bubble tea, because that's how we found it.

Usually we'd be allowed to go ourselves, but the tea place close to Crystal's house closed, so we had to walk ten blocks instead of two. So Crystal's grandma made her cousin Rachel go with us.

"I'm in college," Rachel said. I think I've mentioned this, but she's a freshman at NYU, and she lives with the Wangs and commutes to campus. "I have work to do. I'm not a babysitter."

Crystal's grandma didn't say a word. She just gave Rachel a look.

"Okay, okay," Rachel said, and then glanced at Crystal. "Well, come on. I don't have all day."

229

Rachel walked super fast the entire way there. Crystal and I had to jog to keep up.

When we got to Kiki Tea, Rachel said, "Get me an extra-sweet medium with extra boba."

"You got cash?" Crystal asked, rubbing her fingers together.

"I didn't bring my wallet," Rachel said. "And I walked you here. Against my will. So you owe me." Then she put her headphones in, leaned against the wall, and started watching something on her phone.

Crystal got Rachel's order plus one for herself, and I got a mango milk tea with extra boba.

When we got back outside, I noticed something across the street I hadn't seen when we'd gone in. It was a sign hanging above a door that said "Josephine" in pretty blue script, and below it said "A Pop-up Restaurant, Coming Soon." The door was propped open with a crate of bananas.

I took a sip of my drink and stared at the sign. "What's a pop-up restaurant?"

"Beats me," Crystal said. "Wanna find out?"

I glanced at Rachel, who was still looking at her phone. "Won't Rachel—"

"She hasn't even noticed us come out. Let's go."

Crystal checked for cars and then we jogged across the street.

I knocked on the door. "Hello?"

When no one answered, I said to Crystal, "Should we go in?"

230

"No, you certainly should not."

Both Crystal and I jumped. A man in a black apron with tattoos up his arms was now standing there, staring at us in an unfriendly way. "What do you want?"

"What's a pop-up restaurant?" I asked.

"Go away. I'm busy." He bent down and tugged the crate of bananas inside. But before he could fully close the door, I jammed my shoe in the frame, so the door bounced back.

Crystal slurped her tea. "It's a simple question."

He opened his mouth like he was about to give us a piece of his mind, as you would say, but before he could, I blurted, "I'm a chef, too. Well, kind of." I started telling him a little bit about the Family Cookbook, and that's when the expression on his face changed.

"Wait. What's your name?" When I told him, he snapped his fingers. "I think I've read about you. Are you that kid who was in the *Times*?"

I was so shocked he knew who I was that I stepped back, taking my foot from the door. But he didn't slam it in our faces.

I nodded.

"I loved that article. Family cooking is what inspired me to become a chef."

"So does that mean you're going to tell us what this place is, or what?" Crystal asked. She slurped her drink again.

"Better yet," he said, opening the door wide, "I can show you."

One quick glance over my shoulder told me Rachel still

hadn't noticed we were taking a long time. I hoped this chef wasn't a serial killer. "Okay. Sure."

We followed him inside. It pretty much looked like a normal restaurant, except it was plainer. Nothing was really designed or decorated.

"So, a pop-up restaurant is essentially a regular restaurant, but it's temporary," he explained. He motioned at the space. "There are tons of places like this across the city you can rent for a period of time. I'm trying to launch a new concept, but I wanted to test it out first. So we're going to be running it for two weeks or so, to see what the reception to our food is."

"So you just . . . rented the space, and now you have a restaurant? For two weeks?"

He laughed. "I had to get a permit or two, but yeah. Basically. This space is pretty cheap, too."

I looked around, seeing it with fresh eyes. It was a blank canvas. It could become anything. "Can anyone open a pop-up restaurant?"

"No. Not anyone." Then his face turned thoughtful. "But there was this fifteen-year-old kid, Henry Chapin, who opened one last year. It was up for a week. People went crazy for it. Teen chef and all that. Anyway, want to taste one of the dishes I'm planning?"

I was about to say yes, yes please, but Crystal's phone started buzzing. She put Rachel's drink on the floor, so she had a free hand to take it out of her pocket. "Oops," she said. "It's Rachel. We should go."

"Thanks for showing us around," I said. I couldn't tear my eyes away from the space.

"No problem." He dug a card out from one of the big pockets of his apron. "Come check us out. We open next week."

Nan, I know this is a crazy idea, but . . .

What if *I* opened a pop-up restaurant? Fiona Crenshaw would have to write about that. It's new and exciting enough, right?

We could make some of the best family recipes from my website. I could blow up the family pictures people have submitted and hang them all over the walls. And we'd make it family-style, of course—which means you put everything on big platters on the tables so people have to serve themselves and each other.

And better yet—I could say all Gallaghers could eat for free. Or half off. Or something like that.

I know I have school, the website, homework . . . is it too much? I don't know.

Then again, every time I wonder whether I can do something or not, I see your face, clearer than daylight, telling me, "Mo Gallagher, you can do anything you set your mind to."

So I'm about to go talk to Tate and June about the idea. Wish me luck.

I love you,
Mo

SATURDAY, OCTOBER 28

Dear Nan,

The pop-up restaurant is a go. A yes. An "I can do it!"

June and Tate were excited about the idea when I talked to them about it last Sunday. Well, Tate was excited. June was concerned I won't have time for it with everything I already have going on. And how busy she's been with work.

"But what if I did it just for one weekend? Or one night?" I suggested. "Like maybe the first weekend of November?"

"Mo, that's way too fast," June replied. "There's no way you could launch a restaurant in that amount of time, even if it was just for a day or two."

"Well, what about over winter break?" Tate asked. "New Year's, maybe? That would give us enough time to plan."

I felt like doing a happy dance. Not only because Tate was so supportive of the idea, but because he said "us."

"Winter break would be a great time," I said. "I have two weeks off. No homework, either."

"It's going to be expensive," June said. "And you know how much travel I have over the next month, so I don't want it all to fall on me."

"Junie." Tate put a hand on her shoulder and squeezed. "Relax. It can't be that expensive, especially if Mo only does one night. And maybe Olivia can take care of whatever permits and applications Mo needs. Easy peasy."

"Olivia's going to be busy doing her job," June said. "You know, working for me?"

"Fine," Tate said. "Then I'll do it myself."

June sighed. "All right, fine. I guess I'm overruled."

"So does that mean I can do it?" I asked. I felt bad June wasn't more excited, but I wanted this desperately enough that I wasn't about to take back asking.

Tate nodded. "Sure does, kiddo."

Can you believe it?!

While June was gone this past week, Tate and I spent the evenings searching the internet together. There were lots of pop-up spaces available for rent in Manhattan and Brooklyn, but I couldn't get my mind off the space I saw with Crystal, near Kiki Tea. It's small and cozy and perfect.

And better yet, it's available for the perfect night: December 31. New Year's Eve.

Probably the best thing of all was that Travis overheard me talking to Crystal about it at school. Maybe because it's the only thing I've been able to talk about ever since we came up with the idea.

And on Thursday, he slid into the seat across from me at lunch. "So. What's this I hear about you opening a restaurant?"

"Uh . . . ," I said. "Um . . ."

My face flared. In fact, there was so much heat I'm surprised my head didn't explode off my body, like a rocket. Travis *never* sits with us. He usually sits with the athletic kids, the ones who can run and dribble and play soccer all day long.

"Mo? You okay?" He glanced at Crystal. "Is she choking?"

Crystal gave me a firm pat on the back, which made me cough. "She's fine."

"I'm opening a pop-up restaurant," I managed to say. "One day. For one day. New Year's. In December, I mean. Over winter break?"

"Cool," he said. "That's what I thought I heard."

Crystal eyed him. "What do you want, Travis?"

I don't know if you remember this, but Crystal's had a thing against Travis ever since they were co-leaders for the art club's mural team in fourth grade. They were supposed to come up with a plan for part of the playground wall together, but Travis was too busy with soccer and Crystal ended up doing all the work.

He shrugged. "I don't know. I thought it might be cool to, like, help or whatever."

"What?" I said. "You want—to help? Me?"

Travis took a big bite of his apple. "If that's okay."

I stared at him. "Why?"

I hoped he'd say something like "because I'm in love with you, Mo Gallagher." Well, no, actually. That would have been too intense. But a hint he liked me, you know?

Instead, he only shrugged and said, "I don't know. My brother's in culinary school. We cook together sometimes. It's fun."

Crystal leaned forward and jabbed her plastic fork at him. "That's not good enough. This is important. Maybe the most important thing Mo will ever do. You can't flake out on us. Again."

"Are you still mad about the mural thing?" Travis groaned. "I've apologized about that, like, six times since fourth grade. How many more times do you want me to say sorry?"

Crystal crossed her arms. "Until you mean it."

"It's just . . ." Travis kept crumpling his paper napkin up into a ball and then smoothing it out again. "I won't flake. I promise. With the art stuff, soccer came first. But now that I can't play—I don't know." He glanced over his shoulder where Brian, Hakeem, and the other boys from the team were hanging out. "It feels good to be a part of something. I miss that feeling. So please. Let me help."

Crystal glanced at me. I nodded. She pointed her fork back at Travis. "Okay. *That* was good enough. Welcome to the team."

We all exchanged numbers so we could have our first planning meeting this weekend.

And now this weekend is here. Today. Travis Ortiz is coming here. Which means Travis Ortiz is going to stand in my bedroom. I've changed my outfit fifteen times. Twenty times. I used June's hair dryer to dry my hair but it got too poofy so I scraped it back into a ponytail. Okay, I have to go change one more time because I'm sweating through my shirt. I wish I could stick my head in the sand like an ostrich.

Anyway. I'll let you know how the meeting goes.

Love,
(A Very Nervous) Mo

SATURDAY, OCTOBER 28
(LATER)

Dear Nan,

I know I just wrote to you, but I had to tell you: the planning committee went about ten to fifteen times better than I thought it would.

I was hoping Crystal would get here first, but she didn't. Travis did.

The Townsends' housekeeper, Jessica, answered the door.

"Hi. I'm Travis. Is Mo here?" he asked, stepping into the foyer. Then he spotted me. "Oh. Hey. This place is awesome. You live here?"

"Uh, yes. Yes, I do."

He slipped his shoes off and I noticed he was wearing Pokémon socks, which made me blush. I've only ever seen his feet in shoes.

"Right this way," I said, bowing and pointing.

Jessica turned away, and I could tell she was trying to hide a smile. I would have, too.

Because why, Nan? Why do I turn into a weird English butler whenever I'm nervous? It's so weird. *I'm* so weird.

Travis didn't seem to notice, because he followed me to

my bedroom without saying anything. He plopped himself down in the swivel chair by my desk. I couldn't think of anything to say, so I hovered by the door, weirdly, awkwardly, sweatily.

Thank god the doorbell rang soon after that.

"I'll get it," I said. I hurried to the door, and when I opened it, Crystal was standing there.

"You're late," I hissed.

She tapped the screen of her phone and showed me the time. "Three minutes late, Mo. Chill."

With the three of us in my room, it felt way less awkward. Especially since Crystal flopped onto the bed and immediately opened a notebook.

"My dad said we should make an agenda," Crystal said. "Like, for our plans."

So that's exactly what we did. We have about two months before the restaurant launches, which sounds like a lot of time, but really, it's not.

The hardest part was figuring out the math.

According to the research Tate and I did, it's going to cost us $1,590 to rent the restaurant space for one night. It's so much because they have to clean and prep the space before we get in, and we have to have the kitchen available to us for the entire day for cooking and preparation. The rate gets cheaper if we were to book more days, but I'm not sure I could handle more than one night. My eyes nearly popped out of my skull when I first heard that number, and so did Travis's and Crystal's.

"Wow," Travis said. "That's a lot."

"You could rent an apartment for a *month* for that," Crystal said.

"Yeah, I know. Tate and June said they'll help me cover the cost," I told them, flushing pink.

Travis spun circles in my desk chair. "Wow. Lucky."

I watched him spin. Travis's family is really involved. I've seen them at his soccer games, at school concerts. I bet he could send a single group text, and he could create an entire Ortiz family cookbook in just one day.

"It's even luckier you get to live with your family," I said back.

"No, yeah. You're right. I am lucky for that. I wasn't saying I wanted to trade places." He stopped swiveling and looked around the room. "I just meant that if I was in foster care, I know I wouldn't end up anywhere like this, with all that money flying into my pockets. That's all I was saying."

That made me think about my conversation with that kid, Ricky. I was embarrassed Travis had to spell it out for me like that. I still am. Because he was completely right. So I said so.

"You're right," I agreed. "But the money isn't going to stay in my pockets. I'm going to pay them back. So we need to figure out how much it will cost to buy ingredients, rent tables and chairs, and print out family pictures so we can hang them on the walls."

"My brother said we should also do at least one practice round of cooking," Travis added. "He said sometimes a recipe that serves four gets weird if you try to make it serve more people. Like with the seasoning and stuff."

Crystal nodded. "Yeah. One time my mom tried to make this chicken salad she loves for fifty people and she got the salt all wrong. People were running for water all night."

"And if we can estimate our costs," Travis said, "then we can figure out how much money we'll need to charge people to make it all back."

"That's a lot of math," Crystal said. She glanced over at Travis. "Are you good at math? Because I'm not. And Mo is definitely not."

"Hey. Rude," I complained, sticking my tongue out at her. But I couldn't say anything else, because it's true.

Travis shrugged and grabbed the pen and started scribbling numbers.

And wow—he *is* good at math, because soon we had some calculations. Here's what we came up with:

$1,590 – rental cost
$500 – ingredients for a practice round
   (approximate)
$1,000 – final ingredients (approximate)
$300 – cost to print out pictures/decorations
$300 – cost to advertise
$0 – labor (friends and family)
$3,690 – total cost

Luckily, the space said they have standard tables and chairs we can use, along with dishes and everything, so we don't have to spend any money renting those. According to Travis, if we want to charge people thirty dollars for a meal, we'll have to have 123 guests total.

"That's a lot," I said. "The space isn't that big. I think it only fits fifty people at once."

Travis crossed out a few numbers and said, "Okay, then we'll raise the price. If we charge forty-five dollars per person . . ." He did some math in the margin. "We'd have to have about eighty-two people total. We could do two seatings of forty-five. That would give us a little extra money as a buffer, in case there's anything we have to spend money on that we didn't plan for."

"That sounds a lot better," I said. "But what about Gallaghers eating for free?"

"I don't know if you want to tell *anyone* they can eat for free. It might mess with our budget." He tapped the pen against his lips. (I am never getting rid of that pen.) "How about this—what if any Gallagher can technically get in for free, but with a suggested donation of forty dollars? I bet most people would pay it."

Along with the math, we made a checklist of things we have to do before the restaurant launches. It took us about two hours of brainstorming all in.

"Shoot," Travis said, checking his watch. "I gotta go. It took me and my mom forever to get here and we have to get back downtown for a family Halloween party thing."

He stood up and shouldered his backpack. "But this was fun. I'm excited."

"Okay." I stood up, too. I wiped my sweaty palms on my jeans. "Thanks. You're cool. I mean, this was cool. You are, too. Cool, I mean. Obviously."

Travis smiled. "Yeah, okay. *Cool.* See you at school."

I walked him to the front door, and we high-fived as he left. I hoped he couldn't feel any dampness. I held my breath until I got back to my bedroom, where Crystal was waiting for me with a huge grin and raised eyebrows.

I fell back onto my bed. "He's so stupidly cute!" I yelled. "And I'm just plain stupid."

Crystal started to laugh. "Oh my god, Mo. You literally just swooned."

I jumped to my feet. "You're right. I did."

And then I put the back of my hand against my forehead and swooned again, this time with a long sigh, like the women on the covers of your romance novels.

And then we both practiced our swoons by falling back onto my bed, and we kissed our hands, pretending it was Travis. Well, *I* pretended it was Travis. I guessed Crystal was pretending her hand was Michael Renner. She's had a crush on him since the third grade, even though I saw him eating his own boogers once (she's never believed me).

"Is that Booger Boy?" I asked, grinning at her hand.

Crystal blushed furiously and looked away. "Uh . . ."

She *never* blushes. That's my job. Which meant something was up.

"What?" I asked. "What is it?"

"I . . . actually don't like him anymore."

Nan, even you probably remember Crystal's years-long crush on Michael Renner, so you understand what big news this was to me.

"What? Since *when*? Do you like someone else?"

Crystal smothered her now-beet-red face with a pillow and nodded.

"Who is it?" I yelled. "Tell me, tell me!"

She peeked out one eye only. "Peyton Hall?"

She said it like it was a question, not an answer.

This was the first time Crystal had ever had a crush on a girl—or at least told me about it. That's probably why she was nervous. But I never want her to feel nervous telling me anything, so after a second, I nodded. "I approve. She'd never eat her own boogers. And she's got really nice hair."

"Right?" Crystal said. She sighed and flopped back. "It looks so soft and silky. I bet it feels nice to braid."

"You can always braid my hair," I offered.

She wrinkled her nose. "With those knots? Thanks, but no thanks."

I threw my pillow at her, but she dodged it. Then I clutched my hands to my chest because I wasn't done swooning yet. "Oh, Travis. Your dimples drive me to *distraction*!"

Then I fell back onto the bed.

Crystal jumped up. "Peyton, are you in trouble? I'll save you! But first I must—"

She put the back of her hand to her forehead and

swooned back so dramatically she bounced right off the bed and onto the floor. We laughed so hard I almost peed my pants.

She'd kill me if she knew I was telling you. But I bet you're getting a kick out of this.

Anyway, Crystal's spending the night here. The plan is that we're going to eat Halloween candy and watch *Hocus Pocus 2*. Oh—she just finished showering. Gotta go!

Love,
Mo

Pop-Up Restaurant Checklist

By Mo, Crystal, and Travis

- ☒ Email Fiona Crenshaw at New York Times
- ☒ Get temporary food service permit (Tate did this, it was $70)
- ☐ Get people to help in the kitchen
  - ☒ Crystal
  - ☒ Travis
  - ☒ Mo
  - ☐ June and/or Tate
  - ☐ Marcus (Travis's brother; Travis will ask)
  - ☒ Joe and Carlota (they both said they'll help!)
- ☐ Plan the menu!
- ☐ Make an ingredient shopping list
- ☐ Do a "test run" of menu—early or mid-December?? Where?
- ☐ Print out family pictures to hang on walls
- ☐ Buy red-and-white-checkered tablecloths and candles
- ☐ Advertising
  - ☒ Tell people at school to come

- ☒ Mo to write website post & make video for TikTok
- ☐ Print out color flyers and pass them out
- ☐ Pay someone with lots of followers on TikTok to post about us

Dear Readers,

Thank you so much for all the support, recipes, and notes you've sent after the article about me went up in the *New York Times*! Wow. I never thought so many people would care about family recipes, but then again, I guess food means a lot to a lot of people.

I'm writing with two pieces of news.

My first piece of news is that I am going to be taking a break from posting new family recipes until after the New Year. But don't worry, it's for a very exciting reason.

And the reason is that I'm opening a pop-up restaurant! I plan on making some of my favorite recipes featured here on the Family Cookbook. Once we decide on a menu, I will email everyone and ask their permission first, so don't worry about that. I won't make anything anyone doesn't want me to.

The restaurant will be in Brooklyn, open for <u>ONE DAY ONLY</u>: December 31. Yes, that's right, a special New Year's Eve event. We will do two seatings, one at 6 p.m. and one at 8 p.m. Tickets will cost $45.

If you are interested in coming to my pop-up restaurant, please send me an email at momolovesfamilyfood @gmail.com.

And most importantly: anyone who's a Gallagher who is related to me, you will eat for free. Well, for a strongly suggested donation of $40. Please tell your friends. Especially if their last name is Gallagher.

Hopefully, by the night of the restaurant launch, I, Mo Gallagher, will have a family recipe of my own to contribute.

Thanks for your support!
Mo

From: fcrenshaw@nytimes.com
To: momolovesfamilyfood@gmail.com
Subject: re: I'm doing a pop-up restaurant!!!!!

A pop-up restaurant? Now, that's what I'm talking about.

I'll tweet about it in the next few days, and will add an update to the online piece from before.

Also? Sign me up for two spots for the 6 p.m. seating.

FC

Dear Nan,

You won't believe the reaction we've had to the news of the restaurant. We've already got a lot of reservations, only a couple days later.

Dr. Barb is coming with her husband! I was really happy when I saw that. I was also happy to see that Esther Wu signed up for a seat, too. Esther-from-poker-night Esther. I haven't seen her since your funeral. I didn't know she read the Family Cookbook. Isn't that nice of her? She was always my favorite of your poker-night crew.

Crystal's family is going to come, Joe's brothers and their families are signed up (but not Joe and Carlota, because they'll be in the kitchen with me), and Travis's family is coming, too.

Peyton Hall, her parents, and her brother are signed up for the first seating. When I texted Crystal a screenshot of the email, she sent back a screenshot of a cartoon possum clutching its chest and fake-dying. Which I think is Crystal's way of saying she's excited.

The best are the sign-ups from the internet, from

strangers. I can't believe they want to come, without even knowing me.

Fiona Crenshaw is going to tweet about it tomorrow, and I've got my fingers crossed this will be the final piece of the puzzle. I know it's a long shot, but I can't give up hope. Like Mr. Gregory used to say, I have to keep manifesting.

June is in Paris right now. She's been in Paris a lot for work the past few months. Every time I look at the shared calendar, there are fewer scheduled "household outings" and more new travel dates on there for her. Since she's been gone, Tate and I have FaceTimed with his dad and his brother, and have basically spent all our time watching old football games on YouTube. This weekend, we even watched part of the 2010 AFC Championship game when the Jets lost to the Steelers. I kept cheering for them to win, even though I knew the outcome.

I hope one day I'll have a job that will send me to Paris. I want to eat crepes and say "Oui, oui, merci" while wearing a beret. I'd walk around the city with a baguette for me and a bag of fancy seeds for the swans.

Because I bet they don't have pigeons or ducks in Paris. I bet they only have swans there.

Love,
Mo

SATURDAY, NOVEMBER 4

Dear Nan,

It hasn't even been a day since my article in the food section was updated with the pop-up restaurant information
(and Fiona tweeted about it to her thousands of followers), and already all the spots are filled up. There's even a
waiting list in case we have cancellations.

This means we don't have to print out flyers, which
gives us an extra three hundred dollars of budget to work
with. Maybe we can spend that on chef's hats and jackets.
(*Note to self*: look up cost of chef's hats and jackets.)

I'm saving two spots each seating for potential Gallagher walk-ins. Or hopefully, late-to-the-game Gallaghers
who see the updated article about me sometime tonight,
or tomorrow, or next week.

My biggest hope is one of them will email me to let me
know they're coming—and they'll have a recipe for me to
use, too. I'd love to have a surprise Gallagher recipe as the
pièce de résistance (that's French for "the most important
or remarkable feature"—I've been studying French vocabulary to impress June) of the menu.

But I know I still have to plan an amazing menu without a Gallagher recipe, because the whole thing is a long shot. Which means it's time for me, Travis, and Crystal to start going through all the recipes I've collected to see what will work best.

Just since writing this letter, Travis already texted saying we can use his dad's Costco membership number, so we can buy ingredients in bulk and spend less money.

He's not only cute, but he's smart and thoughtful. And good at math. And isn't flaking out on us at all—even Crystal's admitted that.

UGH.

I have to stop writing this and texting Crystal and Travis at the same time in case I accidentally gush about Travis *to* Travis (the biggest nightmare on earth) instead of writing to you about him.

Love!
Mo

MONDAY, NOVEMBER 20

Dear Nan,

Wow, the past few weeks have flown by. I'm sorry I haven't been writing as much. With planning for the pop-up restaurant and homework, I've been so busy.

Somehow, it's already the Monday before Thanksgiving. June, Tate, and I are going to the Hamptons to celebrate with Tate's mom. She's taking us to her country club, since her chef is taking the holiday off—and June explained, "Bitsy does *not* cook." (That's June's emphasis, not mine. Imagine it with a bit of an eye roll.)

I was hoping we'd be able to go to Boston, to meet June's sister and her family, but June said they don't go to Boston for the holidays. "Not since Terry passed away."

I haven't seen Mrs. Townsend since we went swimming at her house this summer. Tate's been out to see her a couple times, and she came into the city last month to go shopping and take June out to lunch. I didn't find out until after. My feelings weren't even hurt that I wasn't invited. I was just glad I didn't have to make up an excuse about why I didn't want to go.

Anyway, I spent all weekend googling country clubs to try to figure out what to wear and how to act, and if there are, like, extra forks I should know about.

According to my research, it looks like I need pearls and a collared shirt, neither of which I have. Hopefully, June will have something I can borrow. I want to impress Mrs. Townsend this time. I want her to see my rough edges can be smooth, too.

Then again, maybe she'll trip over one of her Republican dogs again and break her other wrist. Or maybe her toilet will explode and she'll have to spend all day with a plumber instead of with us.

Okay. I have to stop writing what I hope will happen before the devil sniffs me out and sends me directly to H-E-double hockey sticks for being a horrible person.

Mo

THURSDAY, NOVEMBER 23

Dear Nan,

Happy Thanksgiving! I discovered a new scientific fact this morning: apparently, if you're dreading something enough, you can make yourself sick. Like, actually sick. Not even a faking-it kind of sick.

Last night I went to bed feeling completely fine, but this morning I woke up all achy and tired. And it wasn't in my head—I had an actual fever. June used their ear thermometer on me three times, and every time it came back the same: 102.3 degrees.

After a lot of back and forth between June and Tate, they decided Tate would go, and June would stay home with me.

June got me all set up in the den, with ginger ale, saltine crackers, and a big fluffy blanket and two pillows from my bed. She also signed up for a subscription to Disney+ so I could watch anything I wanted.

I was feeling better after a long nap, so I asked June if she wanted to get Chinese takeout.

She raised her eyebrows. "On Thanksgiving?"

"My grandma hated turkey and never cooked," I explained. "So Chinese food was our Thanksgiving tradition. We always got noodles and pork ribs."

I could see June thinking about it. I was expecting her to say I needed something healthier since I was sick, but instead she grabbed her phone and said, "Oh, what the heck. Let's do it."

We ordered our exact meal—pork ribs and noodles—from a restaurant close to their apartment. She let us eat directly out of the take-out containers in the den while we watched *Star Wars*. No real plates or metal forks. All of it felt very un-June, but in a good way.

"Are you feeling any better?" she asked me in between bites of dangling noodles.

"I am. A lot better." It was so cozy, and I wasn't feeling so sick that I couldn't enjoy being on the couch instead of at Mrs. Townsend's country club. I did feel bad for June, though. "I'm sorry if I ruined your Thanksgiving."

June smiled as she dug her chopsticks back into the noodles. "Between you and me, I was happy for the excuse to stay here."

I smiled back at her. "Yeah. Me too. Tate's mom is pretty awful, huh?"

June stopped moving her chopsticks, and her smile faded. "I didn't say *that*, Mo."

I only said that because I thought she didn't like Mrs. Townsend, either. She's basically said as much, right?

"She just . . ." I shrugged. "I don't think she likes me very much."

June sighed. "She can be tough. No doubt about that. And honestly, she didn't like me very much when Tate and I started dating."

"Really? She didn't?"

"No. But then she saw how hard I was working. She saw that my fingers were raw from sewing together pieces of leather at night to make samples of my designs while working a day job to pay bills. So she paid off all my student debts. She didn't tell Tate she was going to do it. We weren't even married or engaged. But her help is what made it possible for me to take risks. To start my own company." She swirled her chopsticks in her noodles. "People are complicated, Mo."

After that, we finished eating, and then she told me she was going to clean up and go take a bath. I haven't seen her since. I feel stupid about calling Tate's mom awful. I hope she doesn't tell Tate I said that. I think it would hurt his feelings.

I'm feeling worse, sickness-wise, so I'm going to stop writing and go to bed early.

Happy Thanksgiving, Nan. I would do anything to be eating greasy noodles at Chow on Mein with you right now, even though I feel super crummy. I miss you with all my bones.

Love,
Mo

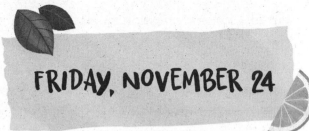

Dear Nan,

Things are much better today. Here's a list of how things have improved:

1. I woke up feeling much better, no fever in sight. Did you talk the big guy upstairs into sending me a one-day illness so I didn't have to go see Mrs. Townsend? If so, thanks.
2. Tate was as happy and relaxed as usual today, and kept asking how I was feeling, so I don't think June told him what I said.
3. I had a phone appointment with Dr. Barb. I always feel better after talking to her.
4. Joe was working today, and he brought me a slice of leftover pie Carlota made. It's a burnt sugar pie with pecans. I thought burnt sugar would make something taste, well, burnt, but no. No, no. It's probably one of the best things I've ever tasted.
5. Crystal, Travis, and I texted all afternoon. It

started as a conversation finalizing our menu (I wrote it out for you on the next page so you can see) and planning for our recipe-testing day, which we're going to do tomorrow. But then it turned to other stuff, like school and TV shows and what we all did for Thanksgiving. I wasn't awkward or weird. I was normal. Could it be . . . Travis and I might actually become . . . *friends?*

Life is weird. One day is down and the next is up. Who knows what's around the corner?

Love you,
Mo

The Family Cookbook:
A Pop-Up Restaurant
Menu (version 1)

AMUSE-~~BOOCH~~ BOUCHE
Pork and Shrimp Dumplings
The Wang Family
Brooklyn, New York

APPETIZER
Rainbow Chard and Butternut Squash Pasta
Gabriel and David Ginsberg-Miller
New York, New York

MAIN COURSE
Manahan Chicken Adobo with Steamed Rice
April Manahan Shriver
Cape Charles, Virginia

DESSERT
*Buttermilk Pie with Vanilla Whipped Cream
and Caramel Drizzle*
Martha C. Walker
Kellogg, Minnesota

SATURDAY, NOVEMBER 25

Dear Nan,

Today was a day.

Or should I say *the* day: we tested all our recipes for the pop-up restaurant. I'm so tired I could sleep standing up with my eyes open, in a full subway car with a mariachi band playing right next to my head.

HOWEVER, I want to write to you about it while it's all fresh. Maybe I'm so tired that if I go to sleep my brain will turn to cotton balls, and I'll forget the details. And I don't want to forget anything.

We started early. So early it was still dark outside when I got up to get changed. That's because it was technically still nighttime. Travis's brother, Marcus, got us a kitchen to use for free at his culinary school, because one of his instructors owed him a favor. But the only time we could use it was from five a.m. to noon. I asked Travis if we should use our extra three hundred dollars of budget to pay Marcus, since he already called in a favor for me, and we don't even know each other.

"Nah. He said he wants to do this because it'll look

great on his résumé. Not many people in culinary school get to say they've already launched a restaurant."

I was all dressed and ready to go, so I knocked lightly on Tate and June's bedroom door. Both of them said they were going to come help me today. Tate came to the door, in sweatpants and a T-shirt.

"Ready?" I asked. "Where's June?"

"Mo, I'm so sorry, but June is absolutely wiped," he said. "One of her main suppliers' factories burned down last night, and she was on the phone until about an hour ago."

"Oh no," I said. "Did anyone get hurt?"

"No, thank god, but it's going to be a very stressful few days for her."

I nodded. "Okay. But are you still coming?"

"Me? Aw, man, Mo, I don't think I would be much help without June there to direct me. I'll take you there, but I kind of feel like I should stay around here in case June needs me after the night she's had. Is that okay?"

We'd planned out the day knowing there were going to be eight people in the kitchen. If there were only six of us, it meant we'd all have to do more work than we planned for.

But then again, I've seen Tate cook, and he's not very good. I did feel a bit of a pang, though. Even if all he did was peel vegetables, I kind of wanted him there. I wanted at least one of them to see me in my element.

"We'll both be there to help on the actual day, Mo," he added, like he was reading my mind. "I promise."

Tate and I took a taxi to Marcus's culinary school together. When we got there, he gave me money to reimburse Joe and Carlota, who were the ones who went and picked up all of today's ingredients.

"We're already sold out, so I'll be able to pay you back for everything," I told him. "I promise."

"Don't worry about that right now. Have fun," he said as I got out. "Just text me and I'll get you an Uber whenever you're ready to come home, okay?"

I nodded. "Okay. Tell June I'm sorry about the fire."

"I will. See you later, kiddo."

I started to feel better as soon as I stepped foot inside the building. Partly because it was freezing and dark outside, and the blast of warmth felt good.

But if I'm being one hundred percent honest, I mostly felt better because Travis and his brother were already there waiting for me.

Marcus is tall and thin, with brown skin a few shades darker than Travis's, a shaved head, and a bunch of gold hoops in one of his ears. Travis looks a lot like him. They have the same nice nose.

I *know* I was blushing when I stuck out my hand to shake Marcus's. "Nice to meet Mo. I'm you. I mean, it's nice to meet *you*. I'm Mo. I think I'm still asleep."

Marcus laughed. "What's up, Mo?"

"See?" Travis said. "Told you she's funny."

Right then, I felt like I floated two inches off the ground.

266

Because Travis Ortiz thinks I'm funny. Funny-on-purpose funny.

The kitchen itself was unlike anything I've ever seen. Everything was twice as big as the stuff in a normal kitchen, made of stainless steel, and sparkling clean. There was a mixer attached to the wall that was so big I could have fit inside the bowl, and a big metal worktable at the center of the room. Black rubber mats were spread on all the floors. Marcus explained they help with back pain, because chefs have to stand all the time.

Marcus was unloading his knife kit (because apparently you need a big bag full of your own sharp knives when you're a chef) when Joe, Carlota, and Crystal got there, almost at the same time. Crystal immediately pulled up a metal stool and put her forehead down on the worktable.

My heart swelled because I know Crystal would rather have a cavity filled than wake up early. But she got up earlier than early to be here. For me.

"Good morning, beautiful people," Carlota sang, whirling into the room with bags of groceries like she'd already been awake for hours. I guess since she works at a bakery, she's used to the early hours. But not Joe.

"Coffee," he grunted, after introducing himself to Marcus and Travis. He ruffled my hair as a hello, probably because he was too tired to say much of anything else. "Is there coffee?"

The rest of the morning was a blur. Marcus and Carlota

sat down together to make our prep list for the day. Everything from "dicing shallots" to "washing and drying rainbow chard" got its own little bullet point on the list.

"It's way easier when you break it all down into single tasks," Marcus explained. "A kitchen during dinner service can be overwhelming, so you want to make sure you're as prepared as possible. This way, when dinner service starts, all we'll have to do is a bit of cooking and heating, so we're not frazzled trying to get everything together."

While we cooked, Marcus put on an upbeat playlist of a guy singing in Spanish.

"Who is this?" Joe asked, after three or four songs. "It's good!"

He lifted his hands in the air and shook his hips in rhythm with the beat. Or at least, he tried. Carlota groaned and covered her face, which only made Joe grin and shake his hips faster.

"Juan Luis Guerra," Travis said. "Our dad's obsessed."

We didn't make the full amounts we have planned for the restaurant—that would have been too much, so we did half batches. But I am glad we tested bigger serving sizes of the recipes, because even as a half batch, the chicken adobo came out way too salty. Now we know to reduce the soy sauce when we make it the night-of.

Everything else went (knock on wood) pretty smoothly, even though there were only six of us instead of eight. When we were done, we all sat down around the metal table and assigned jobs for the night of the pop-up restaurant, so everyone knows their tasks. Then we ate what we cooked.

Marcus asked a bunch of questions about how I got inspired to take on such a big project. And like most things in my life, the story led back to you. Thanks for making me find a hobby, Nan. You were right. Then again, you usually are.

All in all, it was a pretty great day. Tiring, but great. Marcus was meeting his boyfriend at a party, so he took most of the leftovers, but I took some too, so Tate and June could try the recipes. I only wish they could have been there, but they promised they'd be there on the actual day. And that's what matters, right?

Love,
Mo

SUNDAY, NOVEMBER 26

Dear Nan,

The roller coaster of my life keeps chugging up and down and up again, because I have some big news. Some big, sparkling French (that's a hint) news.

Earlier today, I went to refill my water glass in the kitchen.

Tate was there, with his running buddy, Nick. They must have just gotten back from their loop in Central Park, because they were really sweaty, and each of them had a beer. I didn't mean to eavesdrop, but I was there, so I overheard part of their conversation. They were talking about Paris.

"Oh," I said as the ice dispenser on the door of the fridge whirred and ground. "Is June going back to Paris soon? Because of the factory?"

Nick glanced at Tate with a huge smile. "You told her, right?"

"Told me what?" I asked.

"About the sale! You must be excited to go to Paris." He raised his bottle of beer toward Tate, but Tate didn't raise his back. He only pressed his lips together and spun his own bottle in his hands, like he was upset. I noticed, and Nick must have noticed, too, because he immediately put his beer down. "Oh god. Shoot. I'm such an idiot. Did I ruin the surprise?"

"The sale? Go to Paris?" I repeated. I didn't understand.

"Yeah." Tate glanced at Nick, then looked at me. "We were going—we were going to talk to you about this. Later. June sold her company to a huge French clothing brand."

"Wow! That's good news, right?"

"It is. It's very good news. Only thing is, they want her on the team. And their company is based exclusively out of Paris."

I stared at him. I had no idea what to say. I had a million questions. *Paris.* If June was moving . . . did that mean we were going to move, too?

"But don't worry," Tate added quickly. "It would only be for a year, to help smooth out the transition for the rest of her employees. Then she'll get to decide whether she wants to stay with the bigger company, or leave to do something else. We'll keep this apartment, and she's going to rent a place there first. So nothing big will change. Or at least, that's the hope."

"So you and me would stay here?"

Tate nodded. "And she'd be back as much as possible."

"Paris," I said. "Wow."

"Sorry for spoiling it, man," Nick said.

I took my glass of water and turned to go back to my room so I could digest this news on my own.

"Mo," Tate called out before I got back to my room. He'd followed me into the hallway. "I'm sorry. We didn't mean for you to find out like this. June wanted to tell you herself."

I don't know why he looked so tragic about it. Selling her company is great news, right? I mean, of course I'll miss her. But she's already been going to Paris so often. She'll just be gone a little more now.

"Paris," I whispered to myself once I was back in my room. I've always wanted to see the Eiffel Tower. I bet Tate and I will visit June. Nick said as much, right? Maybe we'll spend spring break in Paris. *Christmas* in Paris. Maybe we can spend summer in Paris, too.

The more I think about it, the more excited I get. I'm going to get my own passport! I can't believe just a few letters ago I was daydreaming about going to Paris. And now it's real.

I'm glad I already got that French vocabulary book. I'll have to really study so when me and Tate go to visit, I can ask people for their family recipes, in French. The Family Cookbook, Paris edition. It's the exact refresher my content needs. I hope I don't have to make frog legs or snails. That's French food, right? What else do French people eat? French fries? No, that can't be right. French fries feel American. But then, why would they be called *French* fries? I guess I have some research to do.

Anyway, I'll write soon!

Mo

PS It's a couple hours later, but I started to worry my letter might have made you feel bad that you and me never traveled out of the country. I'd still take a week with you in that basement apartment in Myrtle Beach we rented for spring break in fourth grade over an entire month in Paris. Remember that place? With the leak and the musty smell? I don't think I ever laughed so hard as when you found mice feasting on the Cinnamon Toast Crunch in the cupboard and let out that long scream. You sounded like an opera star. Anyway, if we'd had more time, we would have adventured across the world. We'd have made it to Paris eventually, I know it. Maybe we'd have done it in a motorcycle with a sidecar. I can imagine us in matching pink sparkly goggles, can't you?

FRIDAY, DECEMBER 1

Dear Nan,

It's only been a week since I last wrote, but a lot . . . a lot has happened.

It's almost ten p.m., and I'm writing to you from the subway, on the way to Brooklyn. Alone.

Before you get mad, let me start at the beginning. Maybe then you'll understand.

It's about Paris.

Well, no. That's not quite right. It's more about June and Tate and me than it is about Paris. It happened earlier tonight. They sat me down in the den after dinner. June sat stiffly, her hands on her knees. She must have been pressing her teeth together, because I could see a little hard bump on both sides of her jaw.

"Is everything . . . okay?" I asked.

The second I saw a tear slip out of Tate's eye—even though he brushed it away quickly—I knew it wasn't.

"Negotiations for the sale of my company have changed pretty quickly," June said. "The situation went from only a year in Paris to full-time in Paris. With no end date."

"Okay," I said. My hands and cheeks were starting to feel tingly and buzzy. "So that means . . . what, exactly?"

"It means if I agree to the terms of the deal, we'd be moving to Paris. Full-time. No back and forth." June put her hand on Tate's knee and he put his hand on top of hers. "And we've decided that for us, it's the right decision."

The way June said "us" felt like she meant "me and Tate," not "the three of us."

"I don't think I understand," I said.

Another tear slipped out from Tate's eye. He didn't brush this one away. "We've stayed up every night for the past week, talking about it. Neither of us has slept. We're crazy about you, Mo. You're a fantastic kid. But—"

"No. This is on me," June said quietly. She took a deep breath. "Having to move out of the country has forced us to make certain decisions sooner than we planned to. And one of the biggest things we've realized is that"—she steadied herself—"we aren't ready to be parents. We're not ready for that level of responsibility for the rest of our lives. I guess we just didn't know how much . . ."

She trailed off, shaking her head.

How much what? I wanted to ask. *How much work? How much trouble?*

In that moment, if I could have gone back, I would have uncooked everything I made. Unmade every mess. Figured out myself you can't use high heat with their special sheets so neither of them ever realized I wet the bed, like an idiot, helpless baby.

I wanted to say that. To promise I'd be perfectly be-haved in the future. I'd be quiet, I'd do all my homework, I'd eat only the healthy food June wanted me to.

I'd be *good*.

But what came instead was "I thought you wanted to adopt me."

"That was the goal," June agreed. "But there are so many rules with your situation. It would require huge sac-rifices for us to make the move to Paris work for the three of us. Who knows how long it could take for an adoption to go through? What if Tate were to stay here with you, and I went to Paris alone, and we did long-distance for a year, and then something fell through in the court system? Or they said we couldn't take you out of the country? What if your father finally appeared out of the mist and fought to keep you? I don't want to spend the next however-many-years-of-my-life waiting, separated from my husband. It wouldn't be fair to go through that whole process when I—when *we*—aren't in it with our whole hearts."

I didn't say anything. I was trying to keep myself to-gether. But despite my best efforts, I started to cry.

June started to cry, too. "This is hard for me, too, Mo. When Terry died, I thought—I thought it was my turn. To try to be like her. But I'm not. And now I have to face the fact that I'm not the kind of person I hoped I could be. And that is a horrific feeling." A sob escaped her. "Ex-cuse me."

Tate reached out to her. "June—"

But June was already hurrying out of the room, her face in her hands.

"You deserve so much," Tate said. He had the saddest look on his face. "I'm sorry we can't be the ones to give it to you. Let's pause for now so I can go check on June. Then we'll talk some more, okay?"

I was going to tell him that I didn't want "so much." I just wanted to stay with them.

But before I could say anything, he was already gone.

And . . . I didn't know what to do. I didn't want to sit there and wait. I didn't feel like talking more. I thought about going back to my bedroom, closing the door, and hiding under the covers like the conversation had only been a bad dream. But then it hit me, it's not *my* bedroom anymore. It's just a room I'm staying in. Temporarily.

So I decided to leave, too.

Oh—we're at my stop. I'll write again soon.

Mo

SATURDAY, DECEMBER 2

Dear Nan,

Sorry for another cliff-hanger. I know you hate those.

If you were wondering, I didn't go to Crystal's. When I left June and Tate's, that's where I *thought* I was going. But that's not where I went.

I went to Joe and Carlota's. And that's where I am, right now, in the bathroom. They're waiting for me outside to take me back to Tate and June's.

My walk from the subway station to their apartment last night was freezing cold. And when I reached their door, it started to snow. Little puffy flecks falling out of the sky. The first snow of the year. I thought about all the first snows we had together. Like two years ago, when it happened in the middle of the night, and you made me get my coat on over my pajamas so we could climb out onto our fire escape and catch the flakes on our tongues.

It made me miss you. It made me so, so sad.

They were watching a movie when I showed up. Something about a famous sushi chef who lives in Japan. Nacho and Toast barked at me, but at least this time I knew to expect it.

Joe was confused when he saw me at the door. "Mo? What are you doing here?"

Carlota stood next to him, craning her neck to see into the street behind me, like maybe June or Tate might appear out of the snowy darkness.

"Are you here alone?" she asked. "This late?"

I nodded, and then I burst into tears.

"I'm sorry," I said as I tried to get ahold of myself. "I know I should have called, or texted, or not come at all. . . ."

But then Carlota reached out and put a comforting arm around my shoulder. "Shhh. Whatever it is, it's all right. It's fine you're here, Mo. Don't worry. Come inside."

She led me inside their basement apartment, Joe following behind at a worried distance. The warmth of their small space immediately soaked into my fingertips.

She cleared a blanket away from the couch. "Sit here."

I sat.

Then Carlota went to the stove. The apartment filled with the smell of ginger and the sound of a metal spoon clanking against the sides of a pot. Joe stood between us, cracking his knuckles, glancing toward me and then Carlota every now and then. He didn't say anything, and I'm grateful he let me finish crying.

"Drink this," Carlota said a few minutes later, handing me a mug of sweet and spicy ginger-honey tea.

I took a sip. I felt its warmth sliding down my throat, warming me up from the inside out.

Joe sat down on the edge of their coffee table and put his elbows on his thighs. "Okay, Mo. What happened?"

And so I told them.

I cried so much I spilled some of my tea on the couch. It left a big wet spot. But Carlota told me not to worry. She sat next to me and let me lean my head against her shoulder for a long time.

I must have fallen asleep like that—with my head against Carlota's shoulder—because next thing I knew, it was morning.

I opened my eyes a tiny bit. There was a fuzzy blanket on me, and a pillow under my head. The snow had stopped, and thin gray light was coming in through their barred half-windows. I could see frost gathering in the corners.

Joe and Carlota were also awake. They were hunched at the small dining table, their hands around mugs of coffee. The aroma filled the room, along with the smell of the vanilla-scented candle Carlota likes to burn. And they were whispering.

About me, I realized.

I went completely still. I didn't want them to know I was awake.

"We don't have the space," Joe was saying.

"And we work long hours," Carlota added. "When would we have time to do all that training?"

"She deserves a good home. A family with means," Joe said.

"She does. The best." Carlota sighed unhappily. "I wish I was ready again, after . . ." She steadied herself. "After Isabella. But I don't know if I'll ever be ready."

"I know. Me too." I saw Joe start to glance over at me, so I squeezed my eyes shut again. "Maybe in another life."

"Yes. Another life."

Now it was Joe's turn to sigh. "We should get her back to the Townsends'."

From Carlota, there was a long silence. Finally, she said, "I know."

I'm embarrassed to admit it, Nan, but I thought maybe, just maybe . . .

You know what, never mind. I don't know what I thought.

What I do know is that the world isn't the place you always made me think it was. Filled with sequins and sparkles and love, with an adventure waiting around every corner. It's something else entirely. Something grayer. I think Mom knew that. And I'm starting to know it, too.

Mo

SATURDAY, DECEMBER 2
(LATER)

Dear Nan,

There's been another twist to the story. My story.

Joe and Carlota told me they were going to ride the subway back uptown to the Townsends' apartment, even though I said they didn't need to.

"I made it down here by myself," I told them. "I can make it back okay, too."

I already felt weird and embarrassed I'd come to their apartment in the first place. I didn't want to ask any more of them than I already had.

"What, are you kidding me?" Joe said. "A chance to go out for breakfast on a beautiful December morning after the first snow? Get outta here. Of course we're coming."

"Breakfast?" I asked.

"There's a cute café by the subway station I think you'd love," Carlota said as she wrapped a chunky purple scarf around her neck. She'd called in sick to the bakery so she didn't have to go in for her shift this morning. "Very cozy. It's been run by the same family for thirty years."

And despite everything, I knew I could still eat. In fact, I was starving.

Carlota was right—I did love the little café. It's called Smachno, which means "delicious" in Ukrainian. The laminated menu had a bunch of pictures of the Kovalenko family in the restaurant's kitchen over the past few decades. Family food served at a family restaurant. Exactly my kind of place.

I got breakfast pierogies, which are like little dumplings. They were filled with scrambled eggs, potatoes, and cheese and were so, so good. We also got buckwheat pancakes to share. Carlota slathered them with butter, and dumped nearly the entire pitcher of syrup on them—exactly like you would have done.

When she saw me looking, she winked and said, "Oops. My wrist must have slipped."

While we ate, I could tell they weren't sure how to talk to me or what to talk to me about. Mostly, we said stuff like "Wow, this is good" and "I've never had pierogies before." Carlota kept glancing over at me while she ate. She had this look on her face like she felt sorry for me, and I couldn't stand it. So I made up a lie.

"Everything's going to be fine," I said. "I just need to talk to my uncle. He's probably going to move back and take care of me. We just need to get a few things settled."

"Your uncle?" Joe said. "You have an uncle?"

I guess somehow I'd never told them about Uncle Bill.

Maybe because *I* haven't talked to Billy since August, not since he said all that stuff about you and Mom. He's emailed me a few times, nice emails like things between us are normal, but I haven't responded. I haven't been sure how to.

I'm telling you about all of this because I'm stalling to write about what I'm actually writing to you about—if that makes sense. I'm trying to work through how I feel about it, because I honestly don't know.

When I got back, Tate was waiting for me in the lobby. As soon as he saw us, he hurried toward us. He nodded at Carlota and reached out to shake Joe's hand.

"Thank you so much for getting Mo back safely. Can I pay for your subway fare? Or better yet, can I get you a car to take you home?"

Joe didn't take Tate's outstretched hand. He usually has the happiest face, always smiling, always joking. But the way he looked at Tate—it was like he suddenly became a stranger. An angry stranger with a pinched-shut mouth and cold, not-at-all-like-Joe eyes.

"No," he said. "We don't want your money."

Then he turned to me and put both hands on my shoulders. Thankfully, he looked like himself again. "You good?"

I wasn't good. I wanted them to stay. Or to ask me to come back and spend another night at their apartment. But I knew I couldn't.

So I said, "Yeah. I'm fine. Thanks for breakfast."

He knocked me gently on the chin. "Anytime, kid."

Then Carlota hugged me and gave me a kiss on the cheek. And then they were gone.

Tate blew out a long breath as we got into the elevator together. "We were worried about you, Mo. Really worried. When we came back into the den to talk to you more, after June had collected herself—you were just . . . gone. We combed the building and went outside to look for you. We were about to call the police when Joe called us."

I can't lie—it felt good to hear I'd made them worried. Because at least that means they still care, right? I held my breath, waiting for him to say more. Say something like: "And it made us think how wrong we were. How we want you to stay and get you a dog and all go to Paris together."

But he didn't say that. When I looked up at him, it almost seemed like he was waiting for *me* to apologize.

So I shrugged and didn't say anything. We were standing close in the elevator, but the distance between us suddenly felt huge.

June was there waiting for us in the foyer when the elevator doors opened.

"Oh, Mo," she said. "I'm so glad you're okay."

Her face was the perfect picture of concern, like an actress in a movie. I shrugged again.

"Let's talk in the kitchen," she suggested. "I made a pot of hot cocoa."

The three of us sat at the table, and June was definitely feeling guilty because she gave me three big marshmallows in mine. The Jet-Puffed kind. They must have gone out and bought them earlier in the morning, because June doesn't have stuff like this around unless I need it for a recipe I'm making.

"So, Mo, listen," Tate finally said once we were all sitting down. He cupped his mug between his hands without taking a sip. "You disappeared last night before we were done talking. I know emotions ran high," he said, his eyes going to June, "but our situation doesn't change the fact that we still want what's best for you."

I focused on stirring my cocoa. The marshmallows were dissolving into bubbly blobs. Wouldn't wanting the best for me be . . . you know, keeping me?

"What does that even mean?" I asked.

"Well, because of your food project, we know how badly you've been trying to find family. Right?"

"I've been looking for a family *recipe*," I corrected.

"Sure, but family, too, right?"

"Yeah," I admitted. "I guess so."

June leaned toward me. "This whole time, the agency has been trying to track down your dad, or any other family you might have, but they haven't been successful. So about a month ago, we hired someone to help look. Someone professional. We didn't want to tell you, because we didn't want to get your hopes up, in case he didn't find anyone." She reached out and took my hand. "But he did, Mo. He did some digging and found an older cousin of your grandmother's. Gerry Gallagher. He passed away a few years ago, but he has a daughter. Her name is Margery Callahan, formerly Gallagher, and she's very much alive. She lives in Wichita, Kansas. *And* she wants to meet you. We have a Zoom call set up for the two of you to talk tomorrow morning."

I let her words sink in. Or at least, I tried to.

Margery Callahan. Your cousin Gerry. I don't remember you ever talking about a cousin named Gerry. Maybe you hated each other. Maybe you never even met.

I felt like I was floating above myself. Like I was outside of my body. I thought this would be the kind of news that would make me want to spin on lampposts and dance in the streets, like in the movies. But I barely felt anything.

"Mo?" June said. "Say something."

"Why?" I asked. "Why did you do all of this?"

"Because maybe the two of you—maybe it will be a good fit," June said. "A better fit than us. She's family. Real family."

"Yeah, well, I already have *real* family," I said, thinking of Uncle Bill, "and he doesn't want anything to do with me."

"Maybe this will be different," Tate said lightly.

And . . . I guess I should have been excited. Should *be* excited. Right? Because they're right: this *is* what I've been searching for. Not just a family recipe, but family.

But if I'm being honest, I don't feel the tiniest spark of excitement about meeting Margery over Zoom tomorrow.

Because all I can focus on is that June said they hired someone a *month* ago to find family for me.

Which means they knew they wanted to get rid of me for a whole month.

And I, like a complete idiot, had absolutely no idea.

Anyway. I'll let you know how it all goes.

Love,
Mo

SUNDAY, DECEMBER 3

Dear Nan,

So, it happened. I met Margery (Gallagher) Callahan over Zoom this morning. This might not be very nice to say, but she reminded me of a breadstick.

Maybe I'm not giving her a chance. But all I could think—all I *can* think—is breadstick. Plain, stiff, and flavorless.

When she appeared, she was staring at something on her screen with a frown. And she was wearing a gray shirt. I don't think "gray" was in your vocabulary, let alone your closet, so already I felt like we were off to a weird start. A start like strangers, not like family.

"Hello?" I said, because I don't think she had noticed me yet.

"Oh. Hello, Maureen," she said, refocusing her attention on the screen. "I'm Margery Callahan."

"I actually go by Mo," I told her.

"Mo, then. Hello."

We sat for a moment in silence. Eventually our conversation began to limp forward.

Here's what I learned about her:

1. She's divorced with no kids. She doesn't have any pets, because she's allergic to dander. (She also said she's allergic to soy, dust, and cashews.)
2. She's been the office assistant for the same law firm for fifteen years.
3. She sings alto in her church choir.
4. She lives in a two-bedroom brick house on the outskirts of Wichita.

I asked about you, of course. If she remembered ever meeting you.

"Yes, but not until after I spoke with Tate. I had to go through old photos before I remembered, because it was back when I was a girl. It was a family Christmas. One of the few she ever came to, with her two children in tow."

"My mom and uncle," I offered, leaning forward. I wanted to hear every tiny detail. I wanted to collect any sliver of memory she had of you and memorize it. Of Mom and Billy, too. "What else?"

"The two of them were devilish. Both quite a bit younger than me, but they tortured me. Your uncle wouldn't stop pinching my arms."

"That sounds like Uncle Bill," I said, nodding.

She frowned. "Does it? I suppose he hasn't grown up much if he wouldn't accept the responsibility of caring for you when your grandmother passed."

That shut me right up. I haven't talked to Billy in

months for this exact reason. But when *she* said it, I wanted to reach out and pinch her, too.

She asked me about my favorite subject in school, about my hobbies, stuff like that. Eventually I worked up the courage to ask her for a recipe.

"Food isn't a passion of mine. I'm more of an 'eat to live' kind of person. But I'm sure I have something I can find for you. My father liked to cook. He was passionate about health-supportive cooking."

So there's that.

The conversation petered out. I thought we were going to say goodbye and have that be that, but Margery cleared her throat and said, "As for my visit, I should be all set to come next weekend. I've been corresponding with June's assistant to get my flights set up. This will be my first time to New York."

"Visit? You're coming here?"

She seemed surprised I was surprised.

"Yes," she said. "So we can meet in person."

So I guess that's happening, next weekend. I feel like we exhausted all points of conversation already, so who knows what we'll even talk about.

Anyway. Love you.

Mo

From: margery@goldbergandhannity.com
To: momolovesfamilyfood@gmail.com
Subject: Recipe + arrival details

Hello,

As you requested, I did some digging for a family recipe. These oatcakes were a favorite of my father's (your grandmother's first cousin). They are good for you, and taste nice with a small amount of butter or margarine and apricot jam. If I remember correctly, Dad said his mother used to make them all the time, so there's a chance your grandmother might have tried these at some point as well.

I look forward to meeting you in person this coming weekend. My flight arrives at JFK at 7:31 p.m. on Friday evening, but I'll want to get settled. So I will plan to meet you at your building on Saturday morning.

Regards,
Margery

OATCAKES

(Adapted by Dad from a low-cholesterol cookbook)

Serves 8

1½ cups old-fashioned oats

1 cup whole wheat flour

1 cup unsweetened applesauce

½ teaspoon baking soda

¼ teaspoon salt

¼ cup canola oil

¼ cup buttermilk

Preheat oven to 350°F. Line 2 baking sheets with parchment. Place oats in large bowl. Sift flour, baking soda, and salt into same bowl. Using fingertips, add in oil until mixture resembles coarse meal. Add buttermilk and applesauce; stir until a rough dough forms.

Transfer dough to floured surface, and roll out dough to ¼-inch thickness. Cut out rounds. Arrange on prepared sheets, spacing apart. Gather scraps, reroll, and cut out additional rounds.

Bake oatcakes until edges are pale golden, about 12 minutes. Transfer baking sheets to racks and cool 5 minutes. Transfer cakes to racks; cool completely. (Can be prepared 3 days ahead. Store in airtight container at room temperature.)

THURSDAY, DECEMBER 7

Dear Nan,

So, I finally got my hands on a Gallagher recipe. Not just any recipe—like Margery said in her email, it's one you might have eaten at some point in your life, too.

I made them exactly according to the directions. I've never been more careful with my measurements. I read all the instructions twice.

June came into the kitchen while I was waiting for them to finish baking.

"Oh!" she said. "Sorry. I didn't know you were in here."

"It's okay," I said quickly.

If you can't tell, it's been awkward. We're all moving around the apartment like strangers. Strangers who hold their breath and tiptoe and check rooms before we go inside them. Part of me wants to give them dirty glares and the silent treatment. That's what Crystal would want me to do. (Speaking of, I have to figure out a way to tell her about this. I know I do. This time, I have to. I almost lost her this summer, and I can't risk losing her again.) But the other part of me hopes that if I'm polite and kind, they might change their minds. I still feel painfully hopeful every time one of them calls my name, like they're calling me to tell me that.

I know this is stupid, and they probably won't, but I can't help it. I thought I'd want to talk about everything when I had an appointment with Dr. Barb, but I found myself at a loss for words. Dr. Barb said I didn't have to talk about anything if I wasn't ready to, so I spent the hour making patterns in her sand tray.

Anyway, after June left me alone again and the oatcakes were ready, I poured myself a glass of milk and even put some strawberry jam in a bowl. I really set the scene. I put a thin layer of salted butter on the warm oatcake, and a scoop of jam. And then I closed my eyes and took a bite.

Nan, it was *terrible*. It was like choking on sawdust. I forced myself to eat two of them, in case they grew on me. Spoiler alert: they didn't. A gallon of jam and cream and butter couldn't rescue these hockey pucks.

I tried to imagine you eating them, like Margery said you might have at some point. But all I could imagine was you trying a bite and then tossing them in the garbage. Or slathering them in honey and cayenne pepper, trying to make them taste more interesting.

Honestly, if it wasn't too late to get our deposit back, I'd cancel the pop-up restaurant. There's no point anymore, is there? I've found what I've been looking for. A real, live, homegrown Gallagher family recipe.

And it sucks.

Mo

SUNDAY, DECEMBER 10

Dear Nan,

I spent all yesterday with ~~plain oatcake breadstick~~ Margery. And—well, I didn't like her any more than I did after the Zoom. I wanted to like her. I still do. In fact, I *need* to like her because . . . well, I'll get to why. Thankfully, Joe doesn't work weekends, so I didn't have to explain who she was, or why she was there.

It was bitingly cold out, but we spent most of the day doing touristy stuff outside because Margery has never been to New York City. We went to Times Square, the Empire State Building, and walked a part of the High Line.

She kept making little comments about how crowded, how gray, how loud it was. I told her none of these places fully captured the real New York, but it was clear she didn't want to change the itinerary she had planned, so eventually I shut up and went along with it.

I was more than ready to go inside when Margery finally suggested we stop to get some early dinner. (It was only four. Who eats dinner at four?!) We went to a diner about five blocks away from Tate and June's.

When it was time to order, I got chocolate chip waffles with whipped cream. She ordered—let's see if I can remember it exactly—scrambled egg whites. No salt. And whole wheat toast, served "dry." That means with no butter. She might as well have said, "I'll have a bowl of lukewarm water, please."

But there I go being not so nice again.

We didn't talk much while we ate. Well, not until she set down her fork and said, "The Townsends have explained your situation. It's true, then? That beyond your uncle or continued foster care, you have no other options for guardianship?"

I shook my head and let myself sink lower in the booth. I could have told her about my project. About how I'd spent the past few months trying to find family through food. Trying to find *her*. But suddenly it all felt so weird and jumbled in my brain. This is exactly what I wanted, right? What I *want*? If it is, then why doesn't it feel good at all?

I still had half a plate of syrupy waffles sitting in front of me, but I didn't want them anymore.

"So, I suppose that brings us right to the point," she said. "Today went well enough, I thought. I'd like us to have a few more conversations. To get to know each other more, to make sure we'll be compatible."

"Compatible?" I asked. "For what?"

"For you to come and live with me, of course."

I stared at her. "What? Live with *you*? In Kansas? You're a stranger."

She took a small bite of toast like what she'd asked me was no big deal. Like she'd invited me to the movies instead of to move in with her. "Yes. We are strangers, which is exactly why I *just* said we should take some more time to get to know each other. I see this as my responsibility, as you have no other family willing to step up to the plate. I'm a big believer that charity should extend past your wallet."

Now I'm waiting for Moira to come over. It isn't one of her scheduled visits, so I'm guessing it's so we can talk all of this through.

My mind keeps going back to the word Margery used. "Charity." I know charity is a good thing. I do. But every time I think it, I want to break something.

Because is it so wrong that I don't want to be someone's charity case? I want to be . . . I don't know. I want someone to want me so badly they'd scoop me up in their arms even when those arms are weak and I'm too big to be picked up like that. I want someone to give me kisses that leave behind streaks of pink lipstick, someone who laughs at my bad jokes and takes me to Coney Island on a whim for ice cream sundaes on a school day in the middle of September, just because.

I want someone like you. I want someone like you to want someone like me. Not for charity. Not because taking care of me "is the right thing to do." But because they love me.

Oh—Moira's here. Gotta go.

Love,
Mo

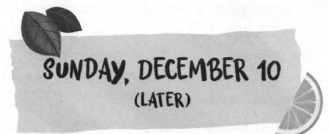

SUNDAY, DECEMBER 10
(LATER)

Dear Nan,

I talked everything over with Moira.

For our check-ins, we usually meet inside Tate and June's apartment, in the den. But this time, I told her I needed to get out of there. She seemed to understand.

"Let's go for a walk," she suggested.

As soon as we were outside, I noticed her feet. She wasn't wearing her old Converse. She had on a new pair of bright-red sneakers.

"Your shoes," I said. "What happened to your other shoes?"

"Oh, those? They finally wore through to the soles," she said. She wiggled one of her feet. "These ones are fun, though, right?"

"No," I said. "They're not."

Moira didn't seem upset, but I still feel bad I said that. It's just—I felt like I could depend on Moira always showing up in her old dirty sneakers. Now even that's changing.

It started sleeting ice-cold rain within a few minutes of us getting outside, so we decided to change our plan.

"Let's pop in here," Moira said. "We can get something hot to drink."

Funnily enough, it was the same diner I went to with Margery yesterday. We sat at a window table this time, because all the booths were taken.

"So," Moira said once she'd ordered us two chamomile teas, one with extra honey (for me). "Let's talk this through."

I pressed my hand against the diner's window front. The glass was freezing cold against my palm. "Do you think if I push hard enough I could break the glass?"

"Mo," Moira said. "I know you're upset. I know none of this is ideal. And I'm sorry things didn't work out with the Townsends. I really am."

"I don't like her that much. Margery, I mean. She's so . . . stiff."

"She's family, though, Mo. And she's willing to take you."

I pulled my hand away from the glass. "So you think I should go?"

Moira sighed. "Well. Honestly, it's a bit of a nightmare for us to transfer your case across state borders. We'd have to do a lot of paperwork to make it happen, and both you and Margery would need to attend meetings and evaluations. I can try to get someone to do some favors for me, to make the whole thing go a little smoother, but the bottom line is that she's willing to accept guardianship. This would be permanent for you. You wouldn't have to move again. Things would stabilize in your life."

"But my life is *here*," I told her. "And she's a stranger."

"We could try to find you another pre-adoptive place-ment, but I can't guarantee you'll click with them," Moira said. "Things can still go wrong. Obviously. Whereas Mar-gery's blood. That's worth something."

"But it's not everything."

"No." Moira sighed. "It's not. But it's what you got, Mo. And that's more than a lot of the kids I work with. A bird in the hand's worth two in the bush."

"What do you mean?"

"It means, she's real. And she's willing to have you come live with her. It's a *yes*, not a maybe."

It was true. I knew I should have felt something—feel something—but I didn't. I don't. I just feel . . . blank.

"Kansas," I said, leaning back into my chair.

I don't know anything about Kansas. Is corn a thing in Kansas? Or no—is that Iowa? I might be mixing up pota-toes and corn. I have no idea. Is there anywhere you can get a decent slice of pizza in Kansas?

I don't know. But I guess I'll find out.

Because I said okay, Nan. I'm moving to Kansas. I, Mo Gallagher, am moving to Kansas. To live with my second cousin once removed, Margery Gallagher Callahan. Maybe if I write it and say it enough, it will start to feel real.

Love,
Mo

301

Dear Nan,

Margery and I talked a few more times this week, over Zoom again. I still feel zero connection to her, even though I'm trying. I keep thinking about what Moira said. About a bird in the hand. Because I don't really have any options, do I?

I sent Uncle Bill a long email asking him to come back home. I wrote out a long list of reasons why it was a good idea. I tried to use logic. I tried tempting him with the idea of eating good bagels and pizza instead of gross army food, that he could grow his hair out and have every last cent of the college fund Rose left for me, if he wanted it.

I knew it was a Hail Mary. But he didn't even respond.

I also decided to finally ask Crystal if she thought her parents might be open to having me come and live with them. *Another* Hail Mary. I knew all week that I was going over to Crystal's house on Saturday, which was yesterday, so my plan was to tell Crystal there, thinking we could maybe talk to her parents together.

On my way over, I felt breathless and anxious about

asking such a big thing, but I also figured, what did I have to lose? If I asked and the Wangs said no, it couldn't be awkward, because I wouldn't be going over to their place anymore. I'd be in Kansas.

Her dad's band was over for a potluck holiday party, and everyone was wearing colorful paper crowns. Throughout the party, I opened my mouth to tell Crystal about the whole mess at least six different times, but I kept chickening out. I didn't want to ruin the fun. Before we ate, Boris—their lead singer, in case you don't remember—had too much mulled wine, and kept belting out Christmas carols in different areas of the house until Crystal's grandma marched him into the kitchen and made him a strong cup of black coffee.

Crystal and I sat on the couch, watching and cracking up.

Then it was time to eat. They had a huge buffet on a folding plastic table I thought might buckle under the weight of all the food.

As we made our plates, Crystal nudged me. "Apparently, Tom has a story about his weird casserole." She pointed to a dish in the back that was lumpy, yellow, and glistening. "Dad says it tastes better than it looks. One of us has to try it. For science."

"You should," I told her quickly. "Definitely you."

"No way. You're the famous food writer opening her own restaurant. You should. You can ask him about the story, too."

Truth was, I didn't want to hear a great story or get an ink-stained card with a handwritten family recipe. Not when I'd already found mine. For bland oatcakes. From an even blander woman. "I'm taking the night off from all that."

"You're just trying to get out of tasting the casserole." She scooped some onto my plate with a wet *smack*.

When we sat back down on the couch to eat, Crystal grabbed my hand and shook it up and down, even though I had a forkful of pasta salad halfway to my mouth.

"Oh, oh!" she cried. "I forgot to tell you! I'm going on a road trip to Florida over spring break with the band. Mom's staying home with Charlie. Isn't that awesome? Dad said we could go to Disney World after their Orlando gig if there's time."

"That sounds so fun."

"You know, Mo could come if she wanted," called out Crystal's dad. He'd just come into the room, balancing a paper plate full of food in one hand and a beer in the other. "I mean, if she's allowed to."

Crystal gasped and swiveled toward her dad. "Are you serious? Are you actually being serious right now?"

He shrugged. "Yeah. The more the merrier, right?" He tipped his beer at me with a smile and then went to check on Boris.

"That would be the most amazing thing to ever happen in my life." Crystal turned to me. "What do you think?"

It was time. I had to tell her now, to ask her. I put my

304

paper plate on the coffee table. My whole body felt like it was buzzing. "Do you think we could go somewhere to talk for a second? Somewhere private?"

Crystal must have been able to sense something was up, because she stood and grabbed my hand. "Yeah. Come on."

Of course, she took me into the coat closet.

"What is it?" she asked.

And so I told her. About June and Tate. About Margery. About Kansas.

"Oh, Mo," she said. And then she wrapped her arms around me and hugged me. "I hate this stupid world sometimes."

When we drew apart, I finally worked up the courage to ask. "Do you think—do you think your parents would ever be open to me staying here? With you? You can say no," I added quickly. "Don't worry. I know it's a big thing to ask. A huge thing."

"Actually, Mo . . . I have something to tell you, too. We already asked."

"What?" I said, sitting back.

"It was my mom's idea. I mean, obviously, it would have been *my* idea if I'd known it was allowed. It was right after we made up, this summer. It was so good to see you, but you seemed . . . I don't know. Not yourself. Like you didn't feel totally at home. When I told my mom about it, she wanted to see if there was any way you could live with us. So she called and asked." Crystal sighed. "But there's a space issue. There are all these rules about it, and beds,

305

and stuff, and we're full up here." She motioned around the dim closet. "I mean, obviously. The only private space we have to talk is in a closet."

I touched my chest lightly with my fingertips. "But you asked. I can't believe you asked."

"Of course we did, you dummy." Crystal reached out and gave me an even fiercer hug than before. "You're my best friend."

"I don't want to go to Kansas," I said into her shoulder.

"Me neither," she said back. "This sucks worse than Tom's casserole."

We both laughed. After a couple more minutes, we went back to the party.

Even with that hope dashed, I feel a lot better. Because the Wangs wanted me. They'd asked to see if it was possible. Even though it wasn't, and I can't live with them, they tried. And that's something. That's more than something.

I love you,
Mo

Dear Nan,

I've been dreading Christmas.

I never in a million years thought I would ever say this about my favorite holiday ever. About *our* favorite holiday ever. The holiday we love so much that we left a Christmas tree up in the corner of our living room year-round.

But here I am, saying it.

Christmas is supposed to be relaxing. It's about sleeping in and ordering those cinnamon rolls from Zingerman's and eating them for breakfast, lunch, and dinner. Watching old movies in our new Christmas pajamas all day long.

Even though June had the apartment professionally decorated, with real pine garlands and everything, and Christmas Eve is now less than a week away, all three of us have avoided talking about Christmas itself. It's been awkward since they sat me down and told me they'd be going to Paris without me, but with Christmas looming, it's been at least ten times worse. June said she and Tate would be "laying low" for Christmas, and of course I was welcome to spend it with them.

Since she said that, June's basically been locked in her office, even for mealtimes. Busy finalizing the sale, she told me apologetically. Tate's been trying to get me excited about my move to Kansas. He's already given me a guide-book for Wichita, and he printed out articles about restaurants he thinks I'd like in Margery's area. In the guidebook, he highlighted a place called the Old Cowtown Museum and wrote, "You'd never be able to see this in NYC!"

And then this morning before school, he said, "Hey, Mo, I have an early Christmas present for you." He handed me a gift bag. Inside was a brand-new Kansas City Chiefs hat.

I could tell how badly he wanted me to like it. His eyes were all big and hopeful. It made me think about how after Billy told me he didn't want me, he gave me his lucky wallet. And now Tate was giving me this stupid hat.

"Thanks," I told him, my voice sticking in my throat. "It's a nice hat. But I'm a Jets fan. For life."

I didn't have the heart to remind him that the Chiefs are based out of Missouri, not Kansas.

"Yeah," he said a little sadly. "That's what I figured."

He hesitated, like he wanted to say more, but then he smiled with his mouth closed and nodded his head and I could tell that was that.

I've been dreading the pop-up restaurant, too. June and Tate promised it would still happen, no matter what. It's funny to think how excited I was about it only a month ago. Everyone else seems to get more excited with every passing day—our planning text chain has grown to include

Joe and Carlota, as well as Marcus and his boyfriend, Jay, who's going to be helping us in the kitchen, too. It's been a whirlwind of activity about who's in charge of printing out the photos; Crystal getting excited because her grandma found blue-checkered tablecloths half off at a fabric store; and Carlota showing us sketches for the menu her graphic-designer friend put together for us for free.

I've been doing the bare minimum. I just want to survive it. Crystal keeps sending me encouraging texts about how great it will be, that I shouldn't worry, and that everyone's going to love it. That even if they don't, *she's* going to love it, and she's the only person whose opinion counts anyway, right? And then a bunch of hair-flip emojis.

And maybe she's right. Maybe people will love it. But honestly, who cares at this point?

Could you send me another day-long sickness next week like you did for Thanksgiving? Or, better yet—can you send me one single day of mono so I can sleep through the entire holiday?

I'll stop asking you for stuff after this, but I could really use your help.

Thanks,
Mo

Dear Nan,

You really are a miracle worker in the afterlife, aren't you?

Right after I finished writing you my last letter, I decided it was finally time to tell Joe that I was moving to Kansas.

"Hey, Joe," I said as soon as the elevator doors dinged open.

"Mo!" he said with a big smile. "What's happenin'?"

We knocked fists and pretended to explode them.

I planned to *say it,* to blurt "I'm moving to Kansas," but he beat me to it.

"Listen, Mo," he said, clearing his throat. "There's something I wanted to talk to you about."

"Oh, really? Me too. But you go first," I added quickly.

"So, I know this is kind of last-minute, but me and Carlota are going to Don's place in Jersey City for Christmas. I don't know how things are going up there"—he motioned at the elevator—"but I figured you might want to be somewhere else for Christmas. We'd be honored if you wanted to join us. My brothers, too. They think you're basically a celebrity after you hustled them at poker."

"You want me to come? For Christmas?"

Joe rubbed the back of his neck. "Yeah. We'd love to have you. Only if you don't already have plans with your uncle, I mean."

I was confused for a minute, but then I remembered how I'd told them Billy was moving back to live with me.

"No! No, I don't have plans yet. I'd actually—I'd love that. If you really don't mind."

"I'm so glad. Carlota's been texting me all morning to see if I'd asked you yet. She'll be thrilled."

"Okay. Cool." I pressed my hands against my cheeks to try to stop myself from grinning ear to ear, then I motioned back at the elevators. "I should probably go ask the Townsends if it's okay."

When I turned back toward the elevators, Joe said, "Hold on—didn't you say there was something you wanted to talk to me about, too?"

I didn't want to ruin the moment. I wanted to enjoy the day knowing I didn't have to spend Christmas with June and Tate and an anxious stomachache. So I decided I'll tell them once Christmas is over. Maybe after the restaurant is done, too. It'll be like ripping off a Band-Aid.

"Never mind," I said. "It's nothing."

And then before the elevator doors shut, I stuck my hand out to stop them. "Hey, Joe?"

"Yeah?"

"How do you feel about cinnamon rolls?"

"Cinnamon rolls?" He grinned. "I love cinnamon rolls."

So maybe Christmas won't be a total wash. I'm not even dreading it anymore. I'm dreading what's going to happen *after*, but like you always said, we can cross that troll-infested bridge when we come to it.

Love,
Mo

~~MONDAY, DECEMBER 25~~
TUESDAY, DECEMBER 26

Dear Nan,

Merry Christmas!

Well, no—the clock just ticked over past midnight, so technically it's not Christmas anymore. But it *was* Christmas all day. I've been up since sunrise and I'm exhausted, but I had to write to you before going to sleep.

Today was equally terrible and wonderful. I never thought you could have a really sad day but be happy at the same time, but I guess I'm learning all sorts of things this year.

It was terrible because it was my very first Christmas without you. There. I said it. I know you don't want me to wallow. You told me that so many times. But it's the truth, and like they say in that movie: at Christmas you tell the truth.

But it was wonderful, too, and that's thanks to Joe, Carlota, and Joe's big, loud family.

The day started at six a.m. Every year on Christmas morning, Carlota and Joe volunteer at their local soup kitchen, which is in the basement of a church around the corner from their apartment.

"I know it's early, so you don't have to come if you don't want to. But I wanted to invite you all the same because it's one of our traditions," Carlota explained to me over the phone.

"No," I said quickly. "I'd love to come. I don't mind waking up early."

Even though it was more than an hour out of his way, Joe took the subway to come get me, and ride back down. I told him he didn't need to, but he waved me off. "Eh, I'm used to it. Plus, no one should have to ride the subway alone on Christmas morning."

I felt guilty, because the real reason I wanted to go was to get out of the Townsends' apartment as early as humanly possible, not because I had a burning desire to volunteer. But I'm so glad I went.

For the early breakfast shift (which is what we were a part of), everyone got assigned a different job. We were all working in a big industrial kitchen, even bigger than the one we used at Marcus's culinary school for our practice round.

Joe was assigned table-setting and water-pitcher refilling, and me and Carlota got assigned French toast service. From seven-thirty to nine-thirty, it was a whirlwind. We doled out more servings of French toast than I thought was possible. I got to wear a Santa hat over my hairnet and I said Merry Christmas at least seven hundred times.

It felt good to think about what other people needed for a while.

When it was over, I didn't feel tired. I felt exhilarated.

Carlota grabbed my hand as we went out onto the street. I was still hot from the busy kitchen, so the icy-cold air felt crisp and refreshing. "Now it's time for fancy coffees."

"Coffee?" I asked, perking up. "For me, too?"

"Of course," Carlota said. "It's tradition!"

So we got mochas with extra whipped cream from a café a few blocks away.

After, we took the PATH to Jersey City to Don's apartment. All the brothers were there except Tony, who was in Florida with his girlfriend. Joe said his family usually celebrates Christmas with a "seven fishes" dinner on Christmas Eve, which I guess is an Italian thing. But since they were only gathering on Christmas Day this year, they decided to make it a "seven fishes" lunch. So there were seven kinds of fish and, of course, a huge bubbling tray of lasagna. When I admitted to Joe I didn't like fish, he winked and scooped me an extra serving of lasagna.

And after *that*, we went back to Joe and Carlota's apartment. They had it all decked out for Christmas—there was a huge wreath made out of red paper coffee cups hanging on their front door; a tiny, pint-sized tree with all sorts of homemade ornaments; and lights strung from the kitchen to the living room. Nacho even had on a Christmas doggy sweater.

Joe slumped down on the sofa without taking his coat off. "Good lord. I'm exhausted."

"We're not done yet," Carlota said, pulling Joe's scarf off from around his neck. "It's time for gifts." Then she went to their mini tree and took out three for Joe, and three for me.

"You didn't need to get me anything." My face flushed as soon as my fingers closed around the presents.

"Of course we did! It's Christmas."

"I got you something, too." I put their gifts for me on my lap and reached into my bag. "It's nothing big. And it's only one thing. It's for both of you."

I handed her the gift, which was all wrapped up in brown paper. She sat down cross-legged on the floor and lifted it at me. "May I?"

I nodded.

She carefully slid her fingers under the tape, so she could unfold the paper without tearing it. I couldn't help but laugh a little.

She looked up and smiled. "Are you laughing at the way I'm opening this? Joe makes fun of me, too."

Joe groaned. "She likes to save the paper so she can reuse it for next year. But then she forgets, and our closets get fuller and fuller of old wrapping paper."

"I'll use it!" Carlota said. "Eventually."

"It's not that," I said. "It just made me think about how my grandma opened presents. She'd rip them into confetti, like she was a hungry squirrel and there were nuts inside."

Carlota smiled. "She sounds like she was quite the character."

"Yeah. She was." That's when I felt the first prickle in the back of my throat. I motioned for her to keep going.

"Oh!" Carlota said when she'd opened it all the way. "Joe, look."

It was one of the pictures I took when I came over to their house for the first time, with Joe's brothers and the lasagna and the candlelit laughter.

"Did you make the frame?" Joe asked, looking it over. "This is great, Mo. I love this."

I nodded. "Yeah. At school."

Joe stood and set the picture up on the shelf above their TV. "There. I only wish you were in it, too."

Then it was my turn to open gifts.

Everything they got for me was perfect. One of the presents was a scarf made out of rainbow wool, because, as Joe said, "You're the most colorful girl we know." (A huge compliment.) Another was a mushroom-in-a-can growing kit, and then, my last gift: a crisp white chef's jacket.

"It's for the pop-up," Carlota explained, beaming. "Try it on, try it on!"

I slipped it on over my sweater. It was a little big on me, so I had to roll up the sleeves once, but otherwise it was perfect. I didn't notice until I had it all buttoned up, but "Chef Mo" was stitched in red thread on the chest, right over my heart.

"Lookin' fresh, kid," Joe said. "You really look the part now."

"Thanks," I said. And then I burst into tears.

Because until now, we'd been so busy I'd barely had time to think about you, or about how my whole life was about to turn upside down—*again*. And in that moment, it wasn't just you I missed. I knew I was going to miss them, too.

"Mo?" Carlota said. "What's wrong?"

"You can take it off if you don't like it," Joe said. "We can throw it in the trash. Or burn it!"

I shook my head and tried to get ahold of myself. "No. I love it. I just miss my grandma."

Carlota nodded, her eyes shining. "We understand. Believe me, we understand. Loss feels sharper on Christmas, doesn't it?"

Of course they understood. Am I the most selfish human on the planet, Nan? I didn't even think about how they also must be feeling extra sad today because of their baby daughter.

Carlota got up and got me a tissue. "I cried in the shower this morning. So we're even."

I laughed a little as I wiped my face. "I also have something to tell you."

I know I said I was going to wait. But it felt like the right moment to come clean. So I explained. They already knew about Tate and June, but they didn't know the rest of it.

Mrs. Business must have a sixth sense, because even though she's a grouch, she slunk onto my lap and curled up as I was telling Joe and Carlota about how Tate and June had tracked down Margery Callahan with her bland-as-cardboard oatcake recipe. About how I was moving to Kansas.

As I talked, I sank my fingers into Mrs. Business's soft fur and felt a little bit better.

"Okay. Okay." At this point, Carlota had ripped a piece of the wrapping paper she'd carefully saved into ragged little bits. "I didn't . . . I thought you said your uncle was moving back to be with you. Here, in the city. After what you told us earlier this month. At Smachno."

I shook my head. "No. I said that because I didn't want you to worry about me. About what would happen to me." I sighed and slumped back against the couch, jostling Mrs. Business by accident. She yowled a complaint, but didn't move off my lap. "And I've been thinking . . . maybe I should call off the whole restaurant thing. I found what I was looking for, right? So there's no point anymore."

"No!" Joe and Carlota both said at the same time.

"No, Mo. You can't," Carlota said. "It's only days away, and we're all ready to go. It would be a mistake to cancel. You've worked so hard for this. We've all worked hard for this."

"And talk about an accomplishment," Joe added. "I mean, how many kids can say they opened a restaurant? Not many, I'd bet."

I know they're right. I know it's a big, exciting accomplishment. And I don't want to let anyone else down, because like Carlota said—I'm not the only one who's been working hard to make the restaurant happen. I just feel bad I'm not excited.

After that, the energy got weird. Not *bad* weird, necessarily. It's hard to explain. We ate cinnamon rolls and laughed and watched *Elf.* Carlota was extra quiet while we watched. She was barely paying attention to the movie, I could tell. She laughed at the funny parts a few seconds too late, like her mind was somewhere else.

I noticed because my mind was somewhere else, too. It had drifted all the way to Kansas.

It's time for me to stop writing and get some sleep. I've yawned, like, eighteen times in the last couple minutes of writing to you. And like you always say, everything feels ten times brighter in the morning. So I'll hope for that.

> Love you, Nan.
> Merry Christmas,
> Mo

THURSDAY, DECEMBER 28

Dear Nan,

I have something to admit that you probably already know: I am extremely nervous.

I feel it in my stomach, in the spot between my eyes, in the way my hands and feet are almost buzzing. Mostly, I feel it in my stomach.

We're opening a restaurant in three days.

Then, it'll all be over. Everything. My time in New York. My best friendship with Crystal. (Well, maybe not that. I won't let that happen.) Knowing Joe and Carlota. Travis.

I want to run away to Fiji and open up a snorkel shop called Dorkel Snorkel, like we always joked about doing together one day. A snorkel shop for dorks, and dorks only.

Clearly, the nerves are affecting my brain, because I'm starting to babble.

I did have one new idea for the pop-up that I think is good. I *hope* it's good. I need to run it by everyone first, though, so stay tuned.

Okay. I've got to go—Joe and I are running to the

printer shop to get the FINAL final menus printed on his lunch break. It's one of our last bits of preparation before the big day.

Which is only *three* days from now.

Fiji, here I come. (I wish.)

Love,
Mo

SUNDAY, DECEMBER 31

Dear Nan,

It's here.

It's eight a.m., but I've been awake since four because no matter how much I tried, I couldn't sleep last night.

It's the last day of what was definitely the worst year of my life. The last day of the year where I'm opening a restaurant to cook dinner for nearly one hundred people.

Last night, Tate knocked on my bedroom door. When I answered, he was holding out two of the tickets Crystal had designed and emailed to everyone who'd already signed up for their spots and paid.

He held them out toward me. "Do you want . . ."

Was he asking if I wanted their tickets back? If I wanted them to come? Of course I wanted them to come. I wanted them to see what I'd done, what I'd made, the fact that I am the kind of kid who can do big things, great things. I wanted them to see me, really see me, and regret everything. But the way he was holding them out, the look on his face . . .

"Oh, thanks," I said, taking the tickets. "We have a waiting list, anyway."

Tate said they'd call me an Uber to take me to Brooklyn. Joe insisted he and Carlota would bring me back at night, even though Tate and June's apartment is completely out of their way.

I'm not sure how much I care if anyone likes the food, or if I do a good job, or if people have fun.

At this point, I just want it to be over.

Mo

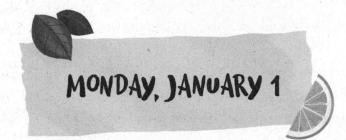

MONDAY, JANUARY 1

Dear Nan,

I know you're probably on the edge of your heavenly seat waiting to hear about how last night went, but here I am the next morning, exhausted, still smelling of cooking oil, my feet sore as heck, and all I can think about is your favorite poem. The one where the guy in the story (can you call a poem a story?) talks about squeezing the universe into a ball.

That's the only way I can think to describe how last night went. My whole universe, squeezed into a single night.

As you could probably tell from my last letter, I wasn't super excited going into it. On the way to Brooklyn, I was ready to hate it. There was bad traffic, so I was already running twenty minutes late, which didn't help my mood. I wanted to go in and throw rocks through the front windows so June and Tate couldn't get their deposit back (I know—I wish I was better than this, too). To call it off.

But as soon as I stepped into the space, everything changed. I was alone in the dining area, but I could hear voices and laughter through the doors to the kitchen. The smaller tables had been pushed together, so they were now three long tables taking up the entire space. Each table had a blue-checkered tablecloth, neatly ironed. A rainbow spray of tulips were already out on half the tables, in bright yellow jars.

I put my backpack on the floor and took out my white chef's jacket Joe and Carlota got me for Christmas. As soon as I slipped it on and buttoned it up, it was like everything just . . . melted away.

Because as much as I tried to pretend like I didn't care about the restaurant over the past month, I did. So, so much.

In that moment, it was exactly where I wanted to be. I wanted to cook. To make these special family recipes stretching back through generations, even though they're not *my* family recipes.

The doors to the kitchen swung open, and out came Joe, carrying a crate with more tulips. He grinned at me, and then called over his shoulder, "The chef is in the building!"

As soon as I stepped into the kitchen, I started to feel like myself again. My *real* self. My rainbow self. My glitter-and-adventures self.

"What's up, Mo?" Travis said, looking up from his cutting board.

"Uh," I said. My face erupted in heat. "Hi. Helloooo."

That's when I knew I was *definitely* myself again.

Then our work began. We had a prep list that was two pages single-spaced with everything we had to do to get ready. It had everything from making the dough for the pie crusts (this was on Carlota's to-do list) to chopping rainbow chard and making three quarts of filling for the dumplings. Each little thing we had to do was planned out and assigned to someone. Some things we did together—like fill and pinch the dumplings, and braiding together dough to make pretty edging for the pie crusts. We tasted everything as we went. Marcus showed me how they taste things in culinary school—you have a main spoon you dip into the big pot, and then use that spoon to drop food onto a tasting spoon. That way you never contaminate what you're cooking.

We must have all been working at the top of our games, because everything I tasted was perfect. The buttermilk pie base was creamy and sweet without even the tiniest hint of graininess, the chicken adobo sauce was syrupy and rich, and the pasta came out perfectly al dente.

I'm *so* glad we were so organized, because time has never slipped by faster than it did yesterday. I thought starting the day in the morning would give us more than enough time for our first seating at six, but it felt like we were all sprinting around the kitchen to get the last bits ready. I'm so happy Marcus's boyfriend, Jay, agreed to come to be an extra pair of hands. Because without him, we never would have gotten it all done.

And then, in the blink of an eye, it was somehow time for our first seating.

Oh, shoot—Crystal's calling. I'll finish writing after I talk to her.

Spoiler alert: it gets better.

Mo

Dear Nan,

Okay. Sorry! We talked longer than I thought we would, because Crystal's mom was out with Charlie, which meant Crystal didn't have to go into the closet to talk.

Where was I?

Oh, yeah—it was right before our first dinner service of the night.

I was supposed to be on welcoming duty at the front door, but I got too nervous, so Travis did it. He's way more charming than me anyway. I peeked from the kitchen, watching the room fill up.

Dr. Barb was there for the first seating, and so was Peyton Hall with her parents and older brother (they were in the section Travis was supposed to be serving, so I made sure to swap his tables with Crystal's). I saw a couple more familiar faces, including Fiona Crenshaw from the *New York Times*, but I was most excited by how many strangers were there. People who don't know me or like me or feel bad for me. People who decided to come because they *wanted to*. How cool is that?

Once everyone was seated, Carlota nodded me toward the main room. "Go say hello. Welcome your guests. This is your night, Mo."

I'd written down some notes on an index card, but my hands had gotten so sweaty the ink smeared. I was so nervous I felt like I was walking the plank on my way out.

"Hello," I said, once the chatter had died down. "I'd like to start by saying some important thank-yous. First, thanks to all of you for coming. I can't wait for you to try the family recipes we've made for you tonight. They're filled with love, and if you read the Family Cookbook, then you know they also come with some great stories."

A few people cheered.

"Next, I'd like to say thank you to my team. The only reason I'm here tonight is because of the help I've gotten along the way. Thank you to Marcus, Jay, Carlota, and Joe. Thank you to my friends Travis and Crystal, who helped me plan this whole thing. But I'd also like to take a moment especially for Crystal."

Crystal was standing off to the side by the water pitchers, and I turned to face her. I hadn't even said anything nice yet, but she already looked embarrassed. "Crystal is the reason the pictures on my website aren't fuzzy or weird. Crystal is the reason I had the guts to go out and start talking to strangers to find new recipes in the first place. Crystal has been along every step of the way for this project, and I could never have done this without her. Crystal, you're pretty much just the best person ever."

The room erupted into applause, and Crystal buried her red, grinning face in her hands.

Now it was time to talk about the part I was most nervous to mention. I'd pitched the idea to the team a couple days ago, and everyone was excited about it, so there was no turning back now.

"So, you might all know that I've been searching for a family recipe, and maybe even some family. But the part of my story that I haven't talked about is that I'm in foster care. It's been . . . not so great." At this point, the room was completely quiet. I felt like I was standing there butt naked. I glanced to the kitchen, and Joe was standing in the doorway, nodding along. He moved his hand in a circle and mouthed, "Keep going!" I looked back at the crowd.

"Um, so, even though my experience hasn't been great, it's been better than a lot of other kids'. I shouldn't be given more just because I'm white, and no one should be given less, just because they're not. But that's what happens. And that isn't fair. The system isn't fair. And the whole point is, since so many of you came, we're going to make some money tonight, and we wanted you to know that whatever profit we make, we're donating to an organization here in New York that helps foster kids. So, if you feel like giving a little extra money tonight, it'll be for a good cause. And actually, I think that it would be an even better idea to give a lot of money instead."

People laughed at that. Even more cheered.

I smiled, feeling looser now that the important part of

my speech was over. "Even if you don't, I hope you enjoy your meal and swap recipes with one another and become like one big family. Because that's the goal for tonight. Thank you!"

Then dinner service started. I stayed in the kitchen with Marcus, Jay, and Carlota while Joe, Crystal, and Travis were on serving duty in the dining room. I swear we didn't stop moving for an hour and a half straight. It's how I imagine the players on the Jets feel, with bright lights shining down on them, working with their teammates. . . .

Nan, it was the best thing I've ever done.

It was hot and busy and stressful, and we made some mistakes along the way, but it was the most amazing, exhilarating hour and a half of my life.

During one calm moment, when the main course had been served, I peeked out from the kitchen. People were laughing and talking and seemed to really like the food. All I could think was, *I did this*. No—the seven of us did. Me, Crystal, Travis, Marcus, Jay, Joe, and Carlota. We created something special, together. The dishes we served tonight were from families with love in their recipes and their kitchens. So many threads were woven together. There was so much history. And I was there, too. I got to be a part of that.

Just as quickly as the first service started, it ended. I wanted to stay in the kitchen while people left, but Joe told me I should go back out and thank people for coming. Which I did, even though my heart felt like it was beating in my throat. I also made everyone come out with me, because the only reason any of this was able to happen was because we were a team. We did this together. We stood and held hands and bowed like we were in a play.

"Thank you all for coming, and being one big family here tonight," I said. I tried to stop my voice from shaking, but I couldn't. "It feels good to be a part of something, doesn't it?"

There was a round of applause, shouts, and whistles. A few people even stood up to clap. It made me smile so hard I thought my cheeks would break. The only thing I could do was laugh and smile and press my hands to my face.

Once everyone from the first seating had gone, I felt like I needed to collapse. Or stick my head in a bucket of ice water. Or run a marathon. Or all three. But I couldn't, because we had half an hour to get cleaned up and ready for our second seating and do it all over again. I settled on going to the bathroom to splash water on my face.

When I went back into the kitchen, Travis was chugging water from a plastic quart container, and Jay was rubbing Marcus's shoulders. Jay had taken off his chef's cap, and his bright red hair was sticking straight up, like he'd been electrocuted.

"Nice work, Chef," Marcus said. "Trav said we raised an extra two hundred bucks to donate."

"We did?" I said. I couldn't believe my speech had worked!

"Yep," Travis said. "Already counted it."

"My feet," Crystal moaned, sitting on the floor. "My poor feet."

"Rookie mistake," Marcus said, nodding at her high-tops. Then he wiggled one of his feet, presenting a bulbous, rubbery slip-on. "Crocs are the only way to survive a night of dinner service."

Crystal looked at his foot somberly. "I'd rather perish."

Travis and I cracked up.

"Mo?" Carlota said. "Can we talk to you for a minute? In private?"

"Sure," I said. "Is everything okay?"

Carlota nodded, but she seemed nervous. So did Joe, which made *me* nervous. I followed them out into the now-empty restaurant. It was mostly clean, but we had some tidying to do before our next seating.

"What is it?" I asked. "Is something wrong?"

"No, no," Carlota said. "Not at all. We wanted to wait until later, but we can't. If I don't say something now I'll explode. Mo, you need to know, you mean the world to us. And after you told us you were moving to Kansas, we haven't been able to sleep. I walk around at night like a ghost. Tell her, Joe."

"It's true. She does."

I waited for one of them to go on. They kept glancing at each other, and I couldn't tell who was more nervous. Carlota was wringing her hands, but Joe was sweating, and kept reaching up to wipe his forehead.

"I feel like I'm about to puke, excuse my language, so I'm just going to say it," Joe said. "We know it's not entirely the way this is all supposed to go, but, Mo—would you consider staying? Here, in New York?"

"But I can't stay," I said slowly. "I told you I can't."

"What Joe's trying to say is that we'd like you to stay in New York with *us*. Live with us," Carlota said. "Permanently. We'd like to become your legal guardians. Your family. If that's something you might want, too."

A buzzing started inside me. Low and thick.

"But—I thought you didn't want that," I blurted. "I overheard you talking about it, before. The night I came and slept on your couch."

"You heard that?" Carlota asked. "That conversation?"

I nodded.

"Oh, Mo. I'm so sorry." She took my hands. "We were so scared. Losing Isabella was the worst thing that's ever happened to either of us, and I was scared to think about being a parent again."

"We both were," Joe said. "But after Christmas, after you told us about moving . . . we both woke up and realized losing you was going to be just as painful. Because, well . . ." He scratched his ear. "Lasagna, Mo."

"Oh, Joe," Carlota said, patting his cheek. "Now's not the time for 'lasagna.' Now's the time for the real words." She turned to me. "What he means to say is that we love you. Between the three of us, we have so much loss. I never thought anything would grow in place of that grief, that pain. But I was wrong, because it has. Love has. We love you so much, Mo. And we don't want to lose you."

"Not to put any pressure on you, because we will respect your decision one way or another," Joe added. "But we want you to stay. We want you to stay more than anything."

"And you won't—" A tear slipped out, but I brushed it away quickly. "You won't change your minds?"

"Never, kid," Joe said solemnly. "Never in a million years."

Right there, in my stained chef's jacket, in the empty restaurant, I burst into tears.

"Yes," I told them, through thick, hiccuping sobs. "Yes."

We hugged and laughed, and I could tell we were all still feeling nervous. But happy. And good.

And then we went back into the kitchen and finished our last dinner service.

I couldn't stop smiling the whole time. Even when I burned my thumb on a hot pan, I smiled.

"What's up with you?" Crystal asked me when they were back in the kitchen refilling water pitchers. She glanced at Travis. "Did you get a kiss or something?"

"No," I said, still smiling. "It's better. I'll tell you later."

And then, finally, it was all over.

After I did my little thank-you-for-coming speech, and we all bowed and waved and were back in the kitchen, I collapsed onto the counter. "I'm exhausted. And I need something sweet more than I've ever needed anything in my life."

"Me too," Travis said.

Crystal caught my eye, and I had to bite down on my tongue to stop from giggling.

Joe went to check the walk-in refrigerator. "Sorry to be the bearer of bad news, but we're out of pie."

"Let's see what ingredients we have left over," Marcus said. "I bet we can make something."

So that's what we did—we went through everything ingredient by ingredient. We had some eggs, some buttermilk, sugar, some extra caramel sauce from the pie.

"Cookies?" Carlota said. "What about buttermilk cookies?"

Crystal got out a giant bowl, and her and Carlota started dumping in sugar, butter, and buttermilk.

"What if we made caramel frosting?" I suggested.

"We should add a tiny bit of soy sauce from the dumplings," Marcus added. "Trust me. Sounds weird, but soy and caramel together is . . ." He kissed his fingers.

We didn't have a recipe or anything like that, but soon we had the cookies in the oven.

And when they came out ten minutes later, we all stood around the stainless-steel island and ate them directly off the hot baking sheet. I know it would have been better to let them cool before frosting them, but none of us could wait.

"Okay. I have to admit, I thought these were going to

be gross," Travis said with his mouth full. "But they're actually good. Like, incredible."

Joe took a bite and closed his eyes as he chewed. "Oh. Wow. Yes."

"Did someone write down what we did?" Carlota asked.

I uncapped a pen. "I will."

And as I started to write down the recipe for our weird cookies, I realized it.

After all this time, looking, searching, I'd finally found it. Or maybe it had found me. Not in the place I'd expected to find it. Certainly not from the people I'd expected to find it with, either.

My first *real* family recipe.

Because I had it all wrong, didn't I? Family traditions don't just have to be about what we love from the past. They can be about what we create for the future.

Oh, Nan. I would have done anything for you to be there.

But you were there, weren't you? I could feel you there. I still can.

I love you, Nan.
Happy New Year.
Mo

<u>BUTTERMILK COOKIES WITH A SOY-CARAMEL FROSTING</u>
Makes 16-18 cookies

For the cookies
- 1/2 cup brown sugar
- 1/4 cup white sugar
- 1 egg
- 1 egg yolk
- 1 stick unsalted butter, softened
- 1 t. vanilla
- 1/2 cup buttermilk
- 2 cups all-purpose flour
- 1 t. baking powder
- 1/2 t. salt

For the frosting
- 1 cup powdered sugar
- 4 T unsalted butter, melted
- 1/4 cup caramel sauce
- 1 t. soy sauce
- 2 T milk (if needed)

Instructions
1. Preheat your oven to 350 degrees. Line a cookie sheet with a Silpat or parchment paper.
2. Whisk together flour, baking powder, and salt until it's well combined.
3. In a different bowl, cream together the sugar and softened butter. That means whip it together until

it gets all light and fluffy. Carlota says the secret to great cookies is to do this part for longer than you think you need to.

4. Next, add vanilla and the egg and egg yolk. Mix that up. Next, slowly add your buttermilk.

5. Slowly add your flour mixture to the bowl with the wet stuff in it. Do it until it's just combined. Don't overmix! Carlota says that's important, too. It's okay if there's a streak or two of flour left.

6. Roll the dough into small balls—about two tablespoons of dough per ball. You can probably fit, like, 9 cookies or so on a pan. I think. Bake them for 9-11 minutes, or until the bottoms are golden brown.

7. While the cookies bake, make your frosting. Marcus says we're adding soy sauce because it adds something called umami. And it's amazing, because you can't actually even taste it, except for its saltiness. Anyway, mix all the ingredients together, except for the milk. That's because you use the milk to thin the frosting, if you need to. That's a step you have to decide for yourself, as a chef.

8. Frost the cookies once they've cooled, so the frosting doesn't melt and turn more into a glaze. They'll still be good, but not _as_ good.

The best way to eat them is standing up, gathered around a kitchen countertop, while you laugh and talk with people you love.

WEDNESDAY, MAY 8

Dear Nan,

Sorry it's been so long since I've written. I've been getting settled. Everything's changed, you know?

Back in January, the conversation with Margery—about me not going to live with her—went so much easier than I thought it would. She asked if I was sure Joe and Carlota were the right fit for me, and when I told her I was sure, surer than anything, she said, "All right. Then I'm happy for you."

I had to stay with June and Tate for six weeks after the pop-up restaurant finished while Joe and Carlota got approved for something Moira called "kinship care." Like the rest of my experience over the past year, this process included lots of phone calls, documents, and other legal things I don't understand. There were court meetings and more strangers. Joe and Carlota had to "jump through a lot of hoops" (those are Moira's words) to get certified and approved to have me come and live with them. I wish it was as easy as one-two-three, but it's been a lot of work for them. But Moira worked hard for us, hard for me. I'm glad to have had her in my corner throughout all of this.

Joe and Carlota said they didn't care the tiniest bit, and that every confusing form and every hour of training was worth it.

I said my final goodbyes to Tate and June in February. Well, I guess it was only a real, in-person goodbye with Tate. June was on her way back from the airport, but was stuck in traffic. Tate was helping me comb the apartment for all my things, and he kept checking his phone screen for the time.

"I'm sure she'll be back any minute," he kept saying. But after he said it for the fifth time, I realized she probably wasn't going to make it.

"She's so sorry," he said, texting something back to her on his phone as I got the last of my stuff. "I can put her on speakerphone if you want?"

I pressed my lips together and shook my head. "No. That's okay. You can tell her I said bye."

"We can keep in touch." Tate kept running a hand through his hair. "If you want. You can email me any-time."

"Okay," I said, even though I knew I probably never would.

He hugged me at their door, holding on to me for a long time.

And that was that.

That same week, Joe quit his job at the Townsends' apartment building.

"Good riddance," he said. He told me he didn't care

that they were moving to France. He said he'd never walked out of a building so fast, and that he whistled all the way to his subway stop.

He took on a maintenance job at another building, and guess what? It came with a raise! I'm going to help out at Carlota's bakery on the weekends. They're even going to pay me.

Right now they're saving up so we can afford an apartment with a slightly bigger bedroom. When we cleared out the nursery together, Carlota cried.

"Are you okay?" I asked.

"I'm happy-sad." She put an arm around my shoulder and squeezed. "I'm sad about finally letting all of this go, but I'm happy because it's for the very best reason."

I understood that. I felt happy-sad about it, too.

A couple weeks ago, the window in my new bedroom started to leak. While we've been waiting on the landlord to replace it, I've been sleeping on the couch—but the secret is I really like it. I might even prefer it.

Joe put up a curtain I can pull closed at night so the living room turns into my softly lit, warm little bedroom. Mrs. Business must like it, too, because she sleeps with me every single night, right on my stomach. There are twinkly lights Carlota keeps in a glass flower vase on the table by the kitchen, and I can see their glow through the sheer curtain. It reminds me of our year-long Christmas tree. It feels good to be here. It feels right. But even so, I still have some bad days. Like last week.

At my appointment with Dr. Barb, I didn't want to talk, and she could tell.

"Why don't we draw today?" she offered.

"I'm not any good," I said, thinking about the lighthouse watercolor painting I did with Tate and June. The memory sent sparks of pain through me.

"That's okay. You don't have to be any good at something to have fun with it."

So I drew. I drew until it was done, without even thinking about what I was making.

"There," I said.

Dr. Barb looked at it. "Do you want to tell me about what that is?"

I pointed. "That's me. On a desert island. Under a palm tree."

"You're all alone. And is that"—she squinted—"a boat in the distance?"

I nodded.

"And who's on that boat?" she asked.

"Tate and June," I said immediately, even though I hadn't really thought it through.

"Oh?" Dr. Barb said. "Can you tell me more about that?"

"It's just . . . sometimes I think about June and Tate and it still hurts. It feels kind of like this. Like, after Billy left, it was the three of us on a boat together. But then they threw me overboard, and they sailed on."

"Hmm." She uncapped a pen of her own and motioned at my drawing. "May I?"

I nodded. Off to the side, she drew another island. She drew little sparkles and shimmers all around it. She drew little stick-figure people. She wrote CRYSTAL and JOE AND CARLOTA and FRIENDS and SCHOOL and COOKING. She drew smiley faces and tall buildings and sunshine. Then she uncapped a red marker, and between the two islands she drew a bridge.

And over the bridge, she wrote TATE AND JUNE.

"I know it's easy to focus on what hurts," she said, "and on the bad things. On the fact that it didn't work out. But there's also good in what you found with them, isn't there? Because without them, you never would have met Joe." She pushed the drawing back in front of me. "What I want you to see is that some relationships are bridges, Mo. They aren't meant to last forever. They take you where you're meant to be."

And she's right, isn't she? Because my relationship with Tate and June *was* a bridge, because it brought me to Joe and Carlota. And my relationship with them isn't a bridge. It's a home.

Things with the official adoption are still up in the air, but not because of Joe and Carlota—it's because of how complicated it all is. Every day Carlota reminds me, "One less day until we can adopt you!" Because we still don't know what the exact date will be. It could take a year or longer. But I can tell she wants me to know every day that they haven't changed their minds. And after a few months of her telling me this, every day, I'm starting to believe it.

Anyway, I'm now on the very last blank page in this journal. That's why I've waited so long to write to you, since my last letter back in January. Because I knew I had to use these final few pages for the right thing. I knew I had to stop writing letters to you like you're still here. And for the past two months, I haven't been ready to let this notebook go. But I think I am now. I think I'm going to be okay.

I'm not sure my heart is as big as a skyscraper *or* New York City, like you said in your letter to me. But it's so much bigger than I thought it was. And you knew that way before I did. You've always been wise, huh? It's so annoying that you're always right.

You know I love you, Nan, with all my heart. And one day, when I'm ready to kick the can, about four hundred years from now (because I think life-extending technology will have gotten really good, and I'll make sure to find a much better health-insurance company than the one you had), ghost/angel Mo will join ghost/angel Nan, and I'll show you all the recipes I gathered over the course of what's sure to be my extremely long and fabulous life.

And through the recipes and the stories that go along with them, I can show you the family I built. The family I found. The family that started with you.

I love you, Nan. I'll see you on the other side of the rainbow bridge.

Go, Jets!
Mo

345

AUTHOR'S NOTE & ACKNOWLEDGMENTS

Many of the recipes in this book come directly from a family cookbook my grandmother gifted me for Christmas in 2019 (including the buttermilk pie, which was a recipe my grandmother's family made during the Great Depression on the Minnesota farm that *she* grew up on!). After reading this book, you can probably understand why it was important to me to keep the recipes here as close as possible to the ones in my family cookbook.

With that said, many of these recipes are not fancy. And what's often not included in recipes like these are the home-cook expert tips that get passed down in person when you help a loved one make a family meal. Like what the *exact* right temperature is for butter, or that you should tent a pie with foil if it's prone to darkening, or that sure, the recipe says one thing, but actually we do it this other way.

I've been to culinary school, and the trained chef in me knows there are aspects of all these recipes that could be improved upon. But the family cook in me knows that they are perfect exactly as they are. If a recipe catches your eye, I invite you, dear reader, to improve it in whatever way you see fit. And then maybe it can become a family favorite of yours.

I would also like to add that while most of these recipes are from my own family, some of them are not. I wanted to celebrate food from different cultures in this book, because food is love the whole world round. I felt the best and most authentic way to include these recipes was to source them from my community, and I am deeply grateful for the wonderful folks who contributed their recipes to this book.

So, thank you to my dear friend Claudio Emma for allowing me to include your delicious lasagna recipe, which we've enjoyed together during many backyard dinners. Thank you to Mae Respicio for the chicken adobo, Karla Valenti (and your dad!) for the bisquets chinos, Jenny Liao (and your fiancé's mom!) for the dumpling recipe. Testing these recipes was the highlight of my research process for this book—and they were all beyond delicious.

I have many other people to thank who made this book possible.

First, my brilliant, kind, patient editor, Nancy. This book was a unique experience in that for so long, it was just the two of us working on it together. You found the seed of potential in the earliest draft, and thanks to you, this book was able to bloom into the best version of itself. Thank you also for coming up with the title, which—in my obviously non-biased opinion—is the best book title ever.

Thank you to my eagle-eyed copy editors, Iris Broudy, Lisa Leventer, Artie Bennett, and Alison Kolani. I cannot believe some of the incredible catches you made! Particular thanks to Iris, whose kind words and early support of this story buoyed my spirits exactly when I needed it most.

Thank you to Jake Eldred, Nathan Kinney, Ken Crossland, Jaclyn Whalen, and the team at Knopf, who work tirelessly to transform Word documents into real (and gorgeously designed) books.

Speaking of gorgeously designed books, thank you to cover artist Julie McLaughlin and art director Suzanne Lee. I will never forget the delight of opening my email with the early sketches and ideas for the book cover, and hemming and hawing over which was my favorite, because even the early designs were all *that* good.

Thanks to my publicist, Joey Ho, for her care and dedication.

Enormous thanks to the entire sales force at Penguin Random House for believing in and championing Mo's story. Lasagna!

Thank you to Pete Knapp, the world's best agent, and the team at Park & Fine, who do so much behind the scenes to make books flourish in the world. Thanks to Stuti Telidevara and Abigail Koons.

Thank you to Jill Benson, whose deep knowledge of

the complexity of the foster care system in New York City helped inform much of Mo's experience. Any mistakes in representation are completely my own.

Thank you to Barbara Perez Marquez and Jessica Sun for your thoughtful and incredibly useful feedback.

Nicole Constantine, thank you for taking such loving care of Langdon (which made much of the actual writing and editing of this book possible) and for insights into the kind of therapeutic techniques that can often be helpful for children.

Thank you to David Bauer, cat dad of the real Mrs. Business. I was spellbound the first time I heard her name and dreamed of one day immortalizing it in a book. I would also like to thank Nick Sudar, Mrs. Business's onetime roommate, who was likely involved in her naming.

Katherine Lin, my ride-or-die author (and life) pal, thank you for reading early drafts of everything I write, including this book.

Thank you to my dog, Mo, both for lending her name to the Mo of this story and for keeping me company during writing sessions and brainstorming walks.

To my parents and my wonderful family, thank you for the unwavering support.

Thank you to my daughter, Langdon, for the flyby office visits that led to many hugs-and-kisses breaks, which is a new—and vital—part of my writing process.

To my husband, Chris, this book would not exist without you. Thank you for taking over all parenting duties of our infant daughter—on top of your own work, in the middle of a pandemic—for a month straight so I could fully focus on finishing the first draft. I am so grateful you are my partner.

And finally, to my grandmother, Gammy. Thank you for all the pink cookies, the tales about beloved farm animals and the friendly chipmunks who would bang on your glass sliding doors asking for breakfast, the books filled with memories and pictures and stories you make for all of us, for your wisdom and humor. This book is, on so many levels, inspired by you. I love you.

On the following pages, you'll find excerpts from my grandmother's homemade family cookbook that inspired this story. I hope you enjoy her stories and recipes as much as I do.

Family Food

Family recipes from the past and present to carry you into the future.

Compiled for Elizabeth, Melissa, and Christopher by their Mom in 2012-2013.

Photo of the Blatz farm as it appeared in the 1940's.

Painting by Teresa Walker

HERITAGE RECIPES

From our earliest years, all of us girls probably had a child-sized table and chair set on which to serve the make-believe food we made on our make-believe stoves. This is a picture of the oldest Blatz sisters, Mildred (Sister Mildred Ann), and Florence (Sister Imogene), sitting at their set when they were very young, in the early 1900's. Society may be changing, and I was delighted when George took over the cooking after he retired, but these little table and chair sets of our childhood point out how we women were programmed to be the cooks in the family from our very beginning, like it or not!

I have included a few of the very old "heritage" recipes from my mother's cookbook, food that I remember loving as a child growing up on the farm. It was a happy time. Food was fresh from the garden without a need for preservatives, and no one knew or worried about cholesterol!

BUTTERMILK PIE

When living on the farm during the Depression, much of how one cooked depended on what ingredients were available. Many of these old family recipes use a lot of eggs, because we could gather them every day, warm and fresh from beneath the hens that laid them. The cow produced rich milk which we skimmed. The rich heavy cream was used for a variety of desserts (some included in this book), and sometimes it was used to churn butter in our old wooded churn. That left buttermilk which needed to be used. The following pie was the result. It has a unique taste and is delicious. One knows it has lemon, but the buttermilk flavor, which is very subtle, is what makes it special.

I have copied my old card below. Our old family recipe didn't give any directions. A similar recipe from the newspaper is more specific, and between the two, it is easy to make and bake. (The old recipe did not have a meringue and it was very tasty without it.)

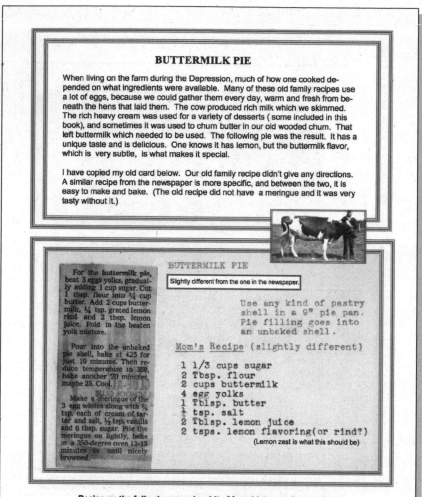

BUTTERMILK PIE

Slightly different from the one in the newspaper.

For the buttermilk pie, beat 3 eggs yolks, gradually adding 1 cup sugar. Cut 1 tbsp. flour into ¼ cup butter. Add 2 cups buttermilk, ¼ tsp. grated lemon rind and 2 tbsp. lemon juice. Fold in the beaten yolk mixture.

Pour into the unbaked pie shell, bake at 425 for just 10 minutes. Then reduce temperature to 350, bake another 20 minutes, maybe 25. Cool.

Make a meringue of the 3 egg whites along with ¼ tsp. each of cream of tartar and salt, ½ tsp. vanilla and 6 tbsp. sugar. Pile the meringue on lightly, bake in a 350-degree oven 12-15 minutes or until nicely browned.

Use any kind of pastry shell in a 9" pie pan. Pie filling goes into an unbaked shell.

Mom's Recipe (slightly different)

1 1/3 cups sugar
2 Tbsp. flour
2 cups buttermilk
4 egg yolks
1 Tblsp. butter
¼ tsp. salt
2 Tblsp. lemon juice
2 tsps. lemon flavoring(or rind?)
(Lemon zest is what this should be)

Recipe on the following page is a bit of farm history as I remember it.

Old Blatz Recipe for Best-Ever Sunday Fried Chicken

Chicken (must be home grown)
Seasoned flour and lard for frying
Large iron frying pan with cover

Directions:

Buy a parcel of land with enough acreage to raise chickens. Purchase the hatching equipment. If hatching equipment is beyond budget, newly hatched chicks may be purchased from a commercial hatchery. They will arrive rather tightly crammed into cardboard cartons with air holes, all cheeping and defecating, and will need to be transferred immediately to their new living quarters. So, before ordering, build as many "brooder" houses as required. These should be well insulated, and also movable, as they must be relocated each year so that the grazing area around them is not contaminated in any way. This means you should also purchase a truck and trailer hitch. (Thinking forward, you might also want to get a cat.) Be sure to have proper water containers in these houses so that the little chicks will not tumble in and drown. Keep the chicks warm, feed them well, and watch them grow.

Uncle Ed (Philip Blatz's brother), caught in the brutal act.

The chickens will outgrow these brooder houses fairly quickly and will have to be moved into larger quarters with roosts and nests and plenty of fenced grazing land on which to roam. When mature enough, (between young pullet size and before becoming an old hen), the chicken you need for dinner is ready to be captured. This can be done with a long wire gadget with a hook on one end to grasp the leg of the startled bird and pull it out from the rest of the flock. Take the squawking chicken to the chopping block, and, holding it firmly by both legs, take a sharp axe, sever the head at the neck with one blow, and release the chicken. If young children are watching, they will think it miraculous that the chicken with its head cut off still leaps around. They will also will think you are a monster. Do not even try to explain what you have done. They will not understand. They will grow up and learn that there are worse things in life, or they will become vegans.

Wait for the chicken to be quiet. (Hopefully your good cat has made off with the severed head so its beady little eyes do not stare up at you in reproach.) Plunge the chicken into scalding hot water and remove all the feathers. Stubble will remain and will have to be carefully plucked by someone. If the traumatized little children can do this, it will calm them, and they may grow up to become contemplatives. It is a mind-clearing chore. At some point, someone with a sharp knife must open the chicken and pull from within all that is slimy and inedible, saving only the heart and the gizzard. When all of this is completed, wash the chicken well, pat dry, and cut it into serving pieces. Roll these in the seasoned flour, brown well in the hot fat, put into a heavy, covered casserole, and bake in a 350 degree oven until fork tender.

This may seem complicated, but if you carefully follow all of the above directions, you will have a chicken that tastes like ambrosia. It will have a superb flavor unlike anything you have ever tasted before and which far surpasses the "free range" chickens which are served in the world's finest restaurants. Believe me. I have tasted. I have watched. I have plucked—and on many a day, I am contemplative.

357

NOTE on the WALKER CHOCOLATE BIRTHDAY CAKE

The recipe for this cake came from an old wartime recipe book called "The Everyday American Cookbook." During the war, shortening was hard to come by, thus the oil substitute, which now, of course, turns out to be a health plus. This is also true of the cocoa which is much better for us than the hard chocolate. I didn't originally pick it for health reasons, but because it was a very moist cake. It just turned out to be a healthy choice.

The filling is one of the flavored cake fillings that we made each week on the farm for the family Sunday dinner dessert—always a layer cake and always baked on Saturday.

The frosting came from a Hershey box and is really the one rich and not so healthy aspect of this cake, but it is really what gives it its sweetness. One has to live a little.

This was the Walker family birthday cake during all the years when my kids were growing up. George did not consider it his birthday without it, and when Missy was married, she introduced it to Jim's family and Jim's father feels just as George did. Liz once entered it in a baking contest in Cincinnati and won first prize.

The three steps are something of a bother, but the three textures of chocolate make it a very special treat. It is really worth getting old for. Missy, who has made it countless times, thinks I exaggerate the difficulty—so give it a try. **You will not regret it.**